D1564552

THE ACCIDENTALS

by USA Today bestselling novelist
SARINA BOWEN

TUXBURY PUBLISHING LLC

OVERTURE

OVERTURE: (n.) *The opening movement of a dramatic composition such as an opera or ballet. Traditionally, the overture is comprised of themes and motifs which will be further developed as the work progresses.*

Chapter One

I WAS in the third grade when I figured out that the man who sang "Wild City" on the car radio was the same one who sent a check to my mother every month. The names weren't exactly the same; the checks said Frederick Richards, while the DJs called him Freddy Ricks.

But I had a good ear, even then. The sigh my mother uttered when she opened his envelopes was exactly the pitch as the one I heard as she switched off the radio.

She wouldn't talk about him even when I begged. "He's a stranger, Rachel. Don't dwell on him."

But everyone else did. Freddy Ricks was nominated for a Grammy when I was ten, and his second album stayed on top of the charts for months. Growing up, I heard his music during TV ads for luxury cars and while waiting in line at Rite Aid. I read interviews he did with *People* and *Rolling Stone*.

I memorized his Wikipedia entry. My name wasn't in it. Neither was my mother's.

Even so, my interest was undiminished. I bought his music with my babysitting money, and I saved every magazine article I could find. I was a rabid little fan girl, and I wasn't nice about it.

Whenever my mother and I fought, I would hang another

photo of him on my bedroom wall. Or else I jammed my ear buds in, ignoring the parent sitting next to me to listen to the one I'd never met.

I was so angry about her silence. Now I would give anything to see her face one more time.

Anything.

But I'll never have another chance to turn the music off and hear my mother's voice. And the guy who didn't bother to show up for almost eighteen years? Supposedly he's waiting at the social worker's office to meet me.

I feel sick as the van pulls up at the office for the Department of Children and Families. My hands are almost too sweaty to unlatch my seatbelt. After wiping them on my denim skirt, I fumble for the greasy door handle.

Every time I ride in this tatty vehicle, which is probably the same one that shows up to remove kids from meth labs, or whatever else social workers do, I think: *This is not my life.*

Although, since a week ago, it is.

Living in a state-run group home is horrifying. But it isn't nearly as bad as hearing my mother's oncologist tell me it didn't matter that her cancer had responded to the chemotherapy, because she'd contracted an infection that might kill her first.

He was right. It did. And nothing will ever be the same.

"I'll pick you up in half an hour," the driver says as I climb numbly out into the sticky Orlando afternoon.

"Thanks," I mumble. One-word answers are the only kind I have these days.

Tasting bile in my throat, I watch the van pull away. But I still have a choice. Although the State of Florida has recently made quite a few decisions on my behalf—and some of them are doozies—I'm pretty sure the legal code can't force me to go inside this building.

I don't *have* to meet the man who abandoned me before I was born. Instead of walking inside, I linger on the hot sidewalk, trying to think.

A thousand times I've pictured meeting Frederick Richards. But never once have I imagined it would happen under the fluorescent lights of the Florida Department of Children and Families.

I turn around, considering my options. The adjacent parking lot belongs to a strip mall. There's a smoothie place, a video game store, and a nail salon. I could saunter over there and get a smoothie and a manicure instead of meeting my father. If I were a braver girl, that's what I'd do. *Take that, Frederick Richards!* My life can go on without ever meeting him. I'll turn eighteen in a month. Then my social-services nightmare will end, anyway.

He'll sit there in Hannah's office, looking at his watch every couple of minutes, while I sip a smoothie across the street.

Right. I don't even like smoothies. Drinks aren't supposed to be thick.

While I take this little mental trip through Crazytown, the Florida sun beats down on me. A drip of sweat runs down the center of my back. And across the way, I catch a man watching me from the driver's seat of a dark sedan. A nervous zing shoots through my chest. But it disappears just as quickly as I realize the man behind the wheel is absolutely not Frederick Richards. He's Hispanic, with salt-and-pepper hair.

I frown at him.

He smiles widely.

Creeper. I turn away, yanking open the door to the social worker's office. A welcome blast of cool air hits me. But the functioning AC is the only pleasant thing about this place. Everything in the room is gray, including the cheap metal office furniture and the dingy walls, which have probably needed a fresh paint job for longer than I've been alive.

"Hi Rachel," the wrinkled receptionist greets me. "You can have a seat, and Hannah will be out to get you as soon as she's ready."

I eye Hannah's door. *Is he really in there?* I don't ask, though, because my mouth is suddenly as dry as toast. Another wave of nausea hits as I steer myself into the battered chair just outside Hannah's office.

Out of habit, I reach into my pocket for my iPod Classic. The steel edges felt cool against my damp fingers. Music has always been my drug of choice. In the palm of my hand, I hold the orderly world, arranged into playlists of my own design. Thousands of examples of prerecorded perfection can be cued up at the touch of my finger.

Some of it was written and performed by the man on the other side of Hannah's door. I've been carrying my father around in my pocket for a long time.

"You've wasted entire months of your life thinking about him," my mother often complained, her laser eyes on the stack of CDs in my room. "And he's never spent five minutes thinking about us. I can guarantee it."

I shove the iPod into my backpack and zip it shut.

Mom was right about everything. And it stings knowing that I'll never have the chance to apologize. Everything stings, all the time. I'm Angry Rachel now. I hardly recognize myself. Even here, glancing around the shabby little office, I want to burn it all right to the ground.

When the door opens beside me, I actually jump like one of those skittish kitties in so many YouTube videos. Whirling around, I see only Hannah and her steady hazel eyes looking down at me. With a frown of concern, she steps forward, mostly closing the door behind her. "Rachel," she whispers. "Do you want to meet Frederick Richards?"

Yes?

No.

Sometimes.

God.

My knees are spongy when I stand up. Hannah opens the door again, and it's only three steps into her office.

And there he is, after all this time, sitting in an ugly chair with metal arms. I would know him anywhere, that face made famous on album covers and in the gossip pages of magazines. Thanks to video, I can picture him singing on stage in L.A. or Rome. I know what he looks like wandering the streets of New Orleans or catching a subway train in New York. That's what Instagram and a couple thousand hours of YouTube can do for a girl.

And now I know what he looks like when he sees a ghost.

He sucks in his breath when I enter the room. For that one moment, I have the advantage. I'd been staring at him forever, but to him, my face is a surprise. Maybe he sees my mother. I've inherited her dark blond hair and brown eyes.

Or, maybe he has no memory at all of what my mother looked like.

Eventually he stands up. He's *tall*. I'm taken aback by the way he fills Hannah's little office. Who knew that music videos don't capture proportion very well?

I'm still rooted in place near the door, my mouth dry. He doesn't know what to do either. He steps forward, taking my clammy hand in his cooler one. "I'm so sorry about your mother. I'm sorry…" He clears his throat. "Well, I'm sorry about a lot of things. But I'm really sorry you lost your mom."

I look down at his big hand holding mine, the long fingers. I couldn't speak at all. People have been saying variations of this for a week, and I can usually stammer out a "thank you." But not this time.

"Rachel," Hannah says from behind her desk. "Why don't you take a seat?"

Hannah's voice is like cool water. I let go of Mr. Frederick Richards's hand and slide obediently into a chair, while he retreats into his.

"This is an unusual situation," Hannah says, folding her hands.

We're still staring at each other. There are creases around his eyes and mouth. His fortieth birthday has just passed, a fact I know from Wikipedia. He's aged over the decade that I'd been following him, but it's still a very handsome face. My mother swooned for him all those years ago. That was her word—swooned. But my mother pronounced it the way her doctor had said "malignant."

"Rachel, Mr. Richards wants to help you. But he has no legal right to care for you. His signature is not on your birth certificate, which complicates things. So he submitted a DNA test and hired a lawyer to help him navigate family court. But the system doesn't move very fast. It's unlikely that he can become your legal guardian before you turn eighteen next month."

Some answer is required of me. "Okay," I whisper. What does that mean, then? Will he just leave?

"Look, can Rachel and I talk?" he asks Hannah.

"You mean alone," Hannah clarifies.

"Yes, I do." He says it curtly, like a man who's used to people listening.

"Today? No," Hannah says. "This is a supervised visit between a child in the state's custody and a stranger. I'm sure this is very difficult for you, Mr. Richards, and an audience doesn't help. But this office plays host to hundreds of difficult conversations a year. I can promise that you will survive it."

Hannah always gives it to you straight. She's delivered plenty of bad news to me in a short amount of time, and all with a complete lack of bullshit.

Hannah didn't sugarcoat the fact that I had to move into the group home. "It's not the Plaza Hotel," Hannah had admitted. "But it's run by good people, and if there's anything really bad about it, you're going to call me right away."

Mr. Frederick Richards sighs in his chair. His hands were nervous, fiddly. In most of his photographs he holds a guitar.

"Since you've come to Florida to offer Rachel your assistance," Hannah says, "why don't you tell us what sort you have in mind? I understand that until now your support has been financial in nature."

He nods. "Yes, it was. I always…" He presses his fingers to his lips. "Before, I assumed that financial support was the only kind necessary." He looks right at me. "I didn't know your mother was sick. Nobody told me."

Again, I know I should say something, but the words just aren't there. My father is going to think his daughter is mute.

"So…" He returns his attention to Hannah. "You said Rachel is headed to boarding school in the fall." His eyes dart toward me. "It sounds like she needs a place to go after she turns eighteen next month."

"Technically, she will age out of our system in August," Hannah agrees. "But she can probably keep her place at the group home until she leaves for school."

I close my eyes, my stomach clenching at the idea of staying there even one minute more. When I open them again, he's watching me. He turns a bit in the too-small chair so that he is facing me. "Rachel, I want to help you. My first choice was to just take you away from here." He waves a hand, taking in either the Department of Children and Families or the entire state of Florida. I don't know which. "But if I can't do that, I'm going to make sure you're being treated well."

"Okay," I whisper.

He turns to Hannah again. "There must be some way I can see her. She isn't a *prisoner* of the state."

"Well." Hannah taps her desktop. "That will be up to Rachel. She goes to summer school, and she has a curfew in the evening. If she wishes to make time for you, she can tell you herself. I'm not at liberty to give out her contact information, but I can give her *your* phone number."

"Please do," he says, watching me.

There's a pounding in my ears. "Pine Bluff High School," I blurt out, surprising all of us. "I'm usually finished by two thirty." I sneak a look at Hannah to see if she disapproves. But the social worker's gaze is steady. "My curfew is seven thirty."

"All right," he says, taking a notebook and a pen out of his shirt pocket. I think I see his hands shaking as he scribbles on the cover.

Hannah glances up at the clock. "We still have a few minutes here. I could make a couple copies of the documents Mr. Richards provided. Should I do that now, Rachel? Or I could wait."

I nod. "Go ahead."

Hannah gets up and blocks the door open with a rubber stopper on her way out.

Frederick sits back in his chair, his head against the wall. "I know that I…" He doesn't finish the sentence. "I don't expect you to understand. But I want you to know how happy I am to see you."

I only nod, because I don't trust myself to speak. I've waited my entire life to hear those words. And yet I would trade them in, in a heartbeat, to erase the last month.

"If it's okay with you, I'll wait in front of your school tomorrow at two thirty."

"Okay." I lick my dry lips. "I'll have homework." It's such an idiotic thing to add. Like homework matters right now.

"I'll only stay as long as you'd like."

In the silence that follows, Hannah breezes back in. "Do either of you have any questions?"

"I just want you to call me if there's any way I can help," he says. "You have my cell, and I'm just at the Ritz-Carlton."

That's when Ray, the van driver, knocks on the door jamb. "Hi Rachel! Are you ready?"

I stand up, ready to flee.

"Rachel?" Hannah's gentle voice stops my exit. "I left you three messages today. Let's make sure we *confirm* our next meeting together, okay?"

"My phone doesn't work anymore. It must have, um…" I don't want to admit it—that it must have been shut off. My mother was sick in the hospital for weeks before she died. Some bills weren't paid. Of all the things going wrong in my life, an unpaid phone bill doesn't even make the top fifty. But it embarrasses me, anyway.

"Oh," Hannah says, her face full of compassion. "Then could I email you about our next meeting?"

I nod.

"Take this," she says, passing me a business card. It reads *Freddy Ricks*. Hannah has just given me something I'd never been able to find before. His personal phone number and email address.

I look at him one more time, just to check that he's real. He stares back at me. His eyes have reddened. "Bye," he whispers. Then, the man whom *Rolling Stone* describes as "eloquence you can dance to" presses his lips together and turns his head away from me, toward Hannah's wall.

———

It's a warm, sticky Florida night, the only kind we have in July. Orlando will be unbearably hot for three more months. By the time it cools off, I plan to be far, far away from here.

I sit on the scratchy bedspread, trying to review a pre-calc homework assignment. Nearby, on the other bed, my roommate Evie conceals herself beneath too-long bangs and monstrous headphones. The music blaring from them is so distracting that I can't imagine how Evie isn't profoundly deaf.

Evie has lived at the Parson's Home for four years. Maybe she doesn't care if she's deaf.

This will be my seventh night here. Inside these walls, reality seems to slip and reshape. I watched my mother die. And even though I'd seen her casket lowered into the ground, I keep expecting her to walk through the door, saying "Rachel, gather your things, we're leaving. And why haven't you taken all your exams yet?"

I flip another page in my math book. Claiborne Prep—where I'm going next year—won't accept a report card full of incompletes. I missed all my final exams the week my mother died. My school arranged for me to take them during the summer session.

And now I'm stuck with this homework and this room and a spinning head. I try one more time to make sense of the equation on the page. But then I hear a car horn outside.

Dropping my pencil, I run from the room. The stairs are carpeted in a shade of brown which tries and fails to hide the dirt of many thousands of feet over several dozen years.

Outside, there's a familiar blue beater at the curb. When I emerge, Haze climbs out from behind the driver's seat. I sit down on the grimy stoop, and he sits down next to me. Haze wraps his tattooed arms around his knees and rests his chin on his biceps. "Evening," he says.

"Hi."

"You didn't call me after. I've been waiting to hear how it was."

"My phone stopped working." And even if it hadn't, I wouldn't have known what to say.

"Did you like him?" He gives me a sidelong glance.

I shrug. *I've always liked him*. "It was really hard. We were both terrified."

"What's he got to be scared of? Except me."

"*Haze*," I warn. We'd been close since I was in the second grade, when I pinched Adam Lewis on the backside so that he'd leave Haze alone. Haze has been my loyal friend ever since, though he no longer needs my protection. The Adam Lewises of the world do not want to run afoul of the nineteen-year-old edition of Haze.

These days, I'm the one receiving all the protection. When my mother was hospitalized, Haze sat there next to me. While I held her hand, he held my other one. Together we'd watched my mother's body slip deeper into illness, with new tubes each day, and a hissing ventilator at the end. During the three-week ordeal, he had ferried me to the hospital and back home. When I was too tired and too afraid to be alone, he had slept on my sofa and cut school.

Haze is stuck in summer school now too, which is basically my fault.

And then, after the end came, as I sat numbly in his car before the funeral, he pulled me into his arms and kissed me for the first time. Even now, it rests here on the grimy stoop between us, this unacknowledged thing that has shifted. Haze has always been quick to throw an arm around my shoulders or pat me on the back. But now I sense a kind of heat rising off him whenever I'm nearby.

At this very moment I'm aware of his fingertips sliding onto my bare knee. And I really don't know what to think about that.

"I don't see how Daddy thinks he can help," Haze is saying. "The man is seventeen years too late."

I know! Angry Rachel privately agrees. Of course I'm mad at Frederick. Still, Haze shouldn't make me defend my decision to meet him.

As I watch, Haze's fingers rub my kneecap gently. There's love in his touch, which I sorely appreciate. But there's also expectation. I reach for his hand, squeezing his fingers to occupy them. And then I change the subject. "Did you hear any news from Mickey Mouse?" Haze is applying for jobs at all the theme parks, hoping to start after we finally graduate.

"Not yet. I've been wondering—what do you think is the worst job there?"

"Is Mickey potty trained? What about Goofy?"

A slow grin overtakes his face. "Did you know the custodial guys have a code for all the bad shit? 'Code V' is for vomit. They clean it up with 'pixie dust,' which is really sawdust cut with charcoal."

"Gross. Don't get stationed by Space Mountain."

"I know, right? Rachel, your curfew is in two minutes."

"True."

"We can hang out after school tomorrow."

I shake my head. "Frederick is coming to see me again." His name sounds funny on my tongue. Formal. But I can't call him "my father" out loud when, as far as I know, he's never called me his daughter.

Haze's face falls. "Why, Rae? You don't need his bullshit. What would your mother say?"

Haze and my mother had always gotten on beautifully together—even after Haze stopped being a cute grade-schooler, and got tattoos, and got left back a grade. "That's just Haze," she'd sigh, after the news of his latest mess. "He's been through a lot." To me, Jenny Kress was a militant taskmaster. But she had a blind spot for Haze. It was one of the enduring mysteries of my life.

"Jenny would say that man is nothing to you," Haze presses.

I stare down at the cracks in the concrete walkway. The truth is that my mother said that very thing many times. Until the night that all changed.

"It was her idea," I say slowly.

"What was?"

My stomach is already cramping. I'm still too raw to think about my mother's final week. Getting through each day requires that I forget those frantic hours, as doctors scrambled to halt her decline, and nurses—my mother's coworkers—came and went with anxious faces.

"It was that night you went out to buy milkshakes, because she said she would eat something." Just the memory of her hospital room pushes me back under the surface of the deep pool of fear I'd been swimming through. "Out of nowhere, she said 'We need to call your father.'"

At the time, I'd tried to brush the idea aside. "Now is not the time," I'd told her.

But she'd said, "Now is well *past* the time." And then she'd let out the saddest sigh I'd ever heard.

That had been the exact moment when I'd really understood how bad things were. Somehow I'd managed to stay positive until right then, even though I'd never seen her so sick. Even though she slept nearly all the time, and her skin felt like hot paper. Even though Hannah the social worker had begun to make regular appearances in my mother's hospital room.

Until that moment, I was able to pretend. And then she burst that bubble. *We have to call your father*. It was the single scariest thing she ever said to me.

"We're not calling him," I'd argued again, feeling like I might throw up.

"Calling who?" Hannah had asked from the doorway.

And that was that.

"Well, shit," Haze says, his voice full of surprise. He clasps one of my wrists and pulls me gently to my feet. "That doesn't mean it was a good idea. What, uh, happened between them, anyway?"

"I have no idea. Except for the obvious thing." My neck heats at the implication of sex.

But Haze just smiles. "That much I figured out. Do you think it was a hookup? Or were they a couple?"

All I can do is shake my head. "Whenever I asked questions, she always said she didn't know him well. That he was a stranger." Although I never quite bought it. Mom seemed angry at him in a way that a stranger might not deserve. Or was that wishful thinking?

I hated the idea that I was the product of a one-night stand. An accidental child.

That awful night my mother told Hannah to summon him had probably been a window—a rare chance to ask questions. But I hadn't done it. I was afraid to break the seal, as if, by acknowledging my worst nightmare, it would come true.

And then it had. My mother's last words were, "It's okay, Rachel."

Haze lifts a hand to rub my back in a way that puts me on high alert. "Rae, you don't have to see that guy again if you're not feeling it."

"I know."

"We were going to drop by your house tomorrow to pick up the things you need."

That's something else I'm afraid to do. "It will wait."

"Okay," he whispers, his eyes going soft. So I know what's coming. He cups my face in his hands, and I stop breathing. Slowly, Haze dips his chin toward mine, bringing our lips together. I become overly aware of his palms on my cheeks, his breath on my face and the quiet *snick* of his kiss.

I pull away as soon as I can without being impolite.

"I'll see you in the morning," he says. Then he turns and jogs toward his car.

Chapter Two

THE FIRST MINUTE of the day is always the hardest.

When I open my eyes, the cracked plaster ceiling overhead usually provides the first clue. And if that doesn't jolt me with the realization that it wasn't all just a nightmare, the gray light filtering through the ratty curtains does the trick. Or the sound of Sister Mary Ruth's warbling voice in the hallway.

My mother is gone, and she's not coming back.

The sick feeling in the pit of my stomach begins then, and it doesn't let up, even if I manage to find the shower unoccupied. Even if Evie doesn't shove anyone in the hallway. Even if nobody steals my piece of toast before it pops, the ache is there.

Before my ordeal began, I didn't know such a place existed. Even summer school was a fuzzy idea, since I've never known anyone to take summer classes except for driver's education.

It's like a hellish, alternate universe was created on the day my mother died, and I'm trapped inside. So, with a pounding heart, I wash and dress as fast as possible.

"Good morning, dear," the nun on duty says as I hustle into the kitchen. She hands me a tiny glass of orange juice, which she dispenses as if it were liquid gold.

"Thank you," I whisper, gulping it down. Then I pick up my

backpack and run outside, where an old blue car sits idling at the curb.

It's sweet relief to sink into Haze's passenger seat. He doesn't waste time with small talk. He doesn't say "good morning" or ask how I slept. He just slides over, wrapping his arms around me. I put my chin on his shoulder and let out a long, shaky breath.

"One month from today," he whispers, naming the length of time until my birthday. I sniff back the tears that threaten to spill. A month is forever. I've only made it eight days so far. "What would happen if you just didn't go back there?" He pulls back, studying me with those dark eyes of his.

"The social worker would come looking for me. And they'd just find me at school, anyway."

"God forbid you blow *that* off," Haze says, putting the car into gear.

I don't bother to explain, because Haze should already know. I need my good grades or I can't switch to Claiborne Preparatory Academy in September. And boarding school is the only thing in my life that didn't implode the day my mother went into the hospital.

Besides Haze. Thank God for Haze.

He lets the subject drop, turning on the radio instead. Sam Smith begins to croon from the speakers, filling up the car with the sounds of someone else's heartache.

———

Later that morning, I'm studying in the media center at school when an unfamiliar email arrives in my inbox. The sender's name is completely unfamiliar. But the subject line is "Welcome to Claiborne."

Dear Rachel,

Hi. I'll bet the last thing you need is a letter from a stranger, reminding you that school will start up again in seven weeks. But you're going to get four of them.

Sorry. I'm just following orders.

I'm Jake, and I've just finished my junior year at Claiborne Prep. Congratulations on your acceptance and all that. Claiborne is awesome, and I'm not just saying that because you already paid your deposit. It is a pretty great place. I've drunk the Kool-Aid, obviously, which is probably why they asked me to write this letter.

Every incoming student receives four letters from a "peer liaison," and so they passed me your name. My email address is talknerdytome@ClaibornePrep.edu but you'll be assigned a normal one with your name, like Rachel.Kress@ClaibornePrep.edu. It's pretty easy to make aliases on the server if you're a geek like me and that kind of thing makes you giddy.

So, yeah. Fun times at boarding school! Do I know how to party, or what? :) When I sat down to write this letter, I wondered if I could pass myself off as a cool guy. Four paragraphs in and I'm pasting that L on my forehead already.

Anyhow.

All they told me about you is: your name, your home address, your former school and your class year. Orlando Florida, huh? Is it weird to live near Disney World? Do you still like going there, or by now would you rather have it firebombed? I've been there a couple of times with my family, like every other kid in America. And I was that kid who threw up after a ride on the tea cups.

True story. In my defense, it was really humid because we went in August to save money. I'm blaming the heat, and the sugary lemonade. My family is never letting me live it down, either. Ten years later I'm still hearing: "Remember the time Jake threw up at Disney World?"

So if you're from Florida, you're going to need to buy some winter clothes. And boots. Don't forget those. It's not all just fluffy snow and rainbows. New Hampshire weather brings plenty of slush and ice. And spring takes forever to arrive. March and April are all about muddy paths and bare trees and the last couple of snow piles that refuse to melt.

I'm really selling it now, right? Claiborne Prep: Land of Bleh Weather and Unnaturally Long Twin Beds. For fifty grand a year, all this can be yours. Join us.

Please feel free to ask me any questions about what to bring or how to sign up for classes. Pro tip: they're not kidding about those extra-long sheets. Regular twin size will pop off the corners all the time. So it's worth ordering them from a catalog. And if you pick a weird color or pattern, you'll never get confused if someone takes your stuff out of a dryer in the laundry room. Mine have snowmen on them. (Thanks mom.)

Feel free to email me at any point.

Jake Willis

Reading Jake's letter is like stepping out of my own reality for a few minutes. I actually laugh out loud when I get to the part about puking on the teacups.

The fact that I'm headed to Claiborne Prep in the fall seems completely surreal.

It was sophomore year when I started begging my mother to send me there. Gazing at their website, I'd fallen in love with the bell tower and the ivy-covered bricks on their website. It looked like something out of a movie. I wanted to kick through piles of real autumn leaves (we don't have those in Florida) and rub elbows with the kind of serious students I imagine go to boarding school.

My mother was unmoved. "We can't afford that," she said the first ten times I mentioned it. "It's a snooty place."

"But what if I win a scholarship?" I'd pressed. That's how my mom had afforded her year there. *Or what if you asked my father for the money?* Even if I didn't voice this request aloud, it always hung there in the air between us.

We had this argument a million times. Both of us pretended that money was the big obstacle. There was a lot more to it, though. When she was my age, my mother also did a year at Claiborne Prep. She grew up in Claiborne, New Hampshire.

And that's where she got pregnant with me.

My mom never said much about her time in Claiborne. And she certainly never spoke of my father. But I knew she hated the idea of her baby girl going so far away. She also didn't want my teenage years to end the way hers did. With too much freedom and then a baby.

I didn't give up, though. I kept working on her. A year at prep school would look good on my college applications, and Mom cared a lot about those.

Finally, she'd said yes. One day she'd left a check on my desk for the application fee, made out to Claiborne Prep. Without asking why she'd changed her mind, I'd sat down and begun my online application.

A week after my application was complete, Mom told me her cancer was back.

Now my fingers hover over the keyboard as I imagine what an honest reply to this friendly note would sound like. *Hi Jake. Right after I applied to your school, my life became a dumpster fire. My mother never wanted me to go to Claiborne, and I think she relented only because she thought she was dying.*

You just can't put that in an email to a stranger.

Dear Jake,

   Thank you for your letter. It's hard to imagine myself there next winter, walking between snow banks. I haven't seen snow since I was three. As for Disney World, I still like the place. Tourist traffic can be a real bummer, but there are perks. My friend Haze and I are good at sneaking into hotels to use the swimming pool. We keep a stash of abandoned key cards to flash when we need to look like we belong.

And you're not the only one who ever puked on the teacups. My intel suggests it happens all the time.

My questions about Claiborne number in the millions. My entire experience with boarding school is reading *Harry Potter* books. What if the sorting hat puts me in Slytherin? Are the elves friendly? Is potions class as hard as it looks?

Seriously though—is it crazy that I'm showing up only for senior year? Maybe it was a dumb decision for someone who's kind of an introvert. Will I have a roommate? That's a little terrifying.

What else? I have a lot of questions about the various music groups. I see a glee club and a choir. Aren't those the same thing? The a cappella singing groups are really interesting to me as well. But I'll probably have to audition, right? Yikes.

My Claiborne email address should be: shegetsstagefright@ClaibornePrep.edu.

Thanks for writing to me. At least I'll know one person at Claiborne.

Best—

Rachel Kress

After I hit "send," I go back to stressing out about seeing my father after school. The last hour of my day is spent staring at a single page of my U.S. Government textbook. By the time the bell rings, my palms are clammy.

In the girls' bathroom, I run a brush through my hair. When I was eight, I spent a month dreaming that Frederick would turn up at the Father-Daughter Banquet at school. Even two months ago, I'd imagined him standing in the back of the auditorium during my solo in the Choir Springtime Showcase.

Each time I pictured meeting my father, I always framed the scene in a flattering light. But now there's only this version of me

—the puffy-eyed, rumpled one in clothes that aren't quite clean enough. I shove my brush in my purse and leave the bathroom, if only to escape my reflection in the mirror.

"Hey." Haze is waiting right outside the door. We fall into step together as we head for the wide front doors. "Are you sure about this?"

"Yeah." *No.*

All the tension I'd felt yesterday in Hannah's office redoubles as Haze opens the door for me. And I don't know whether I'm more afraid that my father won't show up, or that he will.

But there he stands, leaning against a car in the pick-up line wearing sunglasses and a baseball hat. He looks every inch the incognito celebrity. But how else would he look? He can hardly show up wearing a concert tee and his guitar.

I feel lightheaded walking toward him.

Haze puts a hand on my arm, stopping me. "You don't have to see him, you know. You don't have to be civil. He never was."

Haze is right, of course. And yet I'm going to be pleasant anyway. Good girls always are. "I need to do this, okay?"

Haze regards me from beneath a lock of shiny black hair. He has a face built for tragedy, with shaded eyelids and coal-black lashes. "Aren't you angry?"

Why yes, I am. Livid, even. But I can't let Frederick know how I really feel, or he'd just hightail it back to California before I get a chance to… To what, exactly? Get to know him? State my case? Learn the truth?

Make him sorry?

"Just be careful, Rae," Haze says gruffly. "Call me for any reason. I'll come get you." He kisses me quickly, just a peck. Then stalks off, angling close to Frederick Richards, staring him down all the way.

I watch him go. Then I take a steadying breath and start again toward the man who is my father.

Frederick Richards takes off his sunglasses and stows them in his shirt pocket. "Is everything okay?"

"Yes," I say, just standing there, not sure whether he expects me to get into the car or not.

His eyes follow Haze toward the parking lot. "All right. I know it's hot, but do you feel like walking?"

"Sure?"

"If you want, you can stash the backpack in the car." He holds out a hand.

"Okay." I hand it over.

He opens the back door and puts my pack on the seat. Then he closes the door and turns to me.

"You can't park here," I have to point out. "They tow."

"Oh, it will be fine. Carlos will move the car if he needs to." He opens the passenger-seat door. "Stay cool, man. I'll call you."

"Okay, boss," comes a voice from inside.

My father grabs two bottles of water off the seat and hands one to me. Then he shuts the car door and tips his head toward the sidewalk that leads toward the sporting fields. "Shall we?"

My fingers fumble the cap on the water bottle as I keep pace with him.

"So this is your school. How is it?"

This is an easy question. I can do this. I take a swig of water. "Not bad. But Florida isn't known for excellent schools."

"It looks nice to me. My high school looked a lot like a jail, which I found to be a fitting metaphor."

"Not a fan of school, huh?"

My chirpy answer startles both of us. He gives me a quick smile. "Not so much. I was impatient. Thought I had more important places to be."

We are having an actual conversation. The walking is good—much better than sitting on plastic chairs in the social worker's office. Maybe he knew that when he asked me to walk.

"I hear you have big plans for next year," he says.

"Yeah, Claiborne Prep." The acceptance letter had meant everything to me for about a month. And then one morning my mother couldn't get out of bed, and everything went to hell. Frantic, I'd called 911. A couple of weeks later she was gone.

"That's a big decision," he says carefully. The sidewalk stretches toward the baseball diamond.

"Yeah…" I can't tell him my real reasons for wanting to go there. I can't explain that besides the excellent education, I'm dying to see the place where my story began. "My, uh, guidance counselor wanted me to go to private school. There aren't enough honors courses here."

That's true. But it's not the whole truth.

"Well, good for you. Claiborne is a nice town. I went to college there."

Of course I know that already. It says so right on Wikipedia. "It looks nice in the pictures," I say lamely.

He stops. "You've never been there?"

"Not since I was a baby. Then after I applied… It wasn't a good year to travel." My mother spent the winter lying on the sofa, getting thinner and losing her hair. But I hadn't panicked, because the chemo seemed to be shrinking her tumors.

He sucks in a breath. "Right." We continue along the walkway. The baseball team is practicing, but the bleachers are empty and shaded. He walks over to them and sits down, so I sit too. The ball players are engaged in some sort of complicated throwing drill, balls flying everywhere. Every few seconds the coach blows his whistle.

"Rachel…"

It's wild hearing him say my name. His speaking voice has the same rough timbre as his singing voice, and I've been studying the sound of it since forever.

"I can't even imagine the year you just had. And I can't decide whether it's rude to ask you to tell me about it, or rude not to ask."

There's no way I can talk to Frederick about my mother's death. I can barely think about it myself. So I say nothing.

"But I do need to ask you about this place you're staying. Do you feel safe there?"

I don't look at him. "It's not dangerous. It's a little gross, but nobody is trying to hurt me. And I'm the oldest one there."

"How is it gross?"

I look up at his face for half a second, but it makes me nervous. "It's just dingy. The kids that live there are depressing."

"But they leave you alone?"

"Pretty much. They go through my things when I'm not around. I was going to try to get more of my stuff out of our house. But now I think there's really no point. I had my own bottle of shampoo, and it disappeared. Things like that. It's just... little stuff."

"What if you had a trunk that locked?"

"It's not allowed."

He rubs his chin. "Well, that sounds craptastic. And you probably don't feel like yourself."

"Not really. No." As far as I can tell, I'm never going to feel like myself again, and it isn't the group home's fault. "It's a lot of small humiliations. Free lunch tickets. Not enough minutes in the shower." I finger my hair. It's shaggy and terrible.

"What's happening with your place on Pomelo Court?" he asks.

His mention of our house startles me. Of course he knows where we lived—he's been sending us a check there every month. He can probably rattle off the zip code.

It's just that he's never once stopped by.

I realize he's waiting for an answer. "Um, one of my mother's friends is taking care of things. Mary."

"Mary..." he repeats. His eyes are a warm shade of gray. That's something I never could quite tell from pictures of him. "Is this someone you trust?"

"Well, sure. She was Mom's best friend. She runs a salon in South Eola."

"Okay," he says, his face thoughtful. "Look. The social worker

26

and the lawyer tell me that until you turn eighteen in a month, there are only little things I can do for you. If you need to find your stuff, or hit your friend Mary's salon for another bottle of shampoo, I can help with that."

I put a hand to my stringy hair. "I would love to see Mary." In fact, I should have thought to visit her myself. "She's probably working, though."

He shrugs. "So, let's go. If she's too busy to talk today, you can go back tomorrow." He stands up, and I follow him.

I used to be the sort of person who found answers to problems. Now I'm somebody who life leads around by the elbow.

Chapter Three

BACK AT THE CAR, Frederick opens the back door and slides across the seat. I get in next to him.

The driver turns around to look at us, and I recognize him. He's the man who'd smiled at me from the car in Hannah's parking lot yesterday. "Hi, Rachel," he says. "I'm Carlos."

"Hi, Carlos."

"Where to?"

"East Washington Street?"

"Gotcha." He reaches for a GPS on the dash, although I could have told him where to go. "Hey, boss," he says, handing a phone over his shoulder to Frederick. "It's been dancing the Macarena."

"That's unfortunate." The car slides away from the curb while Frederick scrolls through messages on his phone. Then it rings in his hands. He taps the screen and puts the phone to his ear. "Henry. What now?" He listens for maybe two seconds before cutting Henry off. "I know that chaos makes you twitchy. But I've been your easy client for a decade. You've never bailed me out of jail, or FedExed me to the Betty Ford clinic, right? But for once I really need your help, and you act like I owe you something."

I stare out the window, feeling like an eavesdropper.

"I don't have answers for you yet. And I understand that I'm going to look like an asshole before this is over. But it is what it is. I have to go now." Frederick ends the call.

He throws the phone on the seat. "So, Carlos. How are the Dodgers doing?"

"Not good, boss," the driver answers, turning the radio up a notch. "It's going to be another humiliation."

"That seems to be a theme today."

———

The bell tinkles on the salon door when I open it. I don't know the young woman behind the counter. But Mary is in her usual spot near the window, with an elderly woman in her chair. I stop to watch, and Mary looks up.

"Rachel!" She puts down her scissors and comes running. "Oh, honey! Why aren't you in Atlanta with your aunt?"

This is not an easy question to answer, but I don't have to. Because Mary's eyes travel up and over my head, and then she gasps.

I turn around to see Frederick standing there in front of a display of haircare products. Straight-faced, he raises a hand and salutes the two of us.

Mary gets ahold of herself. "Come with me, sweetie. I have someone in my chair, but Megan is going to give you a nice shampoo, and you need conditioner. Then I'm going to trim you up while we talk, okay?" She cups my face in her hands and frowns. "You look awfully tired."

I allow myself be snapped into a salon gown and led to a sink. I tilt my head back onto the neck rest.

"You let me know if that's too hot," the girl says.

"Okay." I close my eyes while shampoo is massaged into my scalp. This is a nice salon, and Mom and I can only afford it because Mary gives us a deal. The shampoo girl takes her time, rubbing her thumbs on my temples, massaging the crown of my head. Her gentle touch has the unexpected effect of making me want to cry. Every swirl of hands through the soap threatens to break me.

"Just one more rinse," she says. And when I finally sit up again, I look around. Frederick has seated himself on a pink divan with a tufted footstool. He has a magazine open on his lap, and he's poking his phone with one finger.

"Come quick," Mary says. "My next client is always late. We can make this work."

"Thank you," I say, sitting in her chair.

Mary swivels the chair around, and the face that comes into view in the mirror looks so hollowed out that I recoil.

It's my own face.

"Oh, sweetie. Are you okay? You have to tell me what's going on. And you look so *thin*, Rachel."

I close my eyes. "I'm okay… It's just hard."

"That's your father?"

I nod. "I met him yesterday."

"Heavens. Your mother once told me who he was. But then she never brought it up again. Forgive me, this is going to sound awful. But I was never really sure she was serious."

Serious as cancer.

In the mirror, I see Mary's eyes sweep to the side as she checks Frederick out. "He sure is a looker. No wonder your mother…" She lets the sentence die.

I don't blame Mary for saying it. I've been trying to picture it myself—a twenty-one year-old Freddy, and a nineteen-year-old Mom. She was biding her time in New Hampshire, saving up for college. And he would have been a local star and a new graduate of the music school, just months away from breaking out nationally.

Somehow they met one night, maybe after one of his concerts. Together, they took off all their clothes and made a baby. And then he left for his first tour before Mom even knew what happened.

The mother I knew wasn't like that. She was the original Good Girl—attending nursing school while working full time, then working double shifts for the overtime pay. My mom could smell an incomplete homework assignment or a dirty dish from a block away.

The mom I knew had a tired smile, and didn't swoon for anyone.

"Since you're here, we should talk about the house," Mary says, her scissors working behind me. "The electricity is the only thing I left on. And the rent is paid up through August fifteenth."

"August fifteenth," I repeat.

Mary sets down her scissors and moves around the chair to face me. "If you need another month, we can tell the landlord. But I didn't think you'd want to spend your money on a house you're not living in."

"No, I…" I'm supposed to be heading to Claiborne soon after that. "That sounds fine."

"I'll pack the place up, Rachel," Mary whispers. "You don't have to do that. But there must be things in your room that you want to sort through, since you're still here. Are you going to Atlanta at all?"

My answer is slow. "I don't think so." My aunt Lisa had come to the funeral. The details of that day are patchy in my memory. The funeral home was packed, mostly with nurses from the hospital where my mother worked. My choir friends were there too, but I hadn't talked to them. I'd sat, numb, in the front row between Haze and the aunt I barely knew.

My mother's sister lives seven hours from Orlando. They weren't close, and I've met her only a couple of times. After the funeral, and a lunch arranged by Mary at which I ate nothing, my aunt Lisa drove back to Atlanta without me. She'd left it to Hannah Reeves to explain.

"You have just a couple of weeks of school left," Hannah had said in her ever-steady voice. "I know that your prep-school acceptance is very important to you, and that you need your grades. And Lisa told me she can't stay on in Orlando without losing her job."

It sounded logical enough until I met Hannah's gaze. It was the only time I'd seen her look anything but self-composed. For the barest moment, Hannah's hazel eyes got wet.

That's when I'd looked out of Hannah's car window for my first view of the Parson's Home for Children.

Hannah had taken a deep breath through her nose. "Rachel, this happens a lot. Your mother didn't expect the end to come so fast. Nobody ever does. She didn't think she'd die before you turned eighteen. And your aunt is in shock right now. I'm going to give her a week, and then I'll call her again to see if you can join her in Georgia when you're done with school."

But then Hannah tracked down Frederick instead, who surprised us both by showing up a few days later. And I still don't know what it means for me.

While Mary blow dries my hair, the next client arrives. Her handbag is an elaborate, quilted monstrosity. "Just one minute," Mary cries. "Listen, you call me any time," she whispers to me. "I'm always home by seven. Seriously, I want to hear from you."

"Thank you."

Mary waves off Frederick's payment.

"How about I leave a tip?" As I watch, he puts five twenties into a tiny salon envelope and leaves it at Mary's station. "Didn't you need shampoo?" he asks, jutting a thumb toward the wall of products.

"Well…" The things in Mary's shop are twenty-five bucks a bottle. My mom and I bought our shampoo at the drugstore, like normal people.

Mary snatches a bottle off a shelf and presses it into my hand. Then she gives Frederick a firm stare. "She needs to eat more often," she says. Then, to me: "Call me, sweetie. Any time."

———

An hour later, I sit on a chaise lounge under an umbrella beside the Ritz-Carlton hotel pool. With my math book in my lap and a pencil in my hand, I could almost be studying.

Except that Frederick is seated a couple of umbrellas away from me, growling into his phone.

Whoever Henry is, Frederick is unhappy with him. "Look, I get that the promoter has your balls in a vice. Otherwise you wouldn't be whining at me like a fucking girl. But this is only going to get worse before it gets better."

There's a lull, and I think maybe they're done arguing. But not yet. "Dude," Frederick says, his voice tight, "I need the calendar cleared, and you need to deal with the fallout. Rip the Band-Aid off, Henry. Do it now, or I'll hire someone who will."

Yikes.

And if Frederick needs his calendar cleared, is that because of me?

A waitress approaches, flashing a set of perfectly pearly teeth. "How are you doing today?"

"Fine, thanks," I say automatically. Her name tag reads *Heidi*. What would Heidi even do if I admitted that I was not at all fine?

"Can I bring you anything? A glass of lemonade? Iced tea?"

"No, thank you." This is a nicer hotel than the ones where Haze and I sneak in to use the swimming pool. A glass of tea is probably six bucks.

"Just wave me down if you change your mind." She gives me another brilliant smile and moves on.

As it happens, I end up ordering that tea an hour later, anyway.

"We're in a bit of a hurry," Frederick tells another smiling waitress as we sit down at a cafe table. "What can we order that comes out quick?"

"Steer clear of the pizza," she advises. "Salads and burgers don't take as long."

"Gotcha. Pizza at a hotel is a pretty dicey proposition, anyway. Okay, I'll have a burger, medium rare. And fries."

I order the Cobb salad. And when she walks away, a silence

falls over us. Frederick fidgets with his roll of silverware. I watch a young father in the swimming pool. He stands in the shallow end, encouraging his little girl. "You can do it! Kick!"

The child is wearing pink swim fins and a Mickey Mouse bathing suit. Frederick notices them too. The swimming dad plucks the little girl out of the water and whirls her around. "Whee!" he says. "Whee!" And then he says it ten more times.

I feel like throwing my overpriced iced tea at them.

That's when Carlos approaches our table with a little black shopping bag. He deposits it in front of Frederick.

"Would you bring the car around in fifteen?" Frederick asks. "We're going to have to dine and dash."

"Sure thing." Carlos gives me a face-cracking smile as he turns away.

Frederick reaches into the bag and pulls out a phone, which he hands to me. "This is for you. So I can get in touch with you."

I look down at the sleek thing in my hands. It's a brand new iPhone, in a jaunty orange case.

"If you want to keep your old number, my assistant can look into that," he says.

I swipe the screen and it flashes to life, the apps popping into view like little jewels. It's the phone that Mom and I never would have splurged on, not in a million years.

A surge of irrational disgust washes over me. I find myself wondering what Frederick would do if I said it wasn't the right color. Or if I turned and threw it into the pool.

Would he yell at me and make a scene? His reaction might tell me something about him that I can't learn from watching carefully edited YouTube videos.

I rub the shiny new thing with my thumb and wonder if Frederick Richards would hightail it out of Florida if his daughter was a spoiled brat. I should have ordered lobster and champagne, just to gauge his reaction. Haze is right, I don't *have* to be nice.

But I feel my father's gaze on me. And I know I won't do any of those things, because I'm not that girl. I don't throw seven-hundred-dollar objects into chlorinated water, or make demands.

And my good manners aren't even the reason. I want Frederick to like me.

And I hate myself for wanting that.

"Thank you," I whisper. Lifting my chin, I say it again. "Thank you. For everything today."

He looks away, his mouth flattening into a line. "It's nothing."

The food arrives, and I eat a little, but mostly push the salad around in its bowl.

"I'll get you home by curfew," Frederick says, putting a french fry back down on his plate. He isn't really hungry either. After he signs the check, I stand up, hefting my backpack. We've taken only one step toward the lobby when a tanned man in a golf shirt walks up, his arm on his son's shoulder. "I'm sorry," he says, smiling, "but we're such big fans. Could we get your autograph?"

"Uh, sure," Frederick says, digging into his pocket for a pen.

The boy looks to be about middle-school age, and he removes his baseball cap and hands it to Frederick. "Thanks," he says, his voice cracking. He looks embarrassed.

But so does Frederick. A wrinkle appears in the center of his forehead. "Who's this?" he says, pointing at a signature on one side of the bill.

The dad laughs. "Ryan Braun."

Frederick nods. "You're Brewers fans? At least you don't root for the Cubs." He signs the hat quickly and hands it back with a wink. "We're in a bit of a hurry…"

"Thanks so much," the dad says, stepping back. His smile is like a toothpaste ad.

"Sorry," Frederick mutters to me as we stride across the lobby. "I see Carlos waiting outside."

"So..." Frederick says as the sedan slides to a stop outside the Parson's Home.

So... I grip the hem of my denim skirt, wondering what happens next. He's about to say that he's booked on the next flight to L.A. And a good chunk of me will be okay with that, because every minute I spend in his presence is as stressful as auditioning for a solo in choir.

"Same time tomorrow?" he says instead.

A knot in my chest unties, and I'm stunned by how relieved I suddenly feel. I don't even know why. I've made it this far without him. He isn't somebody that I ought to rely on. "I need to spend some extra time in the school library on my math review," I hear myself say.

"No problem," he says quickly. "If I picked you up later, I could still make sure you got some dinner."

"They don't starve me here, you know." The ungrateful words just pop out. Though I've waited my whole life for him to invite me to dinner.

Frederick looks past me at the building's gray vinyl siding and dirty windows. He doesn't bother trying to disguise his look of disapproval.

My face gets hot, as if the scuzzy building is my own fault.

He turns his gray-eyed gaze on me. "Have dinner with me tomorrow," he says, "because I'm busy on Saturday."

I fold quicker than a broken umbrella. "Okay. Thanks. I'll see you tomorrow." I opened the door.

"Text me a time," he calls after me. "Carlos put my number and his in your phone."

"Okay!" I run from his car into the Parson's Home at 7:32. The light-blue beater parked at the curb gives an angry stab at the horn as I go inside. But I've run out of time.

It's against the rules to use a phone after curfew, and Evie would happily rat me out. But later, under the covers, my hair smelling like a salon, I fiddle with my new toy. I log into Instagram, and the photos are crisp and bright on the shiny screen.

And this is weird—Freddy Ricks posted a photo of the Pacific Ocean a couple hours ago, just as we were having an awkward meal under a hotel umbrella, more than two thousand miles from the Pacific. *Nice day for a run on the beach,* my father supposedly wrote. The hashtags are #oceanlover and #californiadreaming.

I feel a weird prickly sensation creep across my skull. I've been following his Instagram account forever. And it's not even him?

From memory, I tap Haze's number into my new phone and text him: ***Sorry about tonight. Ran out of time.*** I have to sign it R.K. because Haze won't recognize the new number.

His reply is instant. ***I waited for U. Everything OK?***

I'm fine. It's a terse answer, so I add a heart emoticon. But that's all I write, since I'm too tired to go another round on the subject of spending time with my father.

My phone buzzes a minute later. ***I miss U.***

I close the texting app and spend a couple of minutes adding my email account to my fancy new phone. It populates with a startling number of messages, many of them condolences from teachers I've had over the years. I can't read those right now. If they say anything nice about my mom, I'll end up crying myself to sleep.

Only one message is cheerful. It's from Jake, the boy from Claiborne.

Hey Rachel!

It's not that weird at all that you're showing up just for senior year. A lot of people come for junior or senior year, because CPrep looks good on college applications. And CPrep students have an easier time getting into Claiborne College up the road. Both my parents are professors there, so if I get rejected it's going to be awwwwkward.

My parents are spending the year in Glasgow, so I'll be living in the dorm for the first time. I'm a little nervous about the roommate thing, too. But seniors' rooms are pretty big, which helps.

Music groups—I wouldn't know a glee club from a choir to save my soul. But I do know the a cappella groups have auditions. They treat it like a sorority. You don't "try out" you "rush" them. The only reason I know this is from their overly cute little flyers on the dining hall tables. You'll see.

I hope you're having a nice summer. I'm on Cape Cod with my parents this month and working lots of hours at a clam shack. The pay is good but I smell like fried fish all the time. I keep rewashing the uniform T-shirt, trying to get the smell out. But it's fried onto the cotton. *Sexy.*

The other bummer is that Cape Cod isn't as dark as New Hampshire. I'm an astronomy nut. (Nerd powers, activate!) I brought my telescope all the way here, but there's more light pollution here than I expected. I can't always see the fainter stars, even during a new moon.

I know. First world problems.

Keep the questions coming,

Best,

Jake

It feels like another lifetime since I'd read his first letter. But it has only been a few hours. I tap out a reply with my fingertip.

Dear Jake,

It's nice of you to answer my questions. I still need to know what I should bring with me. Do they send out a packing list?

Astronomy, huh? I don't know any other astronomy buffs. Of course I've been to Cape Canaveral on school trips, and I've seen rocket launches (you can see them from 100 miles away.) But that isn't really the same thing.

Looking through a telescope sounds peaceful. Isn't it true that everything we see in the night sky is really a million years old, or something? That's a comforting thought, actually. Lately my life is happening at warp speed, when I wish it wouldn't.

Bye for now,

Rachel

That's as much truth as I can put into a note to a stranger. After hitting send, I tuck the new phone under my pillow and try to sleep.

Chapter Four

THE NEXT AFTERNOON, I work math problems in the library until the five thirty closing time. The only distraction is Haze, who sits beside me, sulking.

All my exams will be finished in a week or so. And my library job is almost over too. The rest of my summer is about to become a gaping void, with my eighteenth birthday in the middle of it.

My first birthday without Mom. I can't even think about that right now.

I get a new email from Jake, which helps.

Rachel,

It's nice of you to say that astronomy sounds "peaceful" because plenty of other people would say "boring." To me it's exciting, but then again I'm weird. I like that astronomy is both accessible to everyone (Walk outside, look up at the sky) and utterly remote at the same time.

In the way of a true nerd boy, though, allow me to correct your understanding of how old the stuff in the sky is. Like you said, some of the things we can see are really old news. There's a red supergiant called Betelgeuse (not to be confused with the weird

Winona Ryder movie) that's about 640 lightyears away. So tonight's view of it is from 640 years ago.

That star is probably already dead. I'm actually hoping it finally exploded, say, 639 years ago so I'll soon get to see it happen with my own eyes.

On the other hand, Sirius (not to be confused with Harry Potter's godfather) is just 8.6 lightyears away. So our view of that star is from a time when the Nintendo wii was still cutting edge.

When you look up at the stars, you're getting a mixed view of the ancient and new all mashed together. Like someone photoshopped the sky.

Your last message made it sound like your summer isn't going so well. Hope things get better.

You will get a packing list during August. Some people also bring a coffee pot or a popcorn machine, even though it's against the rules. Lots of Claiborne rules aren't followed or enforced.

It's time for me to go sell fried clams to drunk people.

Cheerio!

J.

"Who's that guy?" Haze asks from right over my shoulder, where he's obviously been reading my email.

"He's…" I try to remember how Jake put it in his first letter. "A peer liaison. Or something. From the prep school. To answer my questions."

Even as I stutter out my explanation, Haze's expression goes sour. "Awfully friendly, isn't he?"

"Shouldn't he be?" I challenge. "Would it be better if the people at my new school were assholes?"

"No." Haze grins because he thinks it's funny when I curse. "I guess not. Bunch of preppies, though. They can't be very much fun. Astronomy?" He makes a face.

I close my laptop, feeling irritable. Somewhere there's a boy named Jake standing on a beach in Massachusetts and waiting for a star to explode. I have a picture of him in my mind, staring up at the sky, his hands jammed in his pockets.

My subconscious has made him cute, in a harmless kind of way. With sandy hair and blue eyes. I could probably find a social media account with pictures of him. But I don't think I will. It's more fun not knowing.

Haze closes the book he's supposedly reading and stands up. It's five thirty—time to meet Frederick for dinner.

We walk out of the building, and I'm feeling nervous again.

"You know," Haze says. "You could blow him off today. If you just didn't show up, what could he really say? 'Hey, Rachel! You stood me up! Oh, I'm sorry, Dad. If I do it a thousand days in a row, we'll be even.'"

Six thousand days, I correct. *Or sixty-five hundred.* "I don't think I can make you understand."

"You're right, you can't."

"He's here now, and he wants to help." It sounds better than the truth, which was a more complicated heap of burning curiosity and a decade and a half of waiting to be seen.

"Rachel, *I* help you."

"That is the truth," I admit. "And we will hang out on Saturday, after your shift at the garage."

He walks with me until Frederick comes into view, waiting by the car again. Then Haze stalks away, staring.

"A friend of yours?" Frederick asks when I make my way over to him.

"Yes. Since forever."

"He looks disgruntled."

I slide into the car, smiling at the understatement. "You're right. He's not...gruntled."

In the front seat, Carlos laughs.

"Isn't that weird?" I hear myself begin to ramble. "Some negative words sound like they're the opposite of a positive one, but they're not."

Frederick scratches his chin. "You mean like...nonplussed?"

"Exactly. Not every negative has a positive."

He grunts. "Sure they do. It's just not the positive that you're expecting." He takes his beat-up little notebook out of his pocket, flips it open and begins to scrawl on the page. "But that is a fun idea. I love idiosyncrasies."

"What do you do with those notes?" As I say this, I realized it's the first question I've asked him about himself. The question I really want to ask is, *How did you get my mother pregnant?*

But I'm afraid he won't like me asking. And I'm afraid I won't like the answer.

"A whole lot of nothing, usually," he says, scribbling in the little book. "But once in a while, I get a song out of it."

And then his phone rings, and I listen to another one-sided call with Henry. "Isn't that what we pay Publicist Becky for, to think up this crap?" my father asks him. "You two just pick something, and I don't care what it is. A stomach bug. A drug problem. Tell them I was abducted by aliens. I'm hanging up now."

He ends the call, but his fists are clenched in his lap all the way to the restaurant.

———

Thai food tonight. I sit at another outdoor restaurant table, trying not to fidget. Frederick is across from me, and I still wonder if he's a mirage. This is my third time in his presence. This could go two ways—someday it might seem normal to walk into a room and see Frederick there. Or, more probably, he'll disappear again.

Ten years from now when someone asks me about my father, I might say, "I met him three times when I was seventeen. We had pad thai at a table facing a golf course, and I didn't have the courage to ask him how I was conceived."

Frederick has come prepared with a more neutral topic of conversation. "What classes do you want to take at Claiborne Prep?"

"Well…" I haven't thought about that in weeks. "The English

classes looked cool. There's one for Russian literature. I guess I'll keep taking Spanish for the language requirement." *And music.* But I'm not ready to share that.

Which is funny, because I always imagined that when I met my father, we would talk of nothing *but* music. In my fantasy, he would be touched to discover we had so much in common. And he'd be devastated that he'd wasted so much time.

But now? Music is the last thing I wanted to share about myself. If I tell him I arranged one of his favorites—the Stones' "You Can't Always Get What You Want"—for my junior choir project, in four-part harmony with counterpoint, he'll know exactly how deeply my hero worship runs.

How utterly humiliating.

"I wasn't the student you are," my father is saying. "I almost flunked out my first year of college."

"Did you?" But I know this already, having read it in an interview in *Spin.*

"The required classes almost killed me. But I was able to hang on long enough until they'd let me take all music courses. I scraped by."

I know so much about him already—that he likes old movies and fresh-squeezed orange juice. I'd read that he'd once played for an Obama campaign rally, and that he's allergic to cilantro. I know that his stage name—Freddy Ricks—came about because his friend Ernie thought it sounded "less constipated" than Frederick Richards.

"I wish I'd known there was no need to be so impatient," he says. "I wish I had it to do over again. That and a whole lot of other things."

Like what else? I wait for him to elaborate.

"How's the chicken?" he asks instead.

Angry Rachel lets out a silent scream.

———

"Two things," Frederick says after they clear our plates away. "I'm going to New Orleans tonight."

My stomach drops. "Okay."

"Christ," he says. "I'm coming back." He lifts his chin and looks at the sky. "Not that you'd have any reason to believe me."

My face feels felt hot. I take another sip of my soda.

"Look," Frederick says, picking up his beer. "I canceled a bunch of gigs already. But this one would piss off too many important people. But I think they're done with me by Sunday night."

A concert? I wonder. *Headlining a music festival?* Later I can look this up on his website the way I used to. Hell, I can even use the fancy new phone he gave me.

In a burst of courage, I ask a question. "Why did you cancel some things?"

He takes a swig. "So I could be here in Orlando for a couple of weeks."

"Yes, but *why?*" The question finally flies out of Angry Rachel's mouth. I clamp my jaws together again to prevent five more questions from following it. *Do you really care what happens to me? Did you know my mother at all before you had a one-night stand? Why didn't you call us for almost eighteen years?*

Frederick studies his beer bottle as if the answer is written there. "Last week, Hannah gave you a swab..."

"For a DNA test." I'd been surprised that a Q-tip against the inside of my cheek was all it took. How anticlimactic.

"It was for the judge. I hired a lawyer to try to get custody."

My heart begins to ricochet inside my chest. "But Hannah said that wouldn't work."

"But maybe she's wrong. You want to get out of that place you're staying, right?"

"Of course."

"The lawyer I found was more than happy to try." He reaches around to pull something out of his back pocket. A folded paper.

"No surprises here, but I thought you might want to see the lab report." He smooths the paper onto the table.

The report is titled: "Motherless Paternity Test Results."

Motherless.

"This number here is the only one that matters," Frederick says, pointing to the bottom of the page. *Probability = 99.998.* "So that means…"

"I know what a probability is." It comes out sounding snappish.

"Of course you do," he says softly.

I don't need him to tell me that it's conclusive. I don't need the test at all. If my mother admitted, however grumpily, that Frederick was my father, then he is.

"So…" I clear my throat. "Unless you have an identical twin…" I would have added, *you're stuck with me.* But of course he isn't. He can disappear any time.

He refolds the paper and puts it away. "That's just for court, Rachel. I never had any doubt."

Really? How did you know? And then where have you been?

And—the biggest question in my heart—*how long are you going to stick around?*

Carlos appears beside our table. "Ten after seven, boss."

I thank Frederick for dinner like a good girl.

Chapter Five

I SPEND the first half of Saturday studying in a Starbucks, waiting for Haze to finish a shift at the Jiffy Lube. It's the most civilized escape from the Parson's Home that I could come up with. Unfortunately, I had to bring along a backpack crammed full of books and a giant garbage bag full of my dirty laundry.

I've never felt more like a homeless person than I do right now, concealing my laundry under the cafe table. To cheer myself up, I tap out a reply to Jake's email.

> Jake,
>
> One thing you said put me in a tailspin—that some of the many rules are followed, and some aren't. How does someone with a good-girl complex know what to do?
>
> R.

I've only read a few pages of my book when a new message appears in my inbox. When I see Jake's name, I feel a little rush of happiness. And it's been a pretty long time since I felt that way. After glancing out the window to make sure that Haze isn't here yet, I read it quickly.

Rachel,

Hi again! Sorry to confuse you. But it isn't so tricky.

The academic rules are really important and nobody breaks those. They make you sign an ethics code about cheating and plagiarism and stuff like that. Cheating is a BFD here, so people don't do it.

But the social stuff is squishier. Lots of dorm rules are bent all the time. Example: the dorm curfew rules aren't followed. Anyone who's caught in someone else's room after hours can just say they were working on a group project, because homework is sacred. :)

The rules exist (I assume) so that the flagrant and irresponsible can be punished. Like the lacrosse players last year who were dumb enough to use the school's own messaging system to advertise their kegger in a dorm basement when their resident advisor went home to his brother's wedding.

In my experience, you have to be an idiot to get in real trouble. Anyone who's the least bit careful (or has a good girl streak!) will be fine. -J.

P.S. I'm jealous of your Cape Canaveral access. But Astronomy Nerd Central would be somewhere like New Mexico, with its big telescope arrays and meteorite fields. Trivia: there has never been a meteorite found in New Hampshire. Although I've picked up about a million rocks trying.

I adjust my mental picture of Jake on the beach. Now he's picking up rocks, examining them, then tossing them into the waves.

His messages are like an escape hatch from my real life. They make Claiborne Prep seem like a real place. And when I read his messages, I can almost believe that the earth is still turning around the sun, and that I'm really going to a fancy new school in the fall.

At one o'clock, Haze finally pulls up outside to rescue me. I cram my laundry into his trunk and then fall into the passenger seat.

He moves fast, reaching across the center console to pull me toward him. The kiss takes me by surprise. And maybe because I'm so happy to see him, the slide of his lips over mine has a brand new effect on me—an unexpected zing through my chest.

Haze deepens the kiss, and the taste of him is warm and familiar. The longer it goes on, the more I forget to be nervous.

But then Haze makes a noise. It's a guttural, needy sound from deep in his chest. My comfort stutters. His arms feel more like a vise than a hug, and I stiffen inside them.

Haze releases me then, and we both take a giant breath. "I smell like motor oil," he says, looking down at the mechanic's shirt he's still wearing from his shift at the Jiffy Lube. "Sorry."

Self-conscious now, I sit back and put on my seatbelt. A moment later the car pulls away from the curb.

———

I'd asked Haze to take me to a laundromat because I'd missed the Parson's Home laundry day. He's brought his own too. Side by side, we load our things into washers.

Haze strips off his shirt right there in the Kleen & Bean. And suddenly I didn't know where to put my eyes. Haze used to be a skinny kid with the occasional zit on his chin. But somehow he's become awfully ripped when I wasn't paying attention. All that muscle and smooth, coppery skin.

"Where's Daddy today?" he asks, tossing his shirt into the washer.

"I told him I was busy." The lie just pops out. Nothing good ever comes of discussing Frederick with Haze.

"I just don't get that guy. He's too good for you for seventeen years. And now he wants to spend every afternoon with you? Is there some reason why he waited until Jenny was out of the way?"

"Haze! He didn't know she was sick."

He rolls his dark eyes at me. The lashes are incredibly long for a boy's. "He didn't know, because he never *asked*. And now you're the center of his universe? It doesn't smell right to me."

"What are you saying, Haze? That Frederick is creepy? He's not."

"Are you sure?"

"Okay." I slam my washer door. "In the first place, *ick*. Where do you get these ideas? And in the second place, it's kind of an insult to me if you're saying I wouldn't notice."

Haze puts up both hands defensively. "Easy. Nobody is smarter than you, Rachel. But from where I stand, it looks a little like taking candy from a stranger. Because he is. A stranger, I mean."

Well, that's depressingly true.

"I mean, he's too good to drive his own *car*." Haze laughs. "What's up with that? What does he want from you, anyway?"

I walk over to the change machine so I won't have to admit that I don't know.

Haze has a poor opinion of fathers, anyway. His own had killed himself when Haze was twelve and I was eleven. One day, his dad drove his old blue car over to the Sunshine Skyway Bridge, parked it, and then jumped off.

My mother cried for a week afterward. "At least he didn't do it at home," she said. But she also said, "Men don't think they owe anybody anything. They leave the women to pick up the pieces."

Haze's mom, unfortunately, has not picked them up too carefully. The extra time Haze spent over at my house after that was directly correlated with the amount of wine his mother drank.

The old blue car waited on blocks for four years until Haze was old enough to drive it. In the glove compartment Haze keeps the note his father left for him there. It reads: *Hazario—This isn't your fault. Don't ever let anybody tell you otherwise. Papa.*

The change machine eats the first dollar I put into it, giving nothing in return. I plunge my thumb down on the cancel button, with no result. I stare at that machine for a full minute, wondering if it would be madness to put another dollar in. Having no obvious alternative, I try it. Somehow, four quarters come shooting into the steel cup.

While our washers and then our dryers spin, Haze and I wait on plastic chairs. My math book sits open on my lap the whole time, but my concentration is shot. Since my mother entered the hospital three weeks ago, every minute of every day demands two dollars for four quarters.

———

"It would be great to go swimming right now," Haze says when our clothes are finally dry and folded. "Want to sneak into the Sheraton? I have the key card in the car."

"I don't have a suit."

"Where is it?"

"At my house."

He puts his car in gear and turns right out of the laundromat parking lot, toward our neighborhood.

I have not been down these side streets in ten days. I watch the low roofs and parched lawns slide by; they're as familiar as breathing. But when he pulls to a stop in front of my house, I can only stare at the thing.

"You have the key, right?"

I pull it out, then look back at the little green vinyl house, which my mother had deemed "a half-step up from a trailer." Its windows and doors are shut tight, like a tomb. There are discount fliers moldering on the porch, and the mailbox has a piece of yellow tape on it.

My throat begins to burn. The remnants of my life are waiting inside. On two hooks in the kitchen, our favorite coffee mugs still hang. I can cross the street and walk inside. But I'd be waiting for a familiar voice to call out from the kitchen. *Hi, honey.*

And it won't come.

"Let's not go swimming," I whisper, turning away from the window. "I don't think I want to."

Haze's eyes get soft. He reaches over and puts a hand on my shoulder. "Come here."

I allow myself to be pulled in. I push my face into his hot neck, and he massages my back. I lean into him, his solid frame holding me up, steeling me against all the things that are wrong.

Haze kisses me on the temple. "How about if I go inside and get your suit for you?"

"Okay. I don't think I can do it."

He takes the keys out of my hand. "Where is it?"

I sit up. "Top drawer of my dresser."

"Be right back."

———

The pool at the Sheraton is enormous, and I slip into one of the many bathrooms to change. Haze brought me a tiny bikini. Of course he did.

"Room 305." Haze flashes his key card at a bored guy who hands over two towels.

"Now this is better," Haze says, chucking the towels and his car keys onto a lounge chair. I stash my clothes under the adjacent chair and follow him to the pool's edge. We both jump in, dunking quickly under water to emerge smiling at each other.

"Okay," I agree. "This was a good idea." A Nerf football floats nearby. I pick it up, then look around for its owner. Nobody seems to miss it. "Haze, go deep."

For a solid hour, I forget about everything except playing in the water. The pool narrows in the center, where four concrete lions spit streams of water into the channel. I've always wondered about this design. Lions aren't famous for spitting. When Haze gets near enough to one of them, I give his shoulder a shove at just the right moment. He gets an earful.

"You!" He laughs, splashing me.

"It's just lion spit." His response is to dive under the water and grab my feet out from under me.

He comes up, cradling me in both arms. He shakes the water from his hair like a dog until I laugh. "Now who's going under the lion spit? Hmm?"

"No!" I shriek while he douses me under first one and then another lion.

Then he kisses me on the mouth, and it's a kiss that means business. He pulls me against his chest, and his hands dig into my backside. I feel *caught*, and I don't like it.

Overwhelmed, I pull away as gently as I can. "I don't want to make a scene," I say by way of an explanation.

He exhales. "I wouldn't mind."

We're sitting on lounge chairs, drying off, when Haze clears his throat. "There's something I need to ask you."

"Hmm?" My attention is still on my math book.

Haze puts a hand on my knee. "Rachel, look at me."

I look up into his brooding eyes. "What?"

He gives my knee a meaningful squeeze. "When you turn eighteen, I want you to come and stay with me."

I blink. "Stay...where?"

"With me. Until it's time for you to go off to school."

I try to picture this. Haze lives in a tiny house with his drunk mother. Where would they even put me? On the couch where his mom sits all day long?

Haze's gaze is penetrating, and his thumb strokes my knee.

No—sleeping on the couch isn't his plan at all. "Haze, I'm not sure I can do that."

"You can do anything you want," he whispers.

Now there's a terrifying idea.

"It would only be for a couple of weeks, until you go to New Hampshire." He moves from his chair onto the edge of mine. "Please." He takes my hand and holds it in both of his.

For a second, we just stare at each other. Nothing in my life is ever going to be the same. But he's still here, holding my hand. "I'll think about it," I whisper. And you can bet I will.

And for a few beats of my heart, I get a little stuck in the bright beam of attention he's focused on me. His eyes crinkle at the edges, as if he's on the verge of smiling.

But instead, he leans forward and kisses me again.

————

When I climb into my saggy bed at the Parson's Home Sunday night, it's hard to sleep. My thoughts are like the Astro Orbiter ride at the Magic Kingdom—turning too fast for comfort. My mom, Frederick, Haze, and my little green house all whirled by, daring me to dwell on them.

And tomorrow is my math exam.

Across the room, Evie begins to snore, so I pull my old iPod out from beneath my pillow and press the ear buds into my ears. Setting it to Shuffle, I hit Play.

I've always loved the moment of anticipation before a song begins—that beat of silence that yawns with expectation. There's an eerie intimacy that comes from plugging a song directly into two holes in the sides of your head. Sometimes I can even hear the vocalist take a breath before the first note. The effect is like being in the room with them.

Eyes closed, I wait. And when the first strummed chord charges through those fine little wires and into my ears, I'm not even surprised that it's one of Frederick's. I've been wearing a groove in this song since fifth grade. The opening riff for "Wild City" is as familiar as air.

Then his voice comes in, sad and low:

> She liked to turn the amp up louder
> Her hips would sway and I'd forget the chords.
> Nobody else could wield that power
> I drank it down and begged for more

This music has always been my only connection to him. And in a weird way, he's never let me down. I push Play, and my father shows up every time.

And now? I don't know what will happen. I only know that if Frederick doesn't show up after school tomorrow, this refrain will never sound the same to me.

Late nights in the Wild City
My ears would ring for years
Bright lights in the Wild City
We paid for it in tears

Chapter Six

ON MONDAY AFTERNOON I ace my pre-calc exam. The relief lasts a good fifteen minutes. After that, I go outside to see whether Frederick will really turn up again as he'd promised.

I think I'll *always* wonder—even if Frederick stays in my life after I leave Florida. A little piece of me will always be sitting here on the bench outside school, wondering if today is the day he decides I'm not worth the trouble.

There are three cars in the pick-up circle. And none of them is a black sedan.

Okay. Carlos is probably stuck in tourist traffic.

I check my new phone again. No messages. No texts. But I find a Google news alert on "Freddy Ricks." When I tap on it, the headline stuns me. *Freddy Ricks cancels nine tour stops, including a sold-out show at Madison Square Garden.*

Seriously? I click the link to the article and read:

> Citing tendinitis in the thumb and two fingers of his picking hand, the singer songwriter will be refunding tickets at all locations. "He'll have an outpatient procedure, and some therapy,"

publicist Rebecca Showers told the media.

"Freddy should be as good as new by October."

That's all it says.

In my peripheral vision, somebody waves his arms.

Looking up, I spot Carlos standing beside a tan SUV that I'd never seen before, and gesturing wildly in my direction. I get up and run toward the car.

He showed up again. Fourth time. But I won't get used to it.

When I open the car door, I hear Frederick's phone voice. "Henry, I *would* have more time to speak with you, except the lawyer you hired for me just kept me waiting an hour in his office. So make it quick."

As I slide onto the seat, Frederick raises a hand in greeting, giving me the universal sign for *just a minute.* "Wouldn't it cost just as much to fight the union contracts as it would to just pay them out? Uh-huh. Well, we knew we were going to take a hit."

I arrange my backpack at my feet, all the while sneaking looks at his right hand. As I watch, he makes a fist and beats his own forehead.

"Honestly, Henry. All I care about is whether my Taylor is going to turn up today. No, I'm not rubbing your nose in it. I just need to know. Text Carlos the tracking number? Thanks." With his right thumb, he ends the call and then proceeds to whack the phone against his leg in agitation.

His hand is fine.

He turns weary eyes to me. I've always assumed his life is nothing but fun. Music and adoration all day and all night.

Today he doesn't look like a guy who's having fun.

"Sorry about that," he says. "How was the weekend?"

"Okay. I finished with pre-calculus. I did the laundry."

He gives me a weary grin. "Par-tay."

"It was pretty wild. I have a killer hangover." I watch his reaction. As far as he knows, I might *have* a killer hangover.

He doesn't even blink. "Hey, I thought up a word for you. Inferior."

"Uh, what?" Did he just call me inferior?

"A negative without a positive. You can't be ferior, right?"

"Oh!" I laugh nervously. "Actually, in my case you can. I'm very ferior. Ask anyone."

I get a tired smile before his phone buzzes again. He looks at the display and then shoves it in his pocket.

"The movie on the plane was the last Harry Potter," Frederick says as we walk the grounds at his fancy hotel. "Have you seen those?"

"Sure. But the books are better."

"Right? The *Hobbit* movies were better, though. Even though they didn't stick to the book."

"Yeah?" I wonder what he thinks of the song Ed Sheeran wrote for *The Hobbit*, and whether he's as impressed as I am that Sheeran played every instrument on the recording, except for the cello.

But I'm not ready to out myself as a music nerd, not to a man who hasn't said a single thing about his music to me. "How was New Orleans?" I try. On my new phone, I've already scoped out the music festival where he played over the weekend. His Instagram account has new photographs on it, one of him with his arm around a legendary blues guitar player, and one of a po' boy sandwich. Hashtag: ILoveNOLA.

"It was *hot*," he grumbles. "With mosquitoes the size of your head."

So the concert was outdoors? I swallow back the question. I don't want to sound like a fan girl. And he never brings up his job. Or his *life*. The silence makes me feel as if he's still trying to figure out if I'm worthy of his inner circle.

The phone in his pocket begins to do its angry buzzing thing again, and he plucks it out to glance at the screen. "Aw, Christ," he curses, rubbing the back of his neck. "I'm sorry, Rachel. I have to take this one." He holds the phone to his ear. What he says next makes something go wrong in my stomach.

"Hey, Dad."

Wow.

In the first place, I've never said those words to anybody. And...my grandfather is on the phone? It had occurred to me before that I might have a living grandparent or two. But since Richards is a common name, Google didn't help when I tried searching.

"You saw that headline, huh?" My father chuckles. "Dad, there's nothing wrong with my hand. If I were having surgery, I'd tell you." He steps off the path and into the scrubby trees nearby.

He obviously wants privacy, so I hang back a little. But I can still hear him.

"Dad, listen. There's nothing wrong with me. That was just an excuse to free up my calendar. I've got some things to deal with, and I can't really talk about it right now." My father looks over his shoulder, catching me snooping. "Tell Mom I'm fine. I'll call her soon." He drifts farther ahead. "I'm fine, I swear. Could you please convince Mom? And I'll tell you the whole tale as soon as I can."

He ends the call and then turns around with an expression I can't read. "You have grandparents," he says in a quiet voice. "They're going to want to meet you. There's, um..." He looks out across the fake lake, where an egret is flying past, its long legs trailing in the air. "There's too much going on right now. But we'll make that happen sometime soon."

I felt a little unsteady on my feet just imagining it. And I realize something. "They don't know about me," I blurt out. His own parents don't know he has a kid?

Frederick pinches the bridge of his nose with two fingers and gives his head a slow shake.

"*Wow.*" I can't keep the dismay out of my voice. I'm his deepest, darkest secret. We just stand there for a moment, staring at each other. A golf cart passes us, with two guys inside laughing together.

Do not cry, I order myself as I turn around. I can't look at him right now. I've always felt invisible to him. I'm used to being ignored. But hiding me from his parents feels bigger than that. Like he's *ashamed*. Of me.

Breathing carefully through my nose, I walk slowly back toward the hotel. He falls into step with me. *Grandparents*. I don't have any of those. My mom's mother died when I was four, and I barely remember her. Mom's father had passed before I was born.

Wondering what they might look like, I risk a glance at Frederick. His jaw is set, his mouth in a grim line. If ever there was a moment he regretted coming to Florida to meet me, this is it.

When I think I can speak, I ask a question. It's not the biggest one in my heart, but it's a start. "Why did you lie about your hand?"

"Because canceling concerts makes people angry. I needed a good reason."

"And I'm not a good reason?"

He stops walking. "Of course you're the reason. But I just submitted a petition for custody. If both our faces end up on the *US Weekly* website, I don't think it helps my case."

"Oh," I say stupidly.

We walk the rest of the way back to the hotel in silence. As we enter the lobby, Frederick casts a grumpy look toward the hotel restaurant. "What if we got takeout food tonight? I sent Carlos to UPS for a package."

"Sure, thanks."

Frederick pushes the elevator button. I follow him up to the fourth floor and down a corridor. Are we going to his room? That's a little too much togetherness if he's in such a dark mood.

But when he opens the door, the place is palatial. There's a big living and dining room, and a kitchen area that looks like nobody has ever cooked anything there. The bedroom is through a doorway at the other end of the room.

"There's a balcony," Frederick grunts. "If you want a quiet place for homework."

I hightail it out there with my English take-home exam, leaving the door ajar. I take a seat in one of the two patio chairs pulled up to a glass table.

As I sit, thinking about how to answer an essay question about Kafka's *Metamorphosis*, I hear a knock on Frederick's hotel room door.

"Hey! You found it! *This* is what I need tonight. Let's see if she survived." I swivel around to watch him take a big box from Carlos and carry it over to the gleaming dining table. Carlos hands him a pocket knife, and Frederick slits the tape on the box.

"Quieres burritos?" Carlos asks. "I found this place downtown. If I go now, we can make it."

"Hey, Rachel?" Frederick calls. "How do you feel about burritos?"

I stand up and poke my head into the room. "Si, yo quiero."

Carlos chuckles. "Carne? Cerdo? Pollo?"

"Pork," I choose.

"Surprise me," Frederick says. "I just hope it tastes like L.A."

"Let's not ask for a miracle." Carlos turns for the door.

"Carlos?" my father calls after him. "Text Henry and tell him the guitar he lost is found again."

"Already done," the driver says on his way out.

Frederick bends over his package. "Every time we ship a guitar, I wonder why I thought it was a good idea. So much can go wrong." Inside the box is a black guitar case, and inside the case is a surprising quantity of packing material. From the depths, he pulls a handsome wooden instrument. He turns it over in his hands with the smile of a kid on Christmas.

I watch him dance over to the sofa and sit down with the guitar in his lap. And then he says to the guitar, in his warmest voice, "Come to Daddy."

His odd choice of words propels me back out onto the balcony, where the pages of my English exam are fluttering against the staple. I smooth them down with my hand. From inside comes the sound of strings plucked one at a time as they're tuned.

Then the warm tones of a guitar chord float out the door behind me. The sound raises the hair on the back of my neck. I've heard him play the guitar—both acoustic and electric—on countless recordings. But the strings vibrating at close range send shivers up my spine. I hold my breath while the chords progress and the strumming becomes more elaborate.

The music stops abruptly, but after some small adjustment, it begins again, crashing over me like a wave.

My mother died two weeks ago. I have gotten through each day since with the combined assistance of total numbness, a complete lack of privacy, and the distraction of each strange new thing that's happened. But Frederick's guitar seems to stop time. As he plays, I am confronted by the warm night and the gentle rhythm of a guitar I've been listening for my whole life.

I have to push my school work away and put my face in my hands. The song is unfamiliar. Even so, it begins to shred my heart into little bits. I manage to hold out until he starts humming to himself, his reedy baritone scaling up and down with the melody. Then my tears run down my face and over my hands. I am drowning in them, shuddering silently until the song reaches its end.

In the stillness that follows, I clamp my lips together. I'm a dribbling wreck, trying not to sniff. I hear Frederick moving around in the room behind me, and the sound of water running in the kitchenette. After a minute, he steps out on the balcony and sets a glass of water and a box of hotel tissues on the table. I can't look up.

One warm hand lands on top of my head. It stays there for two beats, then retreats. Frederick goes back inside.

I press my fingers to my eyes, willing them to stop leaking. Behind me, Frederick is cleaning up all the packing paper that came with his guitar. He hums to himself while I dig my finger-nails into my palms and count the leaves on a banana tree in the courtyard below.

———

Eventually, Carlos drops off the food. Frederick comes to the balcony's threshold with two white paper bags. "Do you think you're ready to find out whether a decent burrito can be had in Orlando?"

"Sure," I say in a small voice.

He sits down in the other chair and passes me a bag. "Rachel," is scrawled on it.

We make ourselves busy unwrapping the foil. It smells good, actually. My appetite has been so finicky. Sometimes I can't eat a thing, and other times I'm famished. I take a big bite and chew.

"What do you think?" he asks. He wipes his mouth with a takeout napkin.

The question seems enormous until I realize he's only asking about the burrito. "Pretty good." And it is. The shredded pork mingles with beans and herbs. "Oh!" I make a sound of dismay. "This is full of cilantro!"

The surprise on Frederick's face makes me realize my mistake. He sets down his burrito. Then he takes one of the plastic knives that came with our order and cuts it in half. He picks up one piece and shows it to me. There's not a trace of cilantro inside. "Carlos knows," he says quietly.

"Well. That's handy." My voice is shaky. "He reads *Spin* too."

"*Rolling Stone*," he says. "Hard to forget which reporter you swell up in front of."

There is another minute of silent chewing. I feel drained.

"Can I ask you a question?" he asks.

"Okay?"

He sets down his food. "How long have you known I was your father?"

That's an easy one. "Forever."

His eyes widen. "What did she say about me?"

"Nothing. But whenever your songs came on the radio, she changed the channel. By fourth grade, I knew all of them."

He stands up quickly and slides through the open door. As he reaches for a beer, the refrigerator illuminates him, and I see the look on his face. Like he's been punched.

I don't feel the least bit guilty, either.

Chapter Seven

I'M SITTING in a study hall when Frederick texts me. *New driver today. His car is silver. Don't look for Carlos after school.*

You're picking me up from school? I tap back. Haze will not be pleased. He wants to go for ice cream.

I hope so.

Well, that's just a weird response. *Where is Carlos?* I ask.

He was just here with me as a favor. Had to go home to his family.

Why don't you just rent a car? I ask, hearing echoes of Haze in the question.

I don't drive.

Ever?

Nope. Don't want to. Old dog. New tricks. Not that people don't rib me about it incessantly. Hey—isn't that one of your weird negatives? Because cessantly isn't a word.

But ceasing is, I reply.

Thirty minutes pass without a reply, and like a dope I worry that I've offended him. But then finally my phone vibrates again. Only Frederick's next message makes no sense. It reads: *Motion for Custody Approved.*

Wait. What?

The no-phone-calls-in-school rule means that I have to run out of the building to call him. "What does that mean?" I ask him the second he answers.

"It means I win!" he hollers. "The judge just granted me something called temporary emergency custody. And since you turn eighteen in three weeks, you're done. It's over."

"But...how did that happen?"

"I'll tell you how—Hannah Reeves. She stood there in front of that judge, and told him the way it should be. And he rolled right over. I wanted to give her a big, sloppy kiss."

"Wait... I didn't know about a hearing."

"I didn't tell you about it because I thought I could lose. My lawyer warned me that plain old logic doesn't always prevail. As it turns out, a hot young social worker in a blue suit is what it takes. Meet me in front of school in twenty minutes. Let's spring you from that place."

"Um, technically my school day isn't over for another forty-five minutes."

He laughs in my ear. "It is now legal for me to teach you my slovenly ways. Come out whenever you want, but I'll be there in fifteen. Oh, and Rachel?"

"Yeah?"

"This means we can leave for California just as soon as you take that last test. See you outside." He disconnects.

I don't bother going back inside. I stand there in the sunshine for a while, phone in hand, trying to figure out what just happened. Frederick went before a judge to claim me. He'd told the judge—or at least his lawyer said it for him—"She belongs to me."

It's all I'd ever wanted him to do.

Then he invited me to California. No—he didn't invite me. He'd *informed* me that we're going, as if it's totally up to him.

Which it is, legally.

I can't get my head around it. Did that just happen?

My phone buzzes with a new text, this time from Haze. ***Where R U?***

Outside the east door.

Haze comes out five minutes later. "What's the matter? You never cut out early."

My grin is a foot wide, because the good news is finally sinking in. "I'm done with the Parson's Home, Haze! Forever. Frederick is picking me up."

He frowns. "To go where?"

"Well…" My heart thumps in my chest. "When I'm done with school, he wants to take me to California."

He puts his hands on my shoulders, his face deathly serious. "Please don't leave with him. You don't have to."

My stomach dives. "Haze, I can't stay with you."

"Why not?"

There are about a hundred reasons, and he won't like a single one of them. "I want to see California," I say instead.

At first, the words just echo between us. I'm a little shocked that I've made the decision so quickly. But I've waited my whole life for that invitation. Seventeen years of curiosity cannot be denied. This is my chance to finally understand how Frederick came to be my father.

"No, Rae," Haze whispers. And then he does something I've never seen him do before. He tears up. "You can't just *leave.*"

My throat begins to close up. "I have to," I say. But it's just an excuse. Going to California with Frederick is a choice I'm making, and we both know it.

"You really *don't* have to." His eyes glitter.

I hear the honk of a car horn and turn to look. Frederick has arrived.

"Fuck!" Haze shouts at the asphalt between us. "What I would like to do to that man!" He kicks his gym bag into the school wall.

"Haze," I snap, hating this. "Stop it, okay? I was always going away. You know that, right? I was always leaving in the fall."

He shakes his head. "That's bullshit, Rachel. You would have come back sometimes. Now you never will."

The car honks again.

"You know what?" I say, and my voice gets all high and weird. "It would be really nice if you could be happy for me. When everything went wrong, you were there for me. But when something goes right for a change…" I'm too tired to finish the sentence. And I didn't want to fight. There are things he wants that I can't give, and I don't know the right words to explain it.

I duck from behind Haze's body. Pointing my feet toward the parking lot, I begin to walk.

"Rachel, wait." He hurries to keep up. "Don't walk away like this. Don't choose that asshole over me."

I stop walking, but I'm too upset to look him in the eye. "That is so not fair. Don't put it like that."

He crosses his arms. "Is there any other way to put it?"

"I'm going to California, and you're not going to be nice about it. Are you?"

He hangs his head. With my heart pounding, I walk to the car. An unfamiliar driver opens the door for me. I slide in next to Frederick, who is all dressed up in a suit and tie.

When the car slides into reverse, I close my eyes. Part of me wants to yell, *Stop the car!* It's wrong to walk away from Haze in the middle of a fight. But if I go back to him, we'll just have the same argument over again.

"Remind me why you're nice to that guy?" Frederick asks. "Every time I see him, he's yelling."

That's when I finally snap, because neither of them has it right. "But *he* sat beside me for ten days straight while I watched her die! In that effing hospital!" *And where the hell were you?*

In the silence that follows my outburst, there is only the purr of the engine.

I've earned the startled look on Frederick's face. But even so, it gives me a pang of fear. I turn the other way, looking out the window.

After a minute of quiet, I hear him take out his phone and put it to his ear. "Yes Madeline, I believe you can help me. I'm currently staying in room 408, and I need an upgrade. Can you shake loose a two bedroom suite? My daughter is joining me."

Daughter. It's the first time I've heard him use that word.

"I'm glad business is so good. But please take a look at my account. Who's your best customer this month? *Right.* See what you can do."

On our way out of the parking lot, we passed Haze's old blue car. I wonder if I'll ever ride in it again.

Chapter Eight

LESS THAN FORTY-EIGHT HOURS LATER, I get into the backseat of the car again. This time to leave Florida.

"The airport, if you would," Frederick says to the driver. "Thanks."

The car pulls away from the curb, and a Ritz-Carlton concierge bellhop waves goodbye with a gloved hand.

Once Frederick won his custody suit, everything happened really fast. He contacted the guidance counselor at my high school, who rushed my final grades through. Even my half-finished take-home exam in government was awarded a quick A.

Yesterday, my father's new hired car pulled up outside my old house on Pomelo Court, where a sullen Haze had been waiting to help me pack up my room.

I'd asked my father to wait in the car. "It's a small space," I'd told him.

But the truth was I didn't want him in my mother's house, because it felt like a betrayal. She'd worked so hard to pay for our tiny place so that I could be in the very best school district, and I didn't think she'd want Frederick to step inside.

So he'd read a newspaper in the air-conditioned backseat while I went inside.

Meanwhile, Haze helped me put everything in boxes. I'd thought it would take a long time, but it went depressingly quickly. One box for clothes I wanted at Claiborne. One box for books, etc.

Mary will pack up the rest of the house and put some things into storage for me. I labeled one box for storage, containing what my mother had called "the altar." It was a double stack of all Frederick's CDs.

I'd bought every one of them with my babysitting money. While downloading was fine for other music, for his I'd wanted to read the liner notes.

When I was younger, I'd assumed that every song Frederick wrote was the literal truth. I would listen to a new album from start to finish, and believe that in the past eighteen months he'd broken down by the side of a desert road while reflecting on his life, missed an airplane that would have brought him to his true love, caught his lover leaving him before dawn, and wondered a lot about why young men had to die in Afghanistan.

If he sang, "I meant for you to stay awhile," I assumed that he'd written down the exact words he'd said to someone in real life.

The lyrics were my only way to hear his thoughts, and I took them at face value. It never occurred to me that he might embellish or invent. I even tried to figure out if "Wild City" was a real place.

Shocker, it wasn't.

When I got older, I learned not to take everything so literally. Even so, I'd spent many hours lying on my bed, scrutinizing the printed lyrics to his songs, always listening for allusions to a girlfriend named Jenny or a long-lost daughter.

I never found one.

When my room was packed, Haze taped up the boxes while I tiptoed into my mother's room. It had always been a spartan place, with few decorations. Last year's school picture was framed on the dresser. I didn't like how it had turned out. My smile looked plastic. Beside it, I found my mother's Timex, so I picked that up.

"Make sure you take a few things of sentimental value," Hannah had advised me. "If your mother had a favorite pair of earrings, save them. It might not seem like much, but one day you'll want them. I have my grandmother's gaudy Christmas brooches, and they are some of my favorite things."

The Timex had clocked nursing shifts on my mother's arm for years. Now I'm wearing it on my own wrist. There are two buckle holes with indentations next to them—my mother got thinner as the year progressed.

There was a jewelry box, too, which I hadn't raided since I was a little girl. I flicked open the top. The tray inside held a few pairs of very plain earrings. Underneath, there were pictures. The top one was of me on Santa's knee. Looking at it, I could hear my mother's voice. "Say fuzzy pickles!"

It hurt me just to remember her, and I didn't have time to break down. So I'd put the earring tray back on top of the photos, clicked the box shut, and tucked it into my tote bag, making a mental note to thank Hannah for her advice.

The worst part of yesterday's packing was the look on Haze's face when we were done. I braced myself for another argument, but it never came. Before we went outside, he gave me the fiercest hug I'd ever gotten. And when I kissed him on the cheek, his eyes reddened. But he didn't say a word, except for "goodbye."

Now, on the way to the airport I watch the gaudy Orlando billboards fly by us. This is the landscape of my life, and I don't know when I'll see it again.

Frederick pulls out his phone and taps a number. "Hannah Reeves, please," he says a beat later. "Hello to you, too! Rachel and I are on our way to L.A.," he tells her. "I just wanted to say thank you for all that you do. I guess you're not in it for the money." Whatever she says to him makes him laugh. "I will. Goodbye."

"You laid it on a little thick there," I say when he hangs up.

"Nah. Hannah is good people. Who would want that job? Digging ditches might be easier." He pushes aside the plastic barrier that divides the front seat from the back. "Can you slow down just a little, pal? Thank you." He slides it closed again. "I miss Carlos."

"Carlos is good people too," I agree.

———

My boarding pass reads Seat 2A. I've never flown first class before. As my father approaches the gate with his guitar case in hand, I wait for someone to tell him he can't carry it onboard. But that doesn't happen. Instead, a smiling flight attendant offers to find "a safe home" for it.

My phone chimes repeatedly as we board the plane. I sit down on the slippery leather seat and pull it out. Every text is from Haze.

You can still change your mind, he's written. *If you don't like California, I'll buy you a plane ticket home, okay? Just know that I'm still here for you.*

My stomach tightens just reading it.

Call me before you get on the plane.

I don't, though.

The flight attendant stands over my father, offering him a beer. "Don't mind if I do," he says.

"Would you like some lemonade?" she asks me, extending a glass.

"Yes. Thank you." In first class, the glasses are real, and they arrive the moment you sit down.

I push myself back into the seat. The smell of the filtered airline oxygen is disconcerting. My life in Florida is coming abruptly to an end, like a familiar song shut off right in the middle of the chorus.

My phone chimes again. As my father watches me, I power it down without reading the message.

"You're sneaking out of town, aren't you?" he asks.

"Sort of," I grumble. "You don't like him anyway."

"Rachel, I'm not judging you," he says, his voice low. "I'm famous for sneaking out of town."

DUET

DUET: *1. A piece for any combination of two performers. 2. On piano, two performers on one instrument.*

Chapter Nine

AS I DESCEND the escalator at LAX that night, someone calls my name. And there stands Carlos, waiting beside the baggage claim, wearing one of his trademark smiles. "Bienvenido a California!"

"Gracias, Carlos! Como esta?"

"Bien, bien!" Carlos and I walk over to examine the luggage sliding past on the belt. Frederick hangs back, his phone pressed to his ear. Nearby, two women stand together, whispering, their eyes on Frederick.

I'm getting used to the stares he receives out in public. I make a game of predicting whether people will approach him or not.

These two will, I decide.

Our bags came into view, and I point. At the appropriate moment, Carlos and I lunge for them. We get all four off the belt in one go, although one of them lands on my toe.

"So, I guess I can fit that in on Thursday," Frederick says into his phone, oblivious. "I'll see you tomorrow, Henry." He puts the phone away, and that's when the two women rush him, all smiles and apologies. While Carlos and I stack the bags into two rolling towers, Frederick signs their boarding passes with the Sharpie he keeps in his pocket.

"We saw your show together in Las Vegas!" one of them gushes.

"Last year!" the other one adds.

I turn to Frederick. He wears the telltale forehead wrinkle that crops up when people mob him. "Sir, we have to hurry if you're going to make it to Justin Bieber's party."

Frederick raises an eyebrow at me.

"Oh! Don't let us keep you!" Both the women skitter away.

"Justin Bieber?" His voice is dry. "Aren't you funny."

"I *am*, actually." More than that, I'm giddy over arriving in California. Frederick *is* stuck with me now. I'll get a real glimpse into his life, whether or not he ever meant for that to happen.

When Carlos pulls the car around, I slide into the cool interior next to my father. "It's just a ten-minute ride," he says, scrolling through messages on his phone.

"Really?" I've heard stories about L.A.'s legendary traffic.

"Really. It's one of the great things about Manhattan Beach," he says.

As a little kid, I'd always wondered where my father lived, imagining somewhere magical. My childhood definition of magical had run along the lines of a McMansion with a swimming pool. But the neighborhood Carlos drives into is a different kind of fancy. The homes are stacked close together, and many have stucco walls right up against the sidewalk. But each one has at least one elegant detail—decorative iron gates, or a little jewel of a stained glass window. The houses don't reveal their secrets to the street, they only hint at luxury within.

Just as dusk turns to night, the car slides to a stop in front of a narrow house with a striking zebra-wood door. Carlos pulls our bags out of the trunk while Frederick types a code into the keypad over the doorknob.

"The code is 8-6-7-5-3-0-9," he says. "I'll write it down for you."

"Like the Tommy Tutone song? Who could forget?"

Frederick's eyes widen. "Christ. You weren't even alive when that song was a hit."

"Oldies station, Frederick," I say, following him inside. Of course, "Jenny" was my mother's name. So is that a coincidence?

It must be.

The interior of Frederick's home is not what I expect. "How long have you lived here?"

"Three or four years. I know it's a little barren."

I try to put my finger on why the house feels so lifeless. The lower level is mostly one big room, with a separate kitchen. There's a giant L-shaped sofa in the living room made of pricey leather. There's a sleek coffee table and nickel lamps. In the rear, by a set of sliding glass doors, stands a very elegant grand piano.

But apart from a collection of vinyl records in the corner, the room is as impersonal as the hotel suite we'd just left behind. The only pictures on the walls are landscape photography.

I follow my father upstairs, where there are four doors off a straight hallway. "That will be your bathroom," he points at one door. Then he sets my bag down in the room opposite the bathroom.

Down the hall, I spy the master bedroom, which looks somewhat lived-in, with a stack of books on the bedside table. A third room has black foam on the walls, even over the windows. It's soundproofing. A dozen guitars rest on racks against the walls. The only real furniture is a single stool beside an amplifier.

In my room there's a brand new bed, the tags still hanging off the mattress. A mattress pad, sheets and pillows are stacked, still in their wrappers, on top of it.

I call after my father, who has gone down the hall. "What was in this room before?"

"Nothing," he says over his shoulder. "I never went in there."

———

The next morning I'm wide awake at six a.m. The house is silent as I pull on shorts and a T-shirt. Feeling like a trespasser, I tiptoe down the stairs. But Frederick is already sitting on the sofa.

"Jet lag, right?" he asks, his hair a mess. "Let's go walk on the beach."

I follow him out the door. At the corner, Frederick makes a left turn. Then I can see the ocean—a blue notch between the buildings that taper down the hill. We have to trot down a set of concrete stairs and across a cute little commercial street to reach the beach.

I can see why he lives here. It's kind of glam, and you can walk to everything.

"Ah," he says when we reach the sand. "Now we're talking."

I take off my shoes and let the sand squish through my toes. The breeze off the ocean is cool, making the hair on my arms stand up. There are people walking dogs on the sidewalk behind us. And there are runners and bikers on a path that runs parallel to the ocean.

But the sand stretches out for miles, with barely anyone on it.

Under the lavender sky, I feel transported to someone else's life. As if I've stumbled here in a dream.

———

We buy coffee and then walk into a little neighborhood grocery store. Frederick puts a few things into a miniature cart. "Orange juice, bagels, cream cheese, beer," he says. "That ought to do it." He swings the cart toward the checkout.

"Where do you buy food?" I ask.

He points at the bagels. "I just did. You mean—for later?"

I nod.

"That's what restaurants are for."

"Seriously?"

"What would you add?"

"Bread, something to put on a sandwich. Something to put in a salad."

He turns the cart around. "Go to it."

I put grapes and strawberries into the cart. I choose lettuce and tomatoes, feta cheese and a box of cereal. The prices are horrible, but it has to be cheaper than ordering in. Frederick follows me around with a bemused expression, drinking his coffee.

"Musicians never have to grow up," my mother once said, when I'd been begging for a reason for his absence. It was one of the few little crumbs my mother had ever offered on the subject of Frederick.

I put a half gallon of milk into the cart, and wonder what the hell had happened between them. And if I'll ever trust Frederick enough to ask him.

———

Later that day, the house fills up with musicians. I listen from the landing as Frederick greets them.

"Party's over, Ernie! Now we go back to work. Jesus, Art. I don't know about that mustache."

"It's growing on me," comes the answer.

The front door makes another beep, and then the guys downstairs greet someone named Henry. The infamous Henry—my father's punching bag. I can't help but eavesdrop as they catch up with each other.

"Let's get a picture," Henry says. "I haven't put Freddy's face on Instagram in weeks."

"Jesus," my father grumbles. "The fucking world will stop turning if you don't update Instagram."

"Shut up and put your arm around Ernie. Your *other* arm. I don't want to be able to see the hand that's supposed to be injured."

"You could just injure him for real to make it credible," someone says, and I hear my father's laugh.

I take my time drying my hair and straightening out my belongings. When I run out of things to do upstairs, I put my wallet in my back pocket and descend as quietly as possible. But when I come into view at the bottom of the stairs, all conversation stops.

My father clears his throat. "Guys, this is Rachel. Be nice to her. She's not used to dealing with hooligans such as yourselves." But the joke falls flat, because four guys are staring at me with undisguised curiosity.

"You should see your faces," I whisper.

The guy with the shaved head recovers first, dropping his eyes. "Sorry. It's just that I've been staring at Freddy's mug for a couple decades. I never knew he'd look better as a girl."

"What did I say about being nice?" my father complains.

"You said be nice to *her*," he points out. "Didn't say a thing about being nice to *you*."

"The smartass is Ernie. He plays the bass," my father says. But I already know that. Ernie appears in the liner notes of every album since the very beginning. In interviews, Frederick refers to Ernie as "my best friend." They both grew up in Kansas City, then they went to Claiborne College together. And Ernie's shiny head is visible in most of the music videos.

"Nice to meet you, Ernie," I say. He has soulful brown eyes and wide shoulders.

"And this is Henry," Frederick says, indicating the only preppy guy in the group. "Don't let him boss you around."

But Henry only rolls his eyes and then shakes my hand. "I work for Freddy's management company. Your father *pays* me to boss him around."

After being introduced to a rumpled drummer and a young keyboardist, I flee. "I'm going for a walk," I say, sliding into my shoes beside the door.

My father follows me out onto the front stoop. "Sorry about that," he says.

"It's okay."

"Just to orient you, the beach is that way." He points down the block. "We're on 16th Street right now. North is higher numbers, south is lower numbers. Wait…" He pulls his wallet out. "This is for you."

It's a credit card with my name on it. "What for?"

He shrugs. "T-shirts, coffee. Those groceries you're so fond of. Whatever it is bored girls need on a summer's day."

I turn the card over in my hand. "Thanks."

"There's a bookstore on Manhattan and 9th. You'll see."

"Cool. I'll see you later." I walk down the little front walk. He's still watching me.

"Do you have your phone?" he calls.

The question hits me in a funny way. For the first time, he sounds a hell of a lot like my mom. I turn around. "Why? Is this a dangerous neighborhood?"

He laughs. "No."

"Then bye." I walk away without looking back.

———

It's lovely to be alone. I haven't been alone, with nothing to do, in a very long time. I walk down Manhattan Avenue looking into the shop windows. At least half the storefronts are upscale boutiques, each with a beautiful window display.

I stop to admire some bathing suits, their design managing to be both sporty and sexy at once. The price tags are mostly turned face down, but one is visible. $260, it reads. As I smile, I feel my mother smile along with me. We used to amuse each other with outrageous price tags.

My mother's nose crinkled up whenever she laughed.

Strangely, I feel her presence over my shoulder as I walk all over Manhattan Beach. As far as I know, she'd never been to California. But together, we notice how fit and sporty everyone looks here, and how California smells different than Florida. It's saltier, drier.

I make my way down to the beach itself. The sun has really warmed things up, and I sit down on the sand. The bookstore will be my next stop, but I realize I have another question for my new friend Jake. I tap the texting app and try Jake's email address, in case they're linked. *Hey, it's Rachel Kress. Do you know if there are any books I should read for Sr. Lit? Heading to a bookstore. Thx!*

It's a long shot that he'll be available to answer my question now. But I wait anyway. The ocean is blue and pretty, with little whitecaps. I take a photo and consider whether or not I should text it to Haze. Is that just mean?

Before I can decide, my phone rings in my hand. The number is unfamiliar. "Hello?"

"Rachel?" a guy's husky voice says. "It's Jake."

For some reason I get a warm flutter in my chest at the sound of his voice. "Hi," I say carefully. "Thanks for calling me."

"Hey—no problem!" His voice is so cheerful that I find myself smiling into the phone. "Is your summer going any better now?"

I watch the Pacific Ocean sparkle at the shoreline. "A little? I'm standing on a beach in California right now."

"No way! I'm standing on a beach in Massachusetts. Well, I'm looking out the window at it, anyway. We're, like, patrolling both coasts at once. You see any pirates on your end?"

"No," I say, still smiling like a dope. Phone Jake is even cuter than Email Jake.

"Me neither. Good thing."

"Right."

"So about your bookstore trip…"

"Yeah?" I've already forgotten that this call has a purpose. "I'd love to get a jump on the reading."

"Do you know if you're taking the English lit class first semester, or the Russian one? Any idea?"

"I'd love to take the Russian one, but I don't know if it's up to me."

"Well, I know we'll read *Anna Karenina*. And if you end up in the other English class, they start with Chaucer. I think?"

"Thanks for the tip. Maybe I'll read *Anna Karenina* and hope for the best."

"You'll probably get a class schedule in two weeks or so. You could just wait and find out."

"But I need my very own L to paste on my forehead."

He chuckles into my ear. "Then don't let me stop you. Mine fell off for the summer, but I'll have it superglued up there again in a few weeks."

"Right." I'm hit with a sudden burst of nerves. "It won't be long now."

"You don't sound so happy about that. Are you worried?"

"Yeah." I feel so hollow inside. Like I don't have anything left of myself to make new friends and impress new teachers.

"I'm kind of nervous about next year too," he admits. "For different reasons than you. But my mom always tells me to ask— what's the worst that could happen?"

Mine already happened. It's still happening. "Um, I don't know. You first."

"Easy. The worst thing that could happen is I'll make myself crazy all year trying to impress the astronomy department at Claiborne College. Then I'll get rejected." His voice turns gravelly.

"You really want to get in? Nothing else will do?"

"All my other choices are distant seconds. And it will be really embarrassing if I don't get in."

"Hmm. But if nothing else will do, they'll hear that. Just be crystal clear about how much you want to be there, that counts for a lot. Everyone wants to hear that someone *cares*, you know?"

"You're really smart, Rachel Kress." I hear a smile in his voice.

"People tell me that all the time," I tease.

"Aren't you going to tell me your worst-case scenario?"

"Um…" What to say? "I'll throw up during my a cappella audition."

"But then they'll know you really care."

"Oh shut up!"

He laughs. "All right, so maybe it wouldn't make the right first impression. But I think you can do it. If that's really the scariest thing in your life, you're not doing so badly."

If you only knew…

"It's good to talk to you. I have to get ready for work, though." He sighs. "If it's not too late a night, at least I'll get an hour with my telescope on the beach afterwards. Supposed to be a full moon, unfortunately."

"That's bad?" I guess from his tone. "Wait, are you a werewolf?"

"Wait, you're not?"

We both laugh like crazy people.

"The brightness of the moon hides other objects," Jake explains. "I can't see the smaller stars when the moon is strutting her stuff."

"Oh. Bummer."

"Yeah. Enjoy your vacation at the beach."

"Thanks," I reply a beat too late. *Vacation* is a weird word for my trip to California. But I'm not about to explain right now. "Talk to you soon," I say, hoping it's true.

"Bye!"

———

A bell tinkles on the door of the little bookstore. I like the place immediately, with its wooden fixtures piled high with new books. The bookstore smells of paper and big thoughts.

"Do you have *Anna Karenina*?" I ask the young woman behind the counter.

"Of course," is her answer. "Which translation?"

I falter, having no idea.

"The Pevear is popular."

"Okay. That one, please." I pull Frederick's credit card out of my pocket. *Daddy's credit card.* Haze and I had always scoffed at the kids who threw down their parents' plastic for every desire. Now I'm one of those girls.

"You forgot to sign your card," the sales girl prompts, offering a pen.

"Sorry, it's new." I sign my name on the back in blue ink. RACHEL R. KRESS.

When I was a little girl, my mother told me that the middle initial stood for Rose. For years, I'd written Rachel Rose on papers at school, because I liked the sound of it.

When I was fifteen and applying for my learner's permit, Mom had pulled out my birth certificate to take down to the DMV. That was when I learned that my true middle name is Richards.

The whole thing is weird, really. She named me after someone she didn't know that well—and then changed her mind?

"Do you want a bag?" the sales girl asks.

"No, thank you."

I feel my mother's eyes on me as I walk out of the store.

———

Finding my way back to the zebra door is no trouble. I mount the stoop, ready to type the code into the keypad. But I stop because I hear Frederick's voice, loud and strident.

"We're not going into the studio this month, guys. I know it sucks because you're out the concert pay already. But I'm not ready."

"You'd better *get* ready," Henry argues. "Canceling your summer gigs has already cost you more than a million bucks."

I freeze there, my hand on the door, choking on the number I'd just heard.

"…also very expensive for your reputation," Henry is saying.

"I'm well aware of that," Frederick snaps. "Since you like financial terms so much, just think of this summer as me paying back a debt I incurred in my twenties. It's past due, and the interest penalty I owe is massive. Am I speaking your language now?"

Whatever Henry replies, it's in a voice too low to be heard

over the pounding of my heart. I am stuck there on the stoop like a trespasser, unsure what to do.

But after a minute, someone else says something, and then someone laughs. When it's quiet again, I punch the access code slowly, then rattle the knob as I push the door open.

The conversation stops. And once again, all eyes are on me. The million-dollar summer thief.

"What do you have there?" Ernie asks. "Looks too thick for summer reading."

Embarrassed, I flash the copy of *Anna Karenina* quickly toward the living room and head up the stairs.

"Nabokov?" Another voice says, "Dude, Freddy. She can't be *your*..." He catches himself in time. Right before he says "*daughter.*"

Into the awkward silence that follows Frederick says only, "Art, *Anna Karenina* is by Tolstoy."

———

I got a text around nine o'clock. *I'm mooning you*, it reads. I'm only confused for a second, until Jake's photo resolves onto the screen —a beautifully detailed shot of the bright moon against a dark sky.

Chapter Ten

THE FOLLOWING WEEK, I'm standing at the kitchen counter, sectioning a grapefruit. I perform this operation on a cutting board that I purchased the day before, after discovering that Frederick didn't own one. Apparently, he never cuts anything. Yet he owns a set of fancy German knives in a sleek bamboo block. Go figure.

As I work, I catch myself humming the melody to *Wild City*, and promptly cut the song short. Even though Frederick is showering upstairs, I don't want to be caught singing one of his tunes.

Not for the first time I wonder if that song is grounded in a true story. There aren't any real towns nicknamed "Wild City." And a Google search returns a million lyrics websites, but nothing about the song's meaning.

I've never been able to figure it out. Maybe there's nothing *to* figure out.

Wiping up the counter, I plan my morning. First, reading. And texting Jake. Our messages aren't about school these days. We've been sending each other Youtube links to werewolf videos. And I'll spend part of the day at the beach, where my inner groupie can hum to her heart's content, and where I'm out of the band's way.

It's been hard to get a fix on Frederick's typical day, because there seems to be no such thing. There are days when Henry comes by to drag Frederick to meetings with "promo yokels" and "suits." There are days when Frederick spends his time noodling at the piano, muttering to himself. And sometimes Ernie comes over alone, plugging into the little amp in the living room and playing with Frederick. Those are my favorite days, because I can lurk in my room upstairs and eavesdrop.

Their chatter is as interesting as the music. It's like living inside one of the quieter episodes of *Behind the Music*. Frederick might say, "I think I've got the melody, but I need to try it with more of a pop-radio rhythm. It needs that bounce."

And Ernie will reply with something about back beats or syncopation. And then they'll play the riff again.

I don't know which sort today will turn out to be, since Frederick hasn't come downstairs yet.

From its place on the wall, the land line rings, startling me with its chirp. In the week I've been there, I haven't heard that phone ring even once. I wait to see if Frederick will answer it. After three rings, I wipe my hands on my jeans and pick it up. "Hello?"

"Hello, dear," comes a voice. "Who is this?"

"This is…Rachel." *Who wants to know?*

"Is Frederick at home? Tell him his mother would like to speak to him."

I gasp.

"Hello? Are you there, honey?"

Frederick pads into the kitchen, his hair wet. "Rachel? Is someone looking for me?"

I put my hand over the mouthpiece. "It's your mother," I whisper.

He looks at me for a long moment, and then takes the phone as one might handle a grenade with the pin pulled. "Okay." He sighs. "I guess I'm doing this now." He puts the phone to his ear. "Mom. Hi." He listens. "Yes, she does sound young." He laughs nervously, his expression one of comical terror. "Mom. Mom. Stop talking a second. There's something I need to tell you. Actually, you might want to sit down."

I know I should leave the room and give him some privacy. But I can't tear myself away.

He puts his elbows on the kitchen counter. "Mom, I've been trying to figure out how to say this, but things have happened very fast. It's not going to be easy…" He clears his throat. "Rachel is your granddaughter. She's almost eighteen." He closes his eyes. "Yes, you heard that right."

I don't hear a thing for a minute, and then there's a sort of explosion through the phone. I can hear my grandmother yelling at him.

I turn around and flee the kitchen.

———

From the couch, I can hear half their conversation. Frederick closes the kitchen door, but I can still hear him saying things like, "I know it's a shock." And, "You have every right to be angry."

After ten minutes of that, the front door beeps, and Ernie puts his head inside. "Hi, Rachel!" he says. "Can I come in?"

"Sure." I swing my legs off the couch to make room for him to pass by me.

He puts an instrument case down on the floor. Then he drops the newspaper onto the coffee table and sits down next to me. From the next room, we can both hear Frederick. "I agree with you, okay? It's unforgivable. I am a total asshole."

Ernie raises his chin toward the kitchen. "Freddy having a little trouble in there?"

"He's on the phone with his mother."

Ernie's eyebrows shoot up. "Oh shit."

"Yeah," I say, watching his face.

The bass player closes his eyes for a quick second, then takes a breath and opens them again. He reaches for the newspaper and unrolls it. "Want the music section?"

"You go ahead."

Ernie snorts and then shows me the front of section C. It's a heavily styled group shot of the boy band 1D. "Please tell me they're not your favorite band."

"Nope," I say quickly. *Too busy being my father's fan girl.*

From behind the kitchen door, Frederick starts shouting. "No! You and I are not having *that* conversation right now. No."

"Hey—" Ernie touches my elbow. "Did you feel that earthquake last night?"

I nod. "My first one." Around eight, the sofa had begun to wiggle in a way that sofas generally don't. By the time I'd realized what was happening, it was over.

"That was just a baby earthquake," he says. "We've had some doozies. The aftershocks can go on and on."

It's quiet in the kitchen for a minute. But Frederick does not come out. My heart uses the silence to try to crawl up my throat.

"Do you play any gin rummy?" Ernie asks.

"Rummy?" He's obviously trying to distract me. "Sure."

He takes a deck out of a drawer in Frederick's coffee table and shuffles the cards. I spin around to face him on the sofa as he deals onto the expanse of leather between us.

The front door beeps again and Henry comes in. "Hi guys," he says. "A lot of work getting done here today, I see." He walks toward the kitchen door.

"I wouldn't go in there," Ernie warns.

Henry stops. "What untoward adventures has Freddy embarked upon today?"

A shout comes from the kitchen. "Sure! Let's review every disappointing thing I've ever done."

Henry jerks his thumb at the door. "Who?"

Ernie discards a king of spades. "His mother."

Henry stares down at his phone. "I fear a delay."

I have amazing cards—a long string of spades and three jacks.

Then I draw the jack of hearts. When I discard a king, Ernie winces.

"Now wait a minute! No! No you cannot," comes Frederick's shout. "Not until you cool off. You know what? I'm done here." I hear the sound of the phone slamming into the cradle. Then the kitchen door bursts open. He stops on the threshold. His eyes are pinched and his face flushed. There are sweat circles on his T-shirt.

"Greetings," Henry says.

Frederick scowls. "Henry, what were we doing today? Please tell me your calendar says, 'get very drunk.'"

"We're going over to see the suits."

"No fucking way," he says, sliding past Henry to go upstairs.

Henry looks up at the ceiling and sighs. Then he sets his phone down on the coffee table and follows Frederick upstairs.

"Sorry, Ernie, but I'm going to knock with six." I lay down my cards and cross my arms in front of my chest.

For a long moment, Ernie just stares at me.

"What? Do you have less?"

He lays his cards down on the sofa. "Sorry. You just look so much like your mother that sometimes I'm startled."

"Wait…" *What?* "You knew my mother?"

Ernie's expressive eyes widen. "You didn't know that?"

I shake my head, speechless.

He swallows hard, and for a moment I think he won't say anything more. "We waited tables at the same diner," he says eventually. "In Claiborne. She was going to the prep school. I was in college."

The hair stands up on the back of my neck. "Did Frederick work there too?"

"No. He didn't meet her until later." Ernie clears his throat. "I introduced them at a party."

A party. I'm the product of a party.

From upstairs comes the sound of Frederick shouting. "So we'll be late! I don't fucking care!" A door slams.

Aftershocks.

"I'm getting a drink of water," Ernie says. "Want one?"

"No thanks."

When he gets up to go into the kitchen, my gaze settles on Henry's phone. The screen is still lit.

I grab it off the table and press the menu button, then pull up Instagram. Sure enough, Henry is signed in as @FreddyRicks. I've been watching this account for years, thinking I was seeing the world as my father saw it.

Yet never once have I seen a social media app open on Frederick's phone. I don't even think he has them downloaded.

Later, I won't know why I did it. But I aim Henry's phone at the newspaper and frame a shot. Then I give it a caption. *Just listening to a little 1D at home and reading up on their concert. Sounds awesome. #fanboy*

Then I post it.

———

Frederick spends the evening upstairs in the music room, playing the electric guitar. Alone. There's some very angry playing coming through the ceiling. His mood is no match for the sound-proofing.

I spend the time reading *Anna Karenina* on the couch, too jittery to really concentrate. By my count, I've already cost Frederick a cool million and his mother's approval. It's no surprise that he doesn't want to hang out with me.

Even worse—the Instagram post about 1D got four thousand "likes" and a hundred enthusiastic comments before it was deleted. Nobody's pointed a finger at me yet, but it's only a matter of time.

Someone knocks on the front door, which is odd. Frederick's friends always announce their arrival just by tapping in the code. I pull the door open to find myself face to face with an older woman. Behind her, a taxi is pulling away from the curb.

"Rachel," she whispers, her smile quivering. "I'm Alice."

For a moment, I can only stare back. My grandmother is younger than I'd imagined. She has light brown hair and big hazel eyes.

"Can I come in?"

I jump back and open the door. Alice pulls a rolling suitcase behind her, but it gets stuck on the threshold, and I give it a yank to get it through the door.

"Thank you, dear." She pulls the door closed. "I'm so sorry to startle you. I've just had a nice long flight to get used to the idea of seeing you."

"Does he know you're coming?"

She shakes her head.

"Should I…" I point upstairs.

"What if you didn't?" Alice asks.

"Okay."

Alice glances around at Frederick's living room. "Still living like a college boy, I see." She wheels her suitcase toward the kitchen. Alice has been here before. "Come with me, would you?"

In the kitchen, I watched as Alice unzips her bag. She removes a baggie full of what looks like flour, a stick of butter bagged with an ice pack, and a bag of chocolate chips. After a few more ingredients emerge, she lifts a plastic bowl and a cookie sheet from the bottom.

"Rachel, you and I are going to make cookies. Because that's what grandmothers do. And also so that I don't just stare at you and cry."

"Okay." I'm back to one-word answers again.

Alice dumps the flour into the bowl. I pick up a baggie that contains what looks like both brown and white sugars, and pour those on top.

"There you go," my grandmother says. I look up to see Alice studying me. "Frederick is my only child," she says. "I never expected to have a granddaughter." Her eyes begin to look red.

Alice sniffs. Then she dumps another white substance from a baggie into the bowl. Baking soda and salt, probably.

I take a fork out of the drawer and stir the dry ingredients together.

"I'm very angry with your father. I can't even *say* 'your father' without my blood pressure rising five points. To think that I had a grandchild walking around in the world…" She puts a hand to her chest. "I'm sorry, Rachel. It didn't have to be this way."

Apparently, it did. I keep that thought to myself. "Should I preheat the oven?"

"That's a fine idea."

I tap 375 into the key pad, and then discover that it's also necessary to press "enter" before the oven will heat. Frederick's oven is about twenty years newer than the one in my Orlando house.

"Let's adjust the rack…" Alice opens the oven. "Oh, heavens!" From inside she pulls a cardboard box. It reads: *Accessories.*

"Oh," I gulp. It's lucky that Alice had found that box. "I almost started a fire."

Alice tosses the box on the countertop. Then she puts her head in her hands and laughs. "He's never used his oven." She looks up at the ceiling as if addressing him upstairs. "You are such a *child*, Frederick." She laughs again, and then tears leak from her eyes.

Of course there's no mixer. "We'll just have to mash it with a fork," Alice announces. "It will take some muscle."

"I have a trick," I offer.

Alice waits with liquid eyes.

"If you melt the butter first, it stirs together easily. But then you have to make bar cookies, because they spread."

Alice hands me the butter. "I'm in your hands."

———

The cookies cut from the edges of the pan are crisp, while the ones in the center are gooey. "We have rare, medium, and well done," I say, choosing a soft one and taking a bite. "They're good."

Alice smiles. "Cheers!" She taps her cookie into mine. "You're so skinny."

"I'm not always hungry," I admit. I've been on the lose-your-mother diet for over a month now, and it probably shows.

"Frederick eats irregular meals, I fear."

"Actually, he eats plenty," I say, defending him.

Alice shakes her head. "We can't talk about him or I'll burst." She takes another bite, and then a sorrowful look comes over her face. "I'm so sorry about your mother, honey. I can't even imagine."

There's a moment of silence while we chew.

"Rachel?" It's Frederick's voice, coming down the stairs.

I watch Alice's expression harden.

"Something smells good." He reaches the doorway and stops. "*Mom.*"

Alice's mouth gets tense, but then her eyes fill with tears. "I'm so angry with you, Frederick."

He leans on the door frame. "I know." He looks beaten. But even as he stands there, his T-shirt askew, a few gray hairs glinting in the yellow kitchen light, he looks beautiful to me. It still shocks me every time he walks into the room.

"Frederick," Alice says through her tears. "It's not just *your* life! How *could* you?"

I hold my breath, because Alice has just asked the very thing that I'm afraid to.

But it doesn't matter, because Alice doesn't get an answer. "Where's Dad?" he asks.

"I left him in Kansas City. Crying in front of the Royals game."

———

Grandma Alice sleeps in Frederick's room, forcing him onto the sofa.

"I'll sleep downstairs," I'd offered.

"Oh no you won't," Alice had replied.

Frederick didn't even try to argue. In fact, he leaves us alone. When I get up the next morning, he isn't home. Alice and I take ourselves out for brunch in Manhattan Beach. Then we poke into all the shops.

"Oh this! This is what we need." Alice pushes open the door to a nail salon.

"Manicure pedicure?" asks a woman inside.

"Two, please."

We're soon seated side by side in pedicure chairs, with our feet in warm, soapy water. Until now, I've always considered the idea of paying someone else to paint my toenails a waste of money. As a technician massages my instep with skillful hands, I realize there's a reason people pay for this.

"I've always found it easier to think with my feet in a tub of water." Alice sighs.

"This is nice," I agree. The pedicurist taps my foot, and I realize it's a cue to remove it from the water. The woman rests my foot on the padded edge of the basin and begins buffing my toenails.

"Rachel, do you want to tell me about your mother? Only if you think you can."

I take a deep breath and let it out. "Well, she was from Claiborne. But we moved to Orlando when I was two. She was a nurse at the hospital. On the pediatric ward…" I watch Alice's widening eyes.

"A pediatric nurse." She shakes her head. "That's a tough job. She must have been a wonderful person."

It buoys me to hear Alice say nice things about Mom. "She liked it *most* of the time. She said she never had to wonder whether her job made a difference or not."

Grandma Alice puts a hand on mine. "That's wonderful, Rachel. There aren't many people who can say that. She must have seen some very sad things, though."

It's true. "One time the babysitter dropped me off at the hospital, because Mom and I were going somewhere together. And while I waited, I saw Mom give a white plaque to a crying woman." I swallow. "When a child died at the hospital, one of my mom's jobs was to make a plaster cast of..." I hold my own hands up, fingers splayed.

Alice dabs at her eyes.

"There were about a hundred nurses at her funeral," I tell her as the manicurist pats my feet with a towel.

"It couldn't have been easy," Alice says. "Being a single mom."

"If she hadn't gotten sick..." I can't keep talking about Mom any longer. "I got a scholarship to Claiborne Prep."

"Your mother's genes at work," Alice says quickly. "She never married?"

"She never did." Neither of my parents did, apparently.

"I wish I'd met her. I wish I'd paid more attention. But I didn't meet most of Frederick's college friends. And I thought his music was only a phase." She laughs, but the sound is bitter. "The last I remember, he was dating the drummer of his band."

"Definitely not the same person," I say quickly, and Alice smiles.

But it makes me wonder—if Frederick had a girlfriend, was my mom the other woman? I try that idea on. It doesn't sound like Mom. But it might account for her bitterness. Maybe she thought he'd leave his drummer for her?

And if she was the other woman, she might not have wanted to tell me that.

At my feet, the stylist begins applying pink nail polish to my toes, with a motion so fine and fast that each nail takes only three strokes.

———

Frederick, Alice, and I endure a strained dinner at an Italian restaurant. Frederick barely touches his food, sipping instead from a glass of the bottle of red wine he ordered. And after I go to bed, I can hear strains of his acoustic guitar from the couch.

After a time, I hear Alice emerge from Frederick's room and go back downstairs. Their voices begin low but then escalate.

"But why not?" Alice cries. "She should come immediately. She could finish her summer in a house with two grownups. Two people who haven't neglected her for eighteen years!"

I sit up in bed, my stomach clenching.

"Because I have custody!" he shouts. "Insult me if you want, it will still be true."

Whatever Alice says next, I can't hear it.

"Go ahead and be angry. But she's not going," he says. And then, "No! I already said no."

My heart booms like a bass drum. I can't lie down again until I hear Alice walk back upstairs and close the door to Frederick's room.

———

When Carlos comes to take Grandma Alice away, she hugs me tightly. "I have to fly back now, because I have a job as a librarian, and a husband at home who is almost as helpless as Frederick. But I want you to come to Kansas City for the holidays, if not before," Alice says. "I'm going to tell Frederick."

"Okay," I agree. The holidays seem a hundred years off.

"You are welcome any time. *Any time*, Rachel."

"Thank you." I feel my eyes cloud.

"Oh, honey." Alice squeezes my hand. "You are not alone. I flew here to tell you that."

Carlos gives me a wave before he drives off. Frederick doesn't even come outside.

That night Frederick sits on the sofa with his guitar, which he does not play. Instead he sips from a glass of scotch. I perch tentatively at the other end, my book open in my lap.

"I'm poor company tonight, kid," he says. "I'm sorry."

"I don't mind," I tell him. And it's true. Because he could have sent me away with Alice. He might have chosen to be finished with me. But he didn't do it.

He's just being stubborn, my mother whispers in my ear.

I ignore her.

Chapter Eleven

THE WEEK BEFORE MY BIRTHDAY, I return from the beach to find a powwow in progress. Besides Henry and Ernie, the young keyboardist and drummer are there. But nobody is playing. Instead, Henry paces the room, his sleeves rolled up, and Frederick is drinking a beer, guitar idle in his lap.

"Henry, I know they want the album, like, yesterday," Frederick says. "But I'm not there yet. If I give them some crap and it doesn't sell, that helps nobody."

I tiptoe upstairs, and then listen from the landing.

"This is your last album on this contract. If you become a problem child, they're going to offer you shitty terms on the next one," Henry argues.

"You could always go indie," Ernie puts in. "Maybe you should do that anyway."

"The simplest option is the Christmas record," Henry says. "And it will make Ralph happy."

"Great," Frederick mutters. "We can spend the rest of the summer caroling." He strums his guitar. "Silver bells, silver bells. Freddy's ca-reeeer is in the shitter."

Ernie snorts, but Henry sighs. "Okay, maybe it's not your favorite idea."

That evening, from my hideout upstairs, I hear the front door open and close a number of times. Voices accumulate in the living room, both women's and men's. The conversation mingles with laughter, and someone begins spinning tunes from the vinyl record collection Frederick keeps in a milk crate near the piano.

The self-appointed DJ, whoever he is, has eclectic taste. I heard Coltrane and the Beatles and David Bowie.

I sit there on my bed, feeling forgotten, until my phone chimes with a text. *No pirates here tonight,* it reads. *Still clear on your end?*

My smile blooms like a hothouse flower. *I've abandoned my post to hide in my room.*

Who are you hiding from?

My dad is having a party downstairs.

And you don't like his friends?

I don't know most of them, I admit. Ernie is downstairs, though. I could probably talk him into another game of rummy.

Is there food? Jake asks. *I'll put up with anyone for food.*

I laugh aloud in my empty bedroom. Then I sniff the air. *I think there might be. Maybe Chinese?* Something smells good, damn it. The idea that they're eating down there makes me feel even grumpier and more invisible.

You'd better investigate, Jake suggests.

I will. But I'm not ready to let Jake go. Talking to him is the easiest thing in my life. *What are you up to?*

It's almost time to go to work. For once I'm happy to go and smell like fried clams because my mother has been chasing me around with catalogs, trying to get me to weigh in on khaki pants for school.

I've been worrying about school clothes too. The Claiborne student handbook confuses me. *Can I ask you a question about the dress code? I'm not sure I understand it.*

Sure!

Incoming...

I touch his avatar and hit "call." He answers right away. "Hi," I say, feeling a zing of self-consciousness.

"Hey. The dress code reads strangely, right? I'll tell you why—

it was just redone to eliminate any reference to gender. The girls made a big stink about having to wear skirts a couple years ago. And then the guys piled on saying that ties were sexist." Jake snickers. "A move of pure brilliance, if you ask me. So it was redone in those vague terms to show no gender preference."

"So what do girls wear?"

"Well, you have to stay away from jeans or anything that looks like it's sloppy on purpose. This is my personal rule—if the outfit says 'Fuck you,' they'll call you out. But if it says, 'I tried,' you're fine."

"Okay?" That really doesn't tell me what I need to know. "But what do girls *really* wear?"

He gets quiet for a second. "You mean, like, where do they shop?"

"I only own shorts and T-shirts, Jake. Help me out here."

He laughs. "Well, I don't have sisters, and I don't pay much attention to clothes. That's my disclaimer."

"Noted."

"But J. Crew is sort of ubiquitous. There's plenty of Abercrombie. The super preps like Vineyard Vines. But not everyone is preppy. There are artsy people who wear a lot of black. No idea where they shop, though."

"Okay. I can work with that. I don't have any winter clothes at all."

"The stores on Main Street have coats. Claiborne is right on the Appalachian Trail, so outdoor gear is the one thing you can always buy."

"That is a good tip, Jake. I don't know where I would find a winter coat in Manhattan Beach, anyway."

"I've never been to California. Are there movie stars everywhere?"

"Um, no?" I giggle nervously. *There are probably rock stars downstairs, though.* "I haven't spent much time here. As far as I can tell, it's like Florida, but even more expensive."

"Yeah? I'd better go. Time to serve clams and beer."

"Good luck out there."

"Thanks! Talk later?"

I agree and we disconnected. But now Jake has me thinking about school clothes. I'd seen a J. Crew catalog in Frederick's pile of recycling by the front door.

With the catalog as my mission, I finally venture downstairs.

The scene in the living room is lively, with a dozen or so people standing around talking. The lights are low, and everyone holds a drink, including a handful of unfamiliar women. In spite of all these guests, Frederick stands against the piano talking to his drummer.

"Hey, kid!" Ernie tugs on my ponytail as I take in the scene. "There's a whole lot of Thai food in the kitchen," he says.

"Thanks. I'll check it out."

"Ernie, honey. Come back here." A woman beckons to him from the sofa. Apparently Ernie has other games besides rummy on his mind tonight, because he hustles over to her.

I lean down and dig through the stack of newspapers until I find the catalog I'm looking for. Tucking it under my arm, I head for the kitchen.

Nobody stares at me, like on my first day in California. Tonight they do the opposite. I'm invisible.

The kitchen counters are covered with takeout containers. Two young women in tiny shorts huddle in front of the microwave, their giraffe legs accentuated by impractical platform shoes.

Ignoring them, I grab a paper plate and begin to peer into the various plastic tubs. I pocket a can of Diet Pepsi before a giggle turns my attention toward the girls in the corner. When one of them straightens her back, I glimpse a straight line of fine white powder on the black surface of the countertop.

Fascinated, I watch as the second girl bends low, inhaling powder through a little paper tube.

"We might share," the first girl says, and that's when I know I'm staring. "Who are you here with?"

I just blink at her, shocked by both her hobby and the question.

I grab a paper carton full of some kind of steamed dumpling and flee the kitchen without answering.

Upstairs again, I eat dumplings and flip through the catalog. And it's really a shame I'd been too stunned by the cocaine on the kitchen counter to grab any dipping sauce.

As the night wears on, the front door opens and closes again, but this time the tide is running out. The voices in the living room diminish to only a few, and someone puts on Elvis Costello at a low volume.

I sit crosswise on my bed, flipping through the catalog, until the front door opens once more with a bang, and the quiet conversation downstairs breaks off at once.

"Fucking hell!" a female voice rings out. "I get a text that the party is at Freddy's house tonight. And I think—that's impossible! Because if Freddy was back in town *he would have called me*."

My father's voice says something low and soothing.

"Really?" Her voice is shrill. "Because you don't *look* like a guy who was about to pick up the phone to call me."

I can't hear Frederick's response, but it makes the woman even angrier. "You never told me to keep my voice down *before*. Not when I was screaming your name in bed. Who's going to hear me, Freddy? I can't wait to find out."

And then I hear feet stomping up the stairs.

A few seconds later, a woman walks right past the door to my room, as if heading for Frederick's. But since mine is the only light on upstairs, the woman turns, and a startled face peers into my bedroom.

"What the *hell?*" she yelps. She has shiny brown hair and big eyes, like a doe.

For the second time that night, I'm speechless.

"Liz," my father's voice barks up the stairs. "That's enough already." He sounds tired. "Leave Rachel alone."

She retreats. I don't hear any more of their exchange, but the front door opens and shuts again a minute later. And then Frederick's footsteps slowly climb the stairs. His face appears in the doorway. "Can I come in?"

"Of course." *It's your house.*

He sits on the foot of the bed, and then rolls backward, his hands behind his head. "I'm sorry. That was…"

"Classy?" I supply.

He laughs. "Right."

"But not as classy as the two girls who were blowing coke on your kitchen counter." Even as I say the words, I wonder if *blowing coke* is the right terminology.

Frederick lifts his head. "No shit?"

"They offered me some. I guess if the social worker calls to check on me, I won't mention it."

He jackknifes into a sitting position. "Rachel, you know drugs are for assholes, right?"

I look into his serious face, and try not to laugh. The anti-drug pamphlets they hand out at school would be more entertaining if they were titled: *Drugs are for Assholes*. And his expression is priceless. "Well…" I clear my throat. "I only get high about twice a day. It helps to keep my blues away."

"What?" He gapes at me.

"It's a *song*, Frederick. The rhyming couplet should have tipped you off. I guess you're not a fan of BranVan 3000?"

He flops onto his back again. "Jesus, Rachel. That's not funny."

"I've never even *seen* cocaine before, except on TV."

"Welcome to L.A. So who were these girls?"

"Um, no idea? They had on short shorts and tall shoes."

"Well, that's half of Southern California. How old?"

"Young. Younger than you."

"Well that's *most* of Southern California." He scrapes his face with one hand. "I might need to get out of L.A. for a while. I've been meaning to talk to you about that."

"Why? Where would you go?"

"I was thinking of getting a place in Claiborne this year. If I can buy you a coffee every couple weeks, that seems like a low-key way to make sure you're doing okay."

Nothing he's said to me yet is as shocking as this suggestion. I don't even know where to begin. "Can you *do* that? What about work?"

"I'd only be there about half the time, and traveling the other half. But I wouldn't mind getting away from here for a while. Too many people are pulling on me."

"But… Henry makes it sound like you have a lot to do here."

He shakes his head. "In the first place, you don't worry about that shit, okay? That's my problem."

Well, ouch. For somebody who doesn't know how to be a parent, he's got the leave-it-to-the-grownups line right.

"And anyway, Henry says those things because the record label is pressuring him. But I'm not ready to record. My head is in a hundred places."

"Will they be angry?"

He stretches his arms overhead. "Whatever. Recording artists are always pulling this crap. You wouldn't believe the excuses those guys hear. 'I can't play today, because Mercury is in retrograde,' and 'I have a splinter in my left butt cheek.'"

I smile up at the sloping ceiling. "What about this house?"

"What about it? I'll probably keep it." He rolls onto an elbow. "Tell me what you really think."

"I think that it sounds like a lot of expense and trouble."

"If I stay in California, I might not see you for months. That's not good enough."

Really? It was for seventeen years. My heart rate accelerates, and I ask him one of the questions that's been burning me up inside. "Why did you bring me here anyway?"

His eyes widen just slightly. "Because you asked me to. I mean —Hannah called. But she wouldn't have called if you didn't need a place to go."

This explanation bounces around in my chest like a rubber ball. *Because you asked me to.* Angry Rachel isn't satisfied with this answer. What would have happened if I'd asked him a year ago? Or ten? Would he have come running?

In the silence, I hear my mother whisper a question in my ear. *Why should you have to ask at all?*

"Doing some shopping?" Frederick asks suddenly.

I look down at the forgotten catalog in my lap. "All my clothes are for hot weather. And Claiborne has a dress code."

"Ah, right." He makes a face. "Is it still plaid skirts and clip-on ties?"

"Not quite that bad. You can't wear jeans, and they want collared shirts."

"Better you than me. Carlos could drive you to the mall."

"Which one?"

"Uh." Frederick cups a hands to his mouth and yells. "Henry! We need a consult."

A moment later the manager bounds upstairs, a beer bottle in his hand. "What's shakin?"

"Where do people shop?"

"Shop for…?"

"School clothes," I say slowly. Apparently Frederick never does anything without consulting Henry. So now we're having a school-clothes powwow in my room? Unbelievable.

"The Galleria in Redondo," Henry says without missing a beat. "Macy's, Abercrombie. The Gap." He glances at my catalog. "J. Crew is in that place on Sepulveda."

"Or," Frederick says. "If you hate malls, you can just put that catalog in your suitcase and order one of everything when you get to New Hampshire."

"The reclusive method," Henry says with a smirk.

"Nah." Frederick gives Henry a playful kick. "Just practical."

Henry pulls out his phone. "I'll book you for an afternoon at the mall with Carlos, okay Rachel?" He pokes the screen. "And I see your birthday is coming up. What should I be planning for that?"

"Good point." Frederick turns to me. "Fancy restaurant?"

SARINA BOWEN

That just sounds awkward. "Let's just go somewhere you always go."

"Every Sunday there's a Cuban band playing at a seafood place in Hermosa Beach," my father says.

"Great food," Henry agrees. "But Ernie and the guys might be there."

Live music and a crowd appeals more to me than sitting alone with Frederick. "Let's all go, then."

Chapter Twelve

ON MY BIRTHDAY, I wake up to an email from Haze, and therefore a stab of guilt. I left things so badly between us. His message contains no text, only a photograph of him, arm in arm with Mickey Mouse. Mickey holds a sign which reads, in black marker, *Happy Birthday, Rachel*!

I laugh.

"What's so funny?" my father asks. He's made a run for bagels and cappuccino—his version of making me a birthday breakfast.

I turn my computer so that he can see the picture.

"Cute. So you're still friends."

"I guess so." I begin to labor over my reply.

Haze— I love the pic! What's that uniform you're wearing? Space Mountain? Or the Astro Orbiter? I hope that you're loading old ladies onto the people-movers, because at least that's in the shade. I'm going to spend the day trying not to think about last year's birthday, when my mom took us out to Steak & Ale, and then we all went into the wrong movie theater by accident, and missed the first ten minutes of our show. Once upon a time, that seemed like a bummer, right?

Okay, this message got very heavy all of a sudden. So I'll close by saying, "look, puppies!"

Love always, Rachel.

His reply is a picture of puppies. "Wish I could be there," is all he writes.

———

That night, Ernie pulls up outside the house in a cherry-red convertible.

When I reach for the back door, he shakes his head. "No—the birthday girl sits up front."

"Aw, hell," Frederick complains. But he slips into the back with a smile.

"I look better sitting next to her than you," Ernie says, putting it in gear.

So I ride to the restaurant in style, the salty breeze tangling my hair. A valet steps forward to open our door when we arrive, which makes me worry that my skirt and top aren't dressy enough. But inside, the restaurant is casual.

We're a table of five. By now, I've begun to get a fix on my father's friends. There's Ernie, of course. He's the soulful one, who always thinks before he opens his mouth. The other musicians—like Art, the drummer sitting across the table from me—aren't as close to Frederick. They're like orbiting satellites. Insubstantial.

Henry is more complicated. He's a scrapper, always pacing, spitting out ideas. But I don't understand their dynamic. Henry presses on Frederick, pushing him to see people and make calls. But in turn, Henry seems to do a lot of very menial labor. He orders lunch, he answers Frederick's phone for him. Even now it's Henry who's trying to flag down the waitress.

"Hey, Mari! Can we get a pitcher of sangria?" he asks.

"And a Diet Coke," I say before the woman walks away.

"Nice, Henry. Leave the lady out," Ernie teases.

The manager colors. "I forget that she can't drink."

The waitress brings five glasses anyway, and so my father pours me an inch. "To turning eighteen," he says, raising his glass. They all toast me, which makes me feel incredibly self-conscious.

Frederick orders a dozen things off the menu, and I sample everything from ceviche to stuffed lobster. And when the dishes are cleared away, my father reaches into his jacket and fishes out two little boxes. "This one first," he says, tapping the bigger box.

With four pairs of eyes on me, I untie the ribbon and open it. Inside is a new pair of sunglasses in a leather case. "Hey, thanks!" He must have noticed that mine are beat up and awful.

"Let's see them," Ernie prods.

I put them on.

Across the table, Henry smiles. "That's very L.A. Well done, Freddy."

The other box is even smaller. And after I remove the bow, I see that it reads Cartier in red script.

"Score," Henry says approvingly.

I crack open the box and find a wristwatch inside. It's simple in design, but beautifully sleek. When I lift it out, the metal feels weighty in my palm.

I've never owned anything so expensive.

"It's beautiful," I say. And it's true. Except that now I will be expected to put it on, as I did with the sunglasses. And that means removing my mother's Timex, and replacing it with this gift from my father.

The very idea makes my throat feel thick.

Their eyes are on me. So I lift my purse onto my lap. Carefully, I take off my mother's watch and zip it away in my bag. Then I drape the metal bracelet around my wrist and fiddle with the clasp. "Thank you," I whisper, and Frederick winks.

I put my wrist in my lap, feeling traitorous. The food in my stomach feels like lead. And all I want is to rewind my life to a time where Mom and Haze and I eat a cake in the kitchen and then go to the movies. The restaurant feels too crowded all of a sudden, and my eyes are hot.

It's the music that saves me. The Cuban band starts up with two guitars, bongo drums, a stringed bass, and a beat-up, old trumpet. Their bright rhythms fill the room, and I began to drift on the river of their sound. The lights are dimmed, and drinks refilled, and two women show up—one next to Ernie and one in Henry's lap.

I watch the absorbed expressions on the faces of my father and his friends. I'm envious of the way they lose themselves in the moment, as if the rest of the world has fallen away. I wonder if I'll ever feel like that again, or if grief will always follow me.

———

The sunny L.A. weather the following week offers no clue that summer is drawing to a close. The only sign of change is the flurry of mail from Claiborne Preparatory Academy arriving in Frederick's P.O. box.

I spend hours poring over the information. I learn how to rent a mailbox at the post office and how to connect to the school's computer network. I study the campus map as though cramming for a final exam.

"Another envelope from Claiborne," Frederick announces one morning, handing it over. Inside I find a single sheet of paper, reading ROOMING ASSIGNMENT. My new dormitory building is called Habernacker.

"Good name," Frederick says.

"Do you know where that is?"

He shakes his head. "I didn't wander around the prep school. It's on the other end of town."

"Some help you are." I unfold the paper. "My roommate's name is Aurora Florinda de Garza Garcia. Her address is in Madrid."

"Sounds fancy," Frederick says. "A European girl with four names." Whistling, he leaves the house to get a haircut.

When the door shuts on him, I recite my roommate's name

again. Just the sound of it gives me butterflies in my stomach. So I text Jake. *I'm in a dorm called Habernacker. My roommate is from Madrid.* I type out her name.

No way! comes the quick response. *I'm in Habernacker too. Your roomie's name is not familiar. Probably a transfer? I have two roommates. Both exchange students.*

This is going to be okay, right? I ask, feeling silly.

Sure. And if it isn't, I know the town really well. We can hide their bodies.

Way to be creepy, Jake.

It sounded funnier in my head, he replies.

In the kitchen, I take out a skillet and make myself a grilled-cheese sandwich. While it toasts, I indulge in singing one of my father's songs. "Stop Motion" has been stuck in my head since I heard Frederick and Ernie play it yesterday. I've spent the summer stifling every impulse to sing. But with my father out of the house, I let it rip.

When the sandwich is brown on both sides, I flip it onto a plate and turn around, only to experience heart failure at the sight of someone standing in the doorway. "Geez, Ernie! I didn't hear you come in."

He's staring at me. "I didn't know you could sing."

"Eh…" *Crap.* "I only sing in the shower."

"Bullshit." He crosses his arms. "Does Freddy know?"

Damn. I yank open the fridge, looking for a can of Pepsi. "If you were me, would you want to sing in front of Frederick?"

"If I had pipes like that, I'd want everyone to hear it."

I give him the side-eye. "Maybe you would, and maybe you wouldn't."

Ernie chews his lip. "I really don't get it. You'd pretty much have to be a killer musician with your genes. But fine. We never had this discussion."

"Thank you."

"And you never hit those high notes like you were born to it, or improvised a riff on the bridge."

"You can stop now."

He shrugs. "It sounded great, though."

"You would say that. You co-wrote the song."

"Just the bass line." He squints at me, as if trying to figure something out.

Unnerved, I carry my sandwich past him and up to my room.

———

Later that week, Henry stays for dinner with us—meatball sandwiches ordered from a deli. Every shop in Manhattan Beach delivers. No wonder my father never lights his oven.

Ever since I spoofed my father's Instagram account, I've been waiting for Henry to chew me out over it. Good girls don't pull pranks. We just feel too anxious afterwards.

But Henry doesn't bring it up. There's something else he wants to talk about, instead. "I had a call from publicist Becky," he says.

"Who's publicist Becky?" I ask.

"When your publicist rings," Frederick explains, "there's a small chance you've won an award, and a bigger chance you've fucked up somehow. What did she say, Henry?"

"There's a picture of you and Rachel out there. A blog called to ask if we'd like to provide a name."

Frederick laughs. "No kidding? Another slow news day in Los Angeles."

"Mighty slow."

"Who has it?"

"*Like a Hawk*. It's nobody worth sucking up to," Henry says.

"What are you talking about?" I ask. "What picture?"

"There's a gossip blogger who has a photo of you and me, probably from your birthday," Frederick says. "And they want to post it. But they don't know who you are, so they called my publicist to ask." He takes a swig of his soda. "Henry, tell Becky thanks for the call. But Freddy declines to identify the young woman in the photo."

Henry shrugs. "Fair enough. But you're not going to freak out if they make something up, right? That's the only reason Becky's asking. You know what they do: 'Freddy Ricks hits the town with young model half his age…'"

"That'll be wrong. She's less than half my age. Tell Becky I won't freak out, and feel free to photoshop out my gray hairs."

———

Later, when Henry is gone, the whole conversation is still replaying in my brain. "Why wouldn't you just tell the blogger my name?" I blurt out.

My father looks up from his reading and shrugs. "We could do that. But then some punky blog gets to break a story about—" He makes his hands into quotation marks. "—Freddy Ricks' secret daughter. Why should your life be the thing that boosts their clicks, or page views, or whatever gives them their jollies?"

His eyes go back to the article he's reading on his tablet. But I'm not quite finished. "Is it an embarrassment for you if they put it out?"

His face lifts again, a look of pure surprise on it. "No way, kid. Tell whoever you want. That's not the issue." He offers me his tablet. "Here. Add your name to my wikipedia entry if you want to. Just don't let some asshole make a profit off your tragedy."

I take a step back. "Never mind, I get it."

"Rachel?" he says as I reach the stairs.

"Yeah?"

"Nice job with that Instagram thing. Henry was flapping like a chicken, trying to figure out who did it."

I freeze, my hand on the banister. "It was me."

"No kidding. But Henry doesn't know because Ernie took the fall for you."

"He did? Why?"

Frederick just shrugs, a smile on his face. "Got sick of Henry's bitching, probably. We all thought it was hilarious." He goes back to his article, but I head upstairs, my stomach quivering.

I flop onto my bed, wondering what the blogger's photo of him and me looks like. I have no pictures with him. Not a single one.

OPERA

OPERA: *A drama in which the words are spoken instead of sung. Themes may be tragic and / or comic.*

Chapter Thirteen

WHEN THE BIG DAY ARRIVES, Carlos drives Frederick and I to the airport. When we pull up to Departures, he gets out of the driver's seat and runs around to open my door. I step out, and he tips his head sideways to smile at me. "Adios, señorita."

I surprise him with a quick kiss on the cheek. "Adios, Carlos."

Frederick smacks him on the back. "See you in a couple weeks."

On the flight to Boston, Frederick falls asleep in the first-class seat next to mine, but I can't relax. Even a movie can't distract me. I play games on Frederick's tablet for a while, then tuck it back into the seat pocket in front of him. He's sleeping with his mouth open. I study the lines in his face, and his long hands on the airplane blanket.

"I'm almost used to you now," I whisper.

He does not reply.

———

In Boston, another driver picks us up for the ninety-minute trip to Claiborne. The nerves are gaining on me again. After the tenth time I squirm around on the seat next to him, my father speaks from behind his newspaper. "Hang in there. All you have to do is find some good people. How many kids are in your class?"

"Three hundred."

"No problem, then. There have to be a few good ones, right?"

I'm not so sure.

The car pulls up in front of the Claiborne Inn, where Frederick has booked himself a room. I stand there, blinking on the sidewalk, looking up at the white clapboard building that shouts: "Welcome to New England!" It has a long front porch and rocking chairs.

I wait outside while he checks in and drops his luggage. So this is Claiborne. There are families walking together everywhere, some with boxes or rolling students' luggage. When I dreamt of coming here, I did it because I wanted to see the town where I was born.

But I don't feel any connection. It's just a super-cute town teeming with strangers. And I just want to rewind my life a year and go home.

"All set!" Frederick says, appearing beside me. "You still have a couple of hours until you can pick up your key, right? Let's take a walk and find something to eat."

"Okay." Although eating anything sounds impossible.

He points across the grassy town square. "The prep school is mostly on that side of the green, while the college is that way, up the hill." He points in the opposite direction.

Having studied the map, I already know this. "Does it look the same to you here?" We start down Main Street, which divides the town in two.

"Yes and no. Everyone looks so young." He laughs. "The town wasn't really my stomping grounds. I only cared about the bars and the little clubs between here and Boston."

"Did you ever come to your college reunions?"

"Nope," he says quickly. "Never found the time."

I examine the storefronts on Main Street, with their window boxes bursting with petunias. There are several restaurants, and shops selling spirit wear for both the prep school and the college. You can buy sweatshirts, hats, shorts, or flip flops with either of the schools' insignia. There are two bakeries and a coffee shop, too.

Eventually the town thins, with houses replacing the businesses. We cross the street for our walk back. "This is a very walkable town," I point out.

"You know it. This part, anyway. Stop here a second." Frederick halts in front of the window of a real estate office. There are a dozen listings hanging in the window. "I'll be coming here tomorrow," he says.

"I thought you'd make Henry do that."

Frederick whirls on me with laughing eyes. "I would if he were here. But getting away from him is sort of the point, so I guess I'll have to do one or two things for myself."

On the next block we reach a pub called Wheelock's, and Frederick hoots his approval. "At least this place is still in business. I think I spent all my money here the year I was twenty-one." He pushes open the door with a grin. The interior is all dark wood. There are framed photos on the walls of various sports teams lined up for the camera.

"They're working the college vibe pretty hard," I point out as we take a seat near the window.

"Yeah," Frederick agrees. "Don't look for my mug in any of those football team pictures."

Our waitress has a cow the second she identifies her famous customer. "Oh my God," she gasps at Frederick. "I'm such a big fan. Will you sign my order book?" She thrusts a pad and pen at him.

"Sure thing, Darcy," he says, reading her name tag. "It would be my pleasure." He signs with a flourish and a smile. When she skips away, he smiles at me too. "This town likes me."

Wonderful. But will it like me too?

I'm jittery. And somehow we order the same meal that we did the first time I ever had dinner with Frederick. I pick at the Cobb salad, just like in Orlando. But Frederick devours his burger and enjoys a beer. "They have excellent fries here," he says. "Try one."

I shake my head.

The waitress comes back to our table for the fourth time in half an hour. "Anyone need anything?"

"We're good," I say wearily. All I want right now is to go home to my old, familiar school in Florida.

Why did this ever seem like a good idea?

———

An hour later, a smiling guidance counselor wearing an ASK ME ANYTHING sticker hands me a key card that I accept with a shaky hand. "Welcome, Rachel!" she says. Then we walk through an old iron gate into a pretty courtyard.

Habernacker is a big, U-shaped brick building with dozens of sets of green shutters.

"Fancy," Frederick says, turning around to take it in.

I've been told to go into entryway number two, and now I understand why. The hallways of the old building are vertical. As we climb the stone stairs, we pass just two rooms per floor, with a bathroom on the landing between them.

When we find room thirty-one on the third floor, the door is ajar. It opens with a squeak. A pretty girl with curly black hair stands up from where she's bent over a trunk. "Oh!" She clasps her hands together. "You are Rachel?" She rolls the 'R' in Rachel a bit. Her accent is adorable. "I'm Aurora! I've been waiting to meet you!" She runs over to hug me. "And you are Rachel's papa?" As I watch, Aurora hugs him too.

My father turns on the charm and asks Aurora the questions that I'm still too nervous to stammer out. "Are you a senior as well?"

"Sí!" Then she laughs. "It will take me a couple of days to get used to speaking English again. I am transferring from my

Spanish school for senior year. My father wants me to get into Harvard."

"Ah," Frederick says. "Like me."

"Really?" Aurora squeals.

"Joking!" He beams. "I went to Claiborne up the road, where I majored in music and parental disappointment. But I think you and Rachel are on a different track."

I'm busy inspecting our room, which has wood floors and funky old windows.

"Look!" Aurora grasps my wrist. "This *eez* a very nice room. They put the desks out here in the common room..." She darts through a doorway. "and the beds in here."

I follow Aurora into another little room, where there are two narrow metal beds set in an "L" shape.

"I *did* not make up a bed yet. I thought you could choose."

"Oh, that's nice of you," I stammer, tongue-tied. Over Aurora's head, my father is smiling. His face says: *See? This is going to be okay.*

"What do you *think*?"

"Either one," I say.

———

After verifying that my boxes have arrived from California, Frederick leaves. "Walk me out for a second," he says, ducking into the stairwell.

I follow him down the stairs and into the courtyard, where dusk is deepening the sky.

"It's still okay with you if I look at houses?" he asks.

"Yeah." He's picked the right time to ask, because at this moment it's all I can do to keep from clinging to him like a life preserver.

"I want to get out of L.A. and this place is *really* out of the way. Hard to say whether I'll find a decent house, but I'll look."

"Okay. Sure?"

"I'll poke around and see what I find. Now, you and the roomie have some fun before the homework starts up."

"Right."

"Text me tomorrow for proof of life." He winks and turns away.

"Wait." I surprise myself. I'm just not ready to see him go.

He turns back.

"What are you going to do this week?"

"Look at real estate listings," he says. "Watch the first football game of the season. YouTube. Beer. Chips." He gives me a searching look. "Everything okay?"

"Yup." I swallow. "G'night."

Frederick laughs, but I don't know why. Then he takes three steps forward and puts his hands on my shoulders. He dips his chin and gives me a quick kiss on the forehead. "Go have fun," he says quietly. "I'll see you before I have to go back to Cali." He gives my shoulders a squeeze and then backs away, a patient smile on his face.

I turn around and march back up the stairs.

―――――

Aurora and I spend the next couple of hours arranging our belongings. We put our desks next to one another, leaving one wall of our living room empty.

We also have a generous window seat above an old radiator. "It would be nice to find a cushion to put here," I muse, running my hand along the dark wooden seat.

"*Si*! Also, we need a rug," Aurora says. "And some beanbag chairs. From Ceramic Barn, maybe?"

"Pottery Barn?" I guess.

"Yes! We will order tomorrow." She claps her hands. "And now we'll go out to meet people. There's a list of activities..."

She grabs a sheet of paper off her desk and scans it. But I'm perfectly happy staying here where it's safe. Meeting one new person feels like a good first-day quota.

"Ice cream social at nine," she says. "That's perfect. What shall we do before?" She hands over the list.

"Touch-football is not happening," I grumble, reading the first item. There's a tour of the school's arts facilities starting in ten minutes. That sounds low-key enough.

But then I spot something even more promising.

"I wouldn't mind going to this," I say, pointing at one of the last items on the list. "It's just starting."

Aurora peers over my shoulder. "Telescope Talk? Really?"

"Doesn't that sound nice?" The description reads: *Public viewing hours at the Claiborne telescope. Student astronomers show you the stars.*

"Do you love the science?" Aurora asks. She makes a face. "It will take me a few days to remember English."

"Your English is fine. Science isn't really my thing, but my Claiborne summer pen pal likes it."

My new roommate studies me with smiling eyes. "Is this astronomer a boy, perhaps?"

"Well, sure."

Her grin breaks free.

"But it's not like that," I say quickly.

"Ah." She hooks an arm in mine. "Let's go find this pen pal. He is hot?"

"No idea," I admit. "But he sure is nice."

———

The school telescope is located on top of a brick, castle-like monument on a hill behind the dorms. We walk the last hundred yards in near darkness.

"You are sure this is the right place?" Aurora puffs as we climb a second set of stone stairs.

"Think so." Though my confidence is faltering by the second.

If I were going to film a horror movie on the Claiborne campus, this would make a great setting.

When we reach the top, a boy's voice can be heard. "Who's seen the movie *The Martian*?"

We round the corner to spot a black telescope, shiny in the dim light, and a boy with a blond buzz cut gesturing to a small crowd of students and parents.

"Yeah?" he asks the show of hands. "Who's seen it way more than once?" He raises his own hand, and the adults chuckle politely.

"Wow," Aurora breathes beside me. "Is this your friend? So cute."

He really is. Although I'm not sure it's Jake. The voice seems right. But my pen pal described himself as a super nerd. This boy is sportier looking than that. Even in the dim light it's possible to ogle the muscles bulging in his arms.

He's wearing glasses. And my gaze snags on one detail. His T-shirt reads, *Talk Nerdy to Me*.

"If you're just joining us," the boy says, glancing from me to Aurora, "we're about to look at Mars, which is that red body visible just above the horizon. Mars is visible in the early evenings..." He keeps up his sermon while pulling his phone from his pocket and tapping the screen without looking. "... thirty-four million miles away..."

My phone vibrates in my pocket.

The hair stands up on the back of my neck as I pull it out and check the lock screen. There's a one-word text from Jake. *Hi.*

"Okay!" he says to the crowd. "Let me just check our focus, here." He leans over the eyepiece and adjusts something. "Step up and take a look, but try not to jostle the scope. If it's your turn, and you don't see Mars, let me know and I'll adjust the scope."

One at a time, members of the small crowd begin to take turns at the eyepiece.

"Come on," Aurora says, nudging me. "Don't you want to say hello?"

I do, but I'm not ready. Aurora steps forward, though, and suddenly hanging back is no longer an option. We move closer to Jake and the scope.

My heart booms in my chest as we arrive in front of him. "So I take it that you're Jake?" *Please?*

A smile tugs at his lips. "Aw, Rachel!" He surprises me by pulling me into a tight hug. For one lovely second I'm squeezed against a hard chest. He smells like clean T-shirts and summertime. Not fried clams.

The hug ends almost before it began.

"I guess you didn't look me up on Instagram like I did you! Welcome to Claiborne, Rachel Kress. And you must be Aurora?" He hugs her too, and the two of them begin to chat. But I lose a minute or two of the conversation, jetlagged by that hug, and by the mismatch between the Jake of my imagination and the real-life Jake.

And he looked me up on Instagram. I file that away to think about later.

"Let's look at the moon next," Jake says to the crowd. "Most of the time she just gets in my way, but tonight I'll forgive her for that…"

———

Fifteen minutes later—after I'd learned what a nebula is and peered at lunar craters through the telescope—the talk ends. But Jake is waylaid by a lingering parent's questions.

"We can wait for him," Aurora whispers. "He can go with us to the ice cream social, maybe."

"Okay," I say, feeling pretty awkward about the whole thing. I hadn't expected him to be so…attractive. And therefore hard to talk to.

When he's finally free, he turns to us with a smile. "Ice cream?"

"Of course," Aurora says easily.

So, with a pounding heart and weirdly clammy hands, I follow my two new friends back down the path toward campus.

It's so pretty here. And I don't mean the boy walking beside me. Claiborne in three dimensions is even more charming than on the map, with brick and clapboard everywhere, and endless green shutters on the buildings. The flagstone paths are lit with old-fashioned iron lamps. I could almost convince myself we've gone back in time a hundred years.

Until we reach the crowd on the lawn.

The number of students queued up for ice cream is startling. We add ourselves to a long, chatty line. At the front, cooks in white hats are scooping ice cream into paper bowls.

"So you're from Spain?" Jake asks Aurora.

"Madrid," she says. "My father has warned me about the winters here, but I like to ski."

"Did your father go to Claiborne Prep?" Jake asks.

"Oh yes. He talks about it all the time. He is a fanatic."

"Sounds familiar," Jake says. "My family bleeds green. My brother is the football quarterback. He's a PG this year."

"Oh," says Aurora.

"What's a PG?" I have to ask.

Jake snickers. "Post-grad. He was a senior last year, but he didn't get into the colleges he expected to get into. So he's having a do-over. I can't even gloat because I'm stuck with him another year."

"Your brother is not likable?" Aurora asks, accepting a bowl of chocolate ice cream from one of the servers. "Gracias," she says, moving on to the toppings.

"Eh," Jake says, choosing vanilla. "Lots of people like my brother. He plays lacrosse in the off season, and he's the president of the Gentlemen Songsters." He turns to me. "That's the men's a cappella group." But I know that already. "My brother has many enviable qualities except for one."

"What?" I ask.

"He is a total asshat."

Aurora giggles. "What is *asshat*?"

"When you meet him, you'll know." Jake dumps a spoonful of Oreo crumbs on his ice cream.

When we look for seats, all the tables in the tent are full. So Jake leads us over to a stone wall where we sit three in a row. I'm in the middle. Taking small bites of my chocolate ice cream, I surreptitiously admire the curve of muscle at the top of Jake's knee.

Did he have to be so cute? It's making me self-conscious. I'd pegged Jake for an über-nerd, but I obviously got that wrong.

"So this year is weird for me," Jake is saying. "Most of my friends graduated last year, which kind of sucks. But I thought I'd be rid of my brother…"

"The asshat," I put in.

"Right. But *he's* still here. What a rip-off. And it's weird having my parents across the ocean on sabbatical," Jake admits. "We're renting a ski condo in Vermont for Christmas break, because our house is leased out until June."

"Your father is a college professor?" Aurora asks.

"Yes, of physics. And my mother is too. Sociology."

"Ah. My father is a banker," Aurora says. "And Rachel's father is a famous singer. Freddy Ricks."

I put down my spoon in surprise.

Aurora grins. "I knew him immediately—I saw his concert in Barcelona two years ago."

Jake stares at me. "No way."

And here I thought it wouldn't come up so soon.

"Sorry," Aurora says. "I should let you tell it. But he seems nice, and I'm thinking—what if Rachel was there in Barcelona? Maybe we were in the same room already. Wouldn't that be neat?"

"Well, uh…" I take another bite, stalling. Telling people my story is one of the things I've been dreading. I mean—I *wish* my father had ever taken me to Barcelona.

"What?" Jake asks. "Is your father an asshat?"

It really depends who you ask. "My story is kind of a conversation stopper. I've been wondering what I'll say."

They're both smiling at me, and I have to make a quick decision about how much of my craziness I'm willing to drop in their laps. "I don't usually live with my father," I begin, as my throat inevitably tightens up. "But my mother died about two months ago."

"Oh, *sweetie*," Aurora breathes, laying her hand on my arm.

Great. Now I'm going to make everyone sad. "See? I should have gone with: 'I'm from Orlando.'"

Behind his big spectacles, Jake's blue eyes blink at me seriously. "You didn't, uh, mention that before."

There's a beat of silence. Then Aurora jumps up. "My phone is ringing." She walks away, leaving the two of us alone.

Jake scrubs a hand over his forehead. "I whined about my college applications. Kinda seems stupid now."

"No," I croak. "You were so nice and I didn't know how to bring it up."

He hangs his head. "You said your summer was stressful. I just didn't think…"

"I *know*." My real middle name ought to be *Awkward*. "Look—it was really nice to read letters that weren't about people dying. I needed that."

He lifts his chin and studies me.

"And—just so you know—I really *am* worried about puking during my audition. That was absolutely true."

"You won't." The corners of his mouth twitch. "The universe owes you one."

"Not sure it works that way."

"It should, though." He smiles, and it's such a nice smile that I wish I could just climb inside it and live there.

———

That night Aurora and I lay in our extra-long twin beds, talking in the dark. I learn that Aurora is also an only child, and that her parents divorced when she was six.

"How *did* your mother die?" Aurora asks.

"Breast cancer. She beat it once when I was ten. But not this time."

"That is horrible."

The dark makes everything easier to talk about. "The end came suddenly. People tell me it could have been worse. She wasn't in terrible pain."

"Your papa is lovely."

That's a nice thing to say. But would her opinion change if I told her we met only a few weeks ago? I don't tell her, because it's just so *shameful*. And not just for Frederick. When you don't meet your dad for seventeen years, a part of you believes that you're the reason why.

I used to wonder what was so wrong with me that he didn't want to meet me.

I still wonder it.

"What is he like?" Aurora asks. "What does he do for fun?"

What an excellent question. I rack my brain for details of all those puff pieces I've read about him over the years. "He likes the beach." I've seen shots of him surfing in Australia. And walking at the edge of the Mediterranean in the South of France. "I never lived with him before this summer," I add, feeling guilty about my deception. "My parents lived two thousand miles apart." *Lived.* The past tense will never sound right to me.

"But has your father been good with you since your mother died?"

"Yes, he has." And that's the truth, even if I'm not telling the whole story. People are always going to give Frederick the benefit of the doubt. His Facebook fan page has a million likes.

"I *think*..." Aurora pauses. "In Spanish we say 'no hay mal que por bien no venga.' There is no evil which does not bring some good."

"That is a very nice saying."

"Your life right now is a fairy tale," Aurora says. "The mother dies, and you are sent to your father, who is king of a faraway land."

"Any minute now there will be trolls and dragons," I point out.

"There may be," Aurora agrees, shifting in her bed. "And evil stepmothers. I have one of those." She is silent for a moment. "But every fairy tale has a righteous ending, Rachel. It's guaranteed."

I laugh into the darkness, hoping she's right.

Chapter Fourteen

THE FOLLOWING MORNING I meet Dr. Charles, an elderly guidance counselor who gives me my schedule. "Don't be a stranger, Miss Rachel," he says. "We'll speak more next month when you're ready to start applying to college."

I am so not ready for that.

But my courses look good. I text Jake to tell him that I got the Russian lit class. *All those hours with Anna K are going to pay off.*

His reply: *Nerds of the world, unite.*

Aurora and I have three classes together—government, physics, and calculus. It's nice to know another newbie senior as we weave our way around the beautiful campus, trying to find each new classroom.

As classes get underway, I decide that Claiborne Prep really does feel like the big leagues. The teachers speak quickly and never repeat themselves, and there is a lot less goofing off in classrooms. The worst behavior I see that first week is some surreptitious checking of phones during class.

And the homework assignments! Even during the first week, they're intense.

At mealtime, Aurora and I always go to the Habernacker dining hall together. I love its old-world formality. The chairs are oversized, like heavy wooden thrones. There are red leather banquette seats against the walls.

Those are the good seats. But since the wooden tables are comically long, if you want to claim an empty space in the middle of the bench, you have to either duck under the table or walk along the seat cushion, stepping carefully behind the neighboring diners.

On the third day of school, Jake sets his dinner tray down on the table across from me and Aurora, and my heart leaps. It does that every time Jake appears.

And since he lives in the same entryway of Habernacker—two floors up—my poor little heart gets a frequent workout. I've discovered that if I prop open our door, he'll stop in on his way upstairs to say hi.

"Jake," Aurora says before he can even sit down. "We're going to the showcase concert after dinner. You'll come with us?" The way she says it just assumes he'll say yes. Aurora isn't nervous around Jake the way I am.

"Why not," he says. Today his T-shirt features a couple of triangles. One of them says "You're so obtuse" to the other one.

"Rachel wants to rush a singing group," she adds. "Why is it called 'rush?'"

He shrugs. "It should be called, Kiss Some Ass And Hope They Choose You."

"Auditions start this weekend," I say, feeling my stomach dive. "I'm not ready."

"Sure you are," he says, picking up his fork and stabbing a piece of pasta with it. "You're not going to puke. That only happens in *Pitch Perfect.*"

My phone buzzes in my pocket, and I pull it out. **Survived first 72 hrs?** my father has texted.

I tap my reply. **Unpacked. Found all my classes. Aurora = good people. You?**

Restaurants. Walk. Burritos = meh. Realtor = good people.

Me: *Cool. Having dinner with friends. Got to go.*

Frederick: *Dinner w/ friends. How nonchalant. As opposed to "chalant," which is not a word.*

I grin at the screen. *You've been saving that up, haven't U?*

Frederick: *:D*

"What's so funny?" Jake asks.

"My father made a joke," I say, putting the phone away.

"Did you hear?" Aurora gushes. "He's thinking of finding a place to stay in Claiborne, to be near Rachel."

I drain my Diet Coke. "Father of the year, eighteen years in a row."

If they only knew.

———

"What a crowd," I say as the auditorium fills up for the concert. There are *eight* musical groups at Claiborne, or "CPrep" as Jake calls the school. And it looks like everyone else on campus has shown up to see them.

"Music is a big deal here," Jake says. "And the a cappella groups are the top of the food chain. I used to like a cappella, but Asshat kind of ruined it for me."

The lights go down as the jazz band walks onto the stage. A teacher wearing a red satin dinner jacket and a ponytail takes a short bow to applause. Then he turns toward his crew, lifts his hands, and counts them in. "One. Two. And a one, two, three, four..."

The band erupts into a bouncy, complicated swing tune, the likes of which no band in the history of my Orlando public school could ever have mastered. I know nothing of jazz, but to my ears they sound ready for Lincoln Center.

If all the musical groups are this good, I'm screwed.

The jazz band is followed by the glee club, all forty members. They sing the school fight song in four-part harmony, their voices blending expertly. They finish to wild applause.

"Wow," I say, clapping.

Jake just smiles at me, like I've done something cute.

Next up is the Belle Choir, so I sit up straighter in my chair. There are a dozen of them. They link arms at center stage, making a horseshoe formation. Then a woman with short blond hair hums a note. "She's called the 'pitch,'" Jake whispers in my ear.

The pitch raises her hands, and a dozen girls launch simultaneously into the most accomplished version of "Fly Me to the Moon" that I have ever heard.

I have goosebumps.

"Nice," Aurora says when they finish. But their performance was so much better than nice. As they exit stage left, I itch to follow them.

The jam closes with the Senior Songsters, the boys' a cappella group. "I'll give you ten seconds to pick out Asshat," Jake whispers just as they walk on. "One, two, three…"

"There!" Aurora says, pointing at the fifth guy in line. Even from the back of the auditorium, it's obvious. Jake's brother looks like a bigger, more angular version of Jake, without glasses. And he carries himself like a prince.

"That's the one." Jake sighs. "Consider yourselves warned."

———

I register for the Belle Choir auditions the next day without telling anyone, so that if I'm eliminated in the first round, it won't be so embarrassing. Signing up is as simple as writing my name down for a fifteen-minute time slot, and checking a box for "alto."

When I show up to sing the next afternoon, I find all the girls waiting in their horseshoe formation.

"Welcome, Rachel!" says the blond pitch. "I'm Jessica. We're going to do some arpeggios to warm you up. And then—are you familiar with 'Scarborough Fair?'"

"Sure—the melody," I reply. Would they ask me to sight-read a harmony part? That would be nerve-wracking, but I can manage if I have to.

"The melody is all you need—our arrangement has an alto melody line. That's why we use it as an audition piece."

"Okay."

"We're all going to sing it twice. The first time through, don't worry about blending. We want to hear your voice. The second time through, that's when you blend."

"Got it." It's baby stuff. My shoulders relax during the warmup. And I carry "Scarborough Fair" without even trying.

"We'll be in touch," the pitch says afterward.

I hope it's true.

———

They don't call me the next day. And they don't call the day after that.

Frederick departs for L.A., and I spend a massive amount of time on homework. Since Aurora and I chat too much when we're both home, I pick out a corner of the massive CPrep library to work.

Like everything else at Claiborne, the library is gorgeous, with vaulted ceilings and paneled walls. At night, the main reading room is lit by old chandeliers. But I prefer to work in the stacks, which are less glamorous. There are four floors of shelved books, punctuated with the occasional study carrel.

I sit with my books and listen to the hush. These are the moments when I can feel my mother with me. I know she never lived in a dorm. She was a "townie" as she once called it. But when I'm trotting over the ancient slate flagstones it's as if she's watching from above. When I open my textbook in the library, I feel her beside me, breathing in the smell of old books.

She may have sat in this very corner of the library once. She would have been almost exactly my age.

At Claiborne, I find I'm able to think of her without too much pain. In Orlando I had to squeeze her out of my mind, because I was so scared all the time that thoughts of her might break me.

Here, I miss her in a way that isn't quite so gut-wrenching. Coming to Claiborne alone had been our plan. I was *supposed* to miss her here, in this little world of bricks and leaded-glass windows.

Get that assignment done, Rachel, she whispers to me when I get too lost in my daydreams.

———

Two weeks after my Belle Choir audition, I finally get an email from them. And it sends me running all the way back to Habernacker to find Jake. In our entryway, I keep climbing past my own door until I get to Jake's. Pausing there to get my panting under control, I eventually knock.

There's nobody home.

Defeated, I skip down two flights, only to find him in my own common room, studying with Aurora.

"Help me, Jake," I say, flinging myself onto the fluffy rug Aurora bought for our room.

"He would love to," Aurora says from the window seat.

Jake's color deepens. "Do you come seeking nerd wisdom?" His T-shirt reads *Math Ninja* and pictures a warrior about to karate chop the symbol for Pi.

"I need to know what a rush meal is. I've just been invited to one."

"For the Belle Choir?" He puts down his book.

"Yes."

"*Nice,*" he says. "You'll still talk to us little people after they tap you, right?"

"Only if you tell her what a rush meal is," Aurora puts in.

"Okay. A rush meal is just dinner in the dining hall. But three or four of the singers sit with you and try to figure out if you're cool enough to spend the rest of the year with. It's really all just a popularity contest."

My heart drops to my stomach. "Ugh. I thought it was supposed to be about the music?"

"You'd think." Jake nods. "But you'd be wrong."

"Your audition must have gone well," Aurora points out.

"I guess." But singing is easier than conversation.

———

The next evening I'm tackling some problems for calculus on our window seat. But Aurora is hungry. "I just want to finish this chapter, okay? And then we'll eat," I promise.

She taps her foot on our ancient oak floor. "Can we go now? The homework will wait for you. Your rush meal is not tonight?"

"Nope. Tomorrow."

"Then what are we waiting for?"

Since I prefer not to say, I give in, closing my book. "Let's go, then."

As we trot down the entryway stairs, I hear my phone chime with a text from Frederick. He's back in town, and I've given him his own ringtone now. Every time it rings, I check it immediately. I'm waiting for a text that says, *I found a house.*

If he doesn't, he'll probably go back to L.A. for good. I'm sort of bracing myself. But earlier today he sent a text that said only: *Inane.* It took me a moment, but then I realized he'd added another word to our strange collection of negatives without positives.

Not to be outdone, I'd spent a portion of my Russian lit lecture trying to think of a follow-up. *Feckless* I'd eventually replied. And if the new text in my pocket is another word from Frederick, I'm ready with a follow-up.

At the bottom of the stairs, I throw open the door and almost run right into my father.

"That was quick," he says.

"What?"

"I just texted you to ask if you were free for dinner. Tomorrow, I have to go back to L.A. Henry's got his panties in a bunch."

"Oh." Since he hasn't found a house yet… Is this it? He's throwing in the towel on Claiborne?

I don't ask, because Aurora is standing beside me.

He clears his throat. "So what do you girls feel like? Sushi? Burgers? I've already discovered that burritos are out of the question."

"That bad, are they?" Aurora smiles.

"Whatever you're thinking, it's worse." Frederick rocks back on his heels. "I'm going to eat nothing but Mexican food for the next three weeks. And maybe I'll bring some burritos in my carry-on when I come back."

I replay the words he's just said in my head, and then follow Frederick and Aurora toward Main Street.

We end up at Wheelock's, where Darcy, the exuberant waitress, pounces once again. "You're back!" she shrieks. "Give me two minutes, and I'll have your special table cleared."

"Your *special table*?" I ask when she walks away.

But he only points at me and smiles. "Disheveled," he says.

"Incognito!" I reply.

"What?" Aurora asks.

"It's just a word game we play," I explain.

"Oh, like Friendly Words?"

Frederick winks at me. "Actually, I may have a bit of a Friendly Words addiction."

Aurora's eyes light up, and she digs her phone out of her purse. "What's your handle? Rachel, is he going to crush me?"

Darcy beckons to us.

"We'll see," my father says, leading us to a table. "Rachel has never challenged me to a game of Friendly Words." He pulls out my chair for me. "I think she's chicken."

"What?" I shoot back. "Maybe I'm just trying to save your feelings."

He takes out his phone. "You realize we have to settle this, right? One game, no tears. What's your chat handle?"

"ChoirGirl1998."

I see his eyes rise from his phone to me. "Choir girl?"

Whoops. "It's a movie reference," I lie. "Chick flick."

Aurora gives me a strange look. But Frederick taps on his phone, oblivious.

"Well, hello again!" The waitress puts a beer in front of Frederick.

"Hi, Darcy," Frederick says.

"I assume you wanted your usual. Unless you'd like to mix it up for once in your life."

"If it aint' broken..." he says. This must be their new shtick.

"And what can I bring you girls?"

"Diet Coke, please?"

"Sure, honey."

"Me too," Aurora adds. And when Darcy retreats, Aurora asks Frederick what he's going to do in L.A.

"Meetings. A few hours in the recording studio. More meetings. Mexican food."

"What happens in the recording studio?" she asks. "Wait—do you still need surgery on your hand?"

He shakes out his left wrist. "I'm all set now."

"Strange," I say, flipping my menu closed. "Wasn't it your picking hand?"

"Yep," he says easily. "It's solid now."

"That is lucky," Aurora says. Then she asks him fifty questions about the recording studio, and I hang on every word.

"Still no house yet, huh?" I ask later, putting the question to him as casually as I can, punctuating it by stealing one of his fries.

"It's frustrating," he says. "There aren't many houses for sale. But the realtor is watching for me while I'm gone. The market is a little tight, but she promises something will come up."

"What about renting?" Aurora asks.

"Same story. And I can't live in an apartment because when I practice, it's loud."

Darcy comes by again. "How is everything? Can I bring anyone a refill? Another beer?" While I stare, the woman actually gives my father's shoulders a very brief massage.

"Thanks, Darcy, but I think we're fine," he says.

"Wow," I whisper after she leaves. "That was embarrassing."

"I come here a lot," he says with a tiny shrug.

"She is not so bad," Aurora argues. "It's just that she's not afraid to show affection. You should try it sometime." She steals one of Frederick's fries too, and then points it at me. "Rachel has a thing for our neighbor."

"Aurora!" I yelp. "I do not."

"You are *such* a liar. You *think* I didn't notice you were stalling tonight, because he gets to the dining hall late on Tuesdays and Thursdays?"

Crap. "I needed to ask him for help with my calculus homework."

Both Aurora and Frederick laugh. "Subtle," he says.

Darcy rounds the corner to check on us for the ten-thousandth time. "Check, please," I say a little more forcefully than is strictly necessary.

"You got it, baby." She pats my arm, as if we're besties.

The following night is my rush meal. And I know it will go poorly the moment Jessica opens with, "So, tell us about yourself."

Three faces look across the table at me. In addition to the pitch, who is clearly in charge, there is another Jessica as well. My third interrogator is Daria. Of the three, she has the warmest smile.

"Well, I'm from Orlando." That's going to be my standard opener for the foreseeable future. "I went to a giant school with a big choral program, so there was lots of opportunity for performing."

Their nods are polite.

"We did a bunch of choral competitions." God, could I be any less cool? I'm a big nerd who spends a lot of time on homework. But I can't make that sound cool.

"And what draws you to the Belle Choir?"

"I just really like your sound." *Clunk.* Another dull statement. But it's not easy to put into words how badly I need to stand in that half-circle of girls and feel the warmth of other voices vibrating around me. Singing is my favorite thing in the world, and I need that in my life. Badly. I haven't sung a note in months, and that's not something I can explain, either.

"Are you also auditioning for the Glee Club?" Daria asks.

"Oh! No," I say quickly. But I can see my tactical error on their faces. Rushing *only* the Belle Choir is too presumptuous. "I like your repertoire best," I add lamely. I'm flailing.

"Why don't you tell us about the kinds of music that interest you?" Jessica suggests. "What do you listen to?"

"Right." I'm on firmer footing when I don't have to talk about myself. Then again, I listen to a whole lot of male singer-songwriters my father's age and older. And isn't that just plain weird?

Think, Rachel! "Well, for female vocals, I like the Civil Wars." That's a good start. "Um, Adele has great timbre, but some of her songwriting is a little poppy for my taste."

They're nodding along, so I kept going. "I'm a bit of a nerd about songwriters. Ingrid Michaelson is interesting to me. And Lourdes, because she did everything so young."

"She is cool," Daria agrees.

"For group vocals, I like some older stuff by the Indigo Girls— they always amaze me. Talk about blending voices…"

"Right?" Jessica puts in.

My brain freezes up again. But that's when Aurora sets a cup of coffee on the table and sits down next to me. I've never been so happy to see anyone in my life.

"This is my roommate, Aurora," I introduce her. "This is Jessica and Jessica and Daria."

Aurora beams at them. What I wouldn't do for a tiny bit of my roommate's boundless confidence. "She dragged me to your concert," Aurora says with a smile. "You are getting the very best one with Rachel. Music is in her blood."

I give Aurora a warning look, but she returns it with a wink.

"How's that?" Jessica asks.

"My father is a singer-songwriter," I say slowly. I really hadn't planned on going there.

"Anyone we've heard?" she presses.

"Well...he's Freddy Ricks."

Both Jessicas shriek at once, stunning me. And then they begin to *laugh*.

"I *told* you that was him at the Boat House," the pitch says, pushing Other Jessica's shoulder. "You owe me a smoothie."

"I didn't take the bet!"

"You should have."

They keep laughing, and Aurora gives me a secretive little smile.

"Wow," Daria says slowly, covering her mouth with her hand. "Your dad is *so* amazing."

The tenor of the conversation changes immediately. Both Jessicas lean forward in their chairs. "You must get to meet some pretty cool people," the pitch guesses.

"You could go backstage *anywhere*," Daria adds.

I shrug, feeling sweaty. This line of questioning has its own perils. "His band members are fun. I try not to act like a crazy fan girl, but it's hard." That is certainly true enough.

"Maybe he would arrange a song for us," Daria says.

Oh, crap. "I didn't tell him yet that I was auditioning," I say quickly. I don't add that he's never heard me sing. Not even in the shower.

Jessica looks at her watch. "We have a few more of these meetings tonight. Do you have any questions, Rachel?"

"Just one," I admit. "How many open spots are there? I don't know whether or not to get my hopes up."

"Oh, there's four," Jessica says with a wink. "And two are for altos this year."

"You are definitely getting in," Aurora says after they go away.

With my fork, I toy with my salad. "I dropped Frederick's name. I am a name-dropper."

"I dropped it," Aurora corrects, sipping her coffee. "But do you *think* there are better altos than you?"

"Heck no."

She grins. "And do you think he'd mind?"

"Probably not."

But I mind. And somewhere out in the ether, Mom sighs with disapproval.

"Why do you call him Frederick?" Aurora asks suddenly. And here I'd thought I was done being interviewed.

"It's his name." It's also what my mother called him on those few occasions she'd mentioned him.

"You two weren't close before your mother died?" Aurora asks softly.

"You could say that." I load dishes back onto my tray. "Shall we go?"

"Sure."

Chapter Fifteen

THE BELLE CHOIR doesn't contact me again, but apparently that's normal. Instead of emailing, the competitive musical groups hold something called Tap Night, where they actually run around campus and visit the people they're tapping.

Nobody knows when Tap Night will actually happen, though.

The whole thing makes me nervous. So I dive into my homework with the fervor of a new girl. And I don't worry about making more friends, because I've already found the two best ones.

Jake and Aurora prove to be the sort who are always up for anything. Fake climbing-wall setup on the lawn? They're the first to strap on the crotch-grabbing harnesses and race to the top, Jake ringing the bell before Aurora can catch him. Bong passed around the entryway when the resident advisor is away for the weekend? Aurora and Jake are good for a hit.

I defer, mumbling, "I know, I have a good-girl complex."

Aurora shakes her head, blowing smoke out of her nose. "Never apologize for being a good girl," she says. "It looks good on you."

I hope the Belle Choir thinks so.

Instead of waiting around in my room, hoping they'll show

up, I decide to keep working at the library. Some guy in a soccer jacket has the audacity to sit in my favorite third-floor study carrel, so I have to walk up and down the rows of books until I find an empty one.

When I sit down, my gaze snags on a shelf of books that I wouldn't expect the library to have. It's several years' worth of Claiborne, New Hampshire phone books.

I get right up again and examine them. There's a copy from 1995, and that's the one I pull off the shelf. I flip quickly to the "K" section and scan for my last name.

And there it is. Alana Kress, 154 Armory Street, in the town of Wilder. Alana was my grandmother. She died when I was three, after Mom and I had already moved to Florida.

I jot down the address and look it up on an online map. The house is three miles away. It might take me an hour to walk there.

Someday I will. If my mom lived there, I want to see it.

———

When Frederick returns from L.A., I meet him for coffee on Main Street. Word has gotten out that he's been lurking in Claiborne, apparently. We get some curious looks, which Frederick is very good at ignoring.

Maybe he doesn't even notice people staring anymore.

"What are you doing this week?" I ask him.

"Looking at houses. Avoiding Henry's calls."

"How's that going?"

"Mute is a very useful feature."

"I meant the other thing." I stir the coffee in my cup and try to look disinterested.

"It's a small town, and there's not much available. But the realtor says something will shake loose eventually."

I wonder what will happen if nothing does.

"What's new with you?" he asks.

"Homework, and plenty of it." I never told him about my Belle

Choir audition, and since I haven't heard from them, it seems like I never will.

That Saturday night, Aurora suggests a horror movie that's playing in the student center.

"Let's watch something here," Jake suggests, sitting on the S.L.O.— the squishy Sofa-Like Object that Aurora and I bought. It's a cross between a futon and a giant beanbag, and it fits the three of us, more or less.

"Horror makes you squeamish?" I tease.

"Did you just call me chicken?" He smiles back at me, and I find myself wanting to reach out and measure his dimple with my fingertip.

"Or we could play Hearts," Aurora proposes. "The three-person version."

"Sure," Jake says. "Get the cards."

————

I lose miserably, several times in a row. "Ugh. Can we go out for a snack now?" There's a gelato place that's open until nine on the weekends.

"Nah," Jake says. "Let's stay here." Jake sets the cards on the floor and picks up a copy of the student newspaper off our makeshift coffee table.

I watch him for a second, feeling as if I'm missing something.

"If we're not having gelato, I'm going to make some tea," Aurora says, carrying her electric kettle into the bathroom for a refill.

As I watch, Jake pulls out his phone and checks the time. Then he puts it back.

"What are you waiting for?" I demand.

He shrugs, sticking his face in the paper again.

Outside, I hear voices and the sound of running feet across the courtyard. I go to the window and look down. A group of guys is hustling into the door of entryway 3.

As the door shuts behind them, I feel the hair rise on the back of my neck.

There are several rooms with the lights on over in entryway 3. After a minute I see the group appear in a room on the fourth floor. Aurora, back with her kettle, comes to stand beside me.

"Open the window," she says.

I do, and we can hear the faint sounds of singing—the school fight song, in four-part harmony.

I turn around to look at Jake. "It's tap night for the singing groups, isn't it?"

His eyes lift from the newspaper and he nods. "Worst kept secret on campus."

"Oh." I go to sit next to him on the S.L.O. "So... I guess I'm waiting, aren't I?"

Jake puts his hand on top of mine for about a nanosecond. Then he takes it back again.

"Thank you for not telling me earlier," I say in a low voice. "I'd be a wreck."

From her desk chair, Aurora snorts. "Jake is excellent at not telling."

The minutes tick by. Aurora busies herself with flipping through a magazine, and I busy myself with feeling ill. Every minute that goes by is a minute when the Belle Choir is busy tapping someone who is not me.

Eventually there's the sound of running feet in the courtyard again. The three of us look at each other, but I don't get up to see which entryway they're approaching. Then, over the thudding sound of my heart, I heard footfalls in our stairwell.

Aurora jumps off the couch. "They're coming for you!" She throws open our door. Jessica rushes in first, followed by Daria, Other Jessica, and nine other girls. They made a quick horseshoe in front of me and began to sing "Our Glory Years," a traditional Claiborne song.

I just stand there, open-mouthed, while the sounds of twelve blended voices reverberate off the walls. When it's over, Jessica beckons me to the end of the horseshoe and puts an arm around me. "Rachel, would you like to be a member of the Belle Choir?"

"Heck, yes!"

There's a cheer from the hallway and I turn to see a small group of our neighbors peering in.

Twelve girls hug me quickly. And then the Belle Choir begins to file out of the room, on their way to tap somebody else.

I close the door, then turn to see my two friends smiling at me. Aurora claps her hands. "Don't you want to call your dad and tell him?"

But hearing his name is not what I need right now. Because I'll never know whether I would have gotten in if I wasn't Freddy Ricks's daughter. "It can wait," I say.

———

October arrives, and the trees all over town are painted in glorious colors. The maples turn an astonishingly bright shade of red, and the yellow elm leaves look lit from within.

The sun begins to set very early, which means it's already dark when my Belle Choir rehearsals end each evening.

I walk back to Habernacker alone, humming whatever tune we've sung last. We're working on Jessica's arrangement of John Lennon's "Imagine." She's made it into an ensemble piece, bringing in voices one by one until it rises to a great crescendo. The climax of the song makes chills run up and down my back, in the best possible way.

Jessica—the pitch—runs the Belle Choir with an iron fist. During the first couple of rehearsals I was a little afraid of her. Maybe that's silly, but I want to do well.

When she gives me a solo stanza of "Imagine," though, I start to relax. Rehearsal is my favorite thing to do. Life is basically perfect between seven and eight p.m. on weeknights.

The Saturday before Halloween, I play a Belle Choir recording while Aurora and I sit painting each other's toenails on the S.L.O.

"If you get sick of hearing this music, just say the word," I insist. "I'm still trying to learn the repertoire. But...hold still! You wiggle too much."

"I can't help it," Aurora claims. "I'm very *teecklish*."

There's a knock on our door.

"Come in, Jake!" Aurora calls.

"How'd you know it was me?" he asks, opening the door.

"X-ray vision," I supply. But who else would it be?

The smile he gives us is devilish. "Looks like I'm interrupting something kinky."

"Oh, you wish," Aurora scoffs. "Rachel, that looks fine. Really."

"Well, you don't make it easy." I cap the polish and Aurora swings her legs onto our makeshift coffee table.

"Have a seat, Jake."

He climbs past Aurora and sits in the middle. His T-shirt reads: *Insufficient Memory*. "Anyone have plans tonight? Hot dates?"

"We were going to look at the movie listings," I say. My phone rings, and I get up to answer it.

"Don't smear the polish!" Aurora calls.

I walked four steps on my heels while the phone continued its trill. "Hello?"

"Rae," a soft voice says.

"Haze?"

He lets out a breath. "I just really needed to hear your voice."

"Are you okay?" My friends are watching me from the couch.

"Yeah. I just really miss you."

I give up on heel-walking and hurry into the bedroom. "I miss you too," I say as I close the door.

"Liar." He laughs gently. "You're busy."

"I *have* been busy. I should still have called you, though. But it's good not to think too much about last year."

His sigh is heavy. "Okay. I guess it would be. I could have called you too."

An excellent point. "What's new with you? How's the job?"

"I found it, by the way. The worst job at the theme park."

"Really? Which one?"

"Remember the race cars in Tomorrowland? I've been refueling them. No shade anywhere. And at the end of the day you smell like both sweat and diesel."

"Oh Haze, I'm sorry."

"It's not so bad. The pay is awesome and my pass gets me into any park. I've been on Tower of Terror about a thousand times."

There's a knock on the bedroom door.

"Just a second." I open it.

"We're thinking of going to the hockey game instead of a movie," Aurora says. "Is that okay with you?"

"Hockey? I guess. I'll be right there."

"Hockey?" Haze repeats. "That sounds fun."

"Does it? I thought they fight."

He laughs. "At your school? That would be some serious nerd-on-nerd violence. That I'd like to see."

"When you put it that way, I guess it doesn't sound so bad."

"So. Do you have a boyfriend yet?"

"No."

"You hesitated."

"I did not." *But I don't want to have this conversation.*

"I know you're far away, Rachel. But I think about you all the time."

"I'm sorry." It's the only reply I can give that's both true and also kind.

"Naw. Don't be. Have fun at the hockey game. And call me sometime."

"I will," I promise, hoping I'd follow through.

When I come out of the bedroom, Jake's eyes follow me across the room.

"Who was that?" Aurora asks.

"My best friend from Florida."

Jake stands up. "I'm going to get my coat. Face-off is in half an hour."

───────

"Come, on, SHOOT! *Aw!*" Jake collapses back into his seat.

Aurora and I exchange amused glances. Who knew that our favorite astronomer could get so worked up over sports?

There are two minutes left in the game. When Jake told me there were three periods, I didn't believe him at first.

"Of course there's three," he says. "Why is that weird?"

"I'm from football country. We like even numbers."

"Hockey players have enormous backsides," Aurora points out.

"That's padding. They're basically, like, bubble wrapped in there— NOOO!"

Jake, and half the other people in the student section, stand up to peer at our goal. "Phew. That was close. Our goalie should get the Medal of Honor."

"I need some of that padding," Aurora complains. "My derriere is cold."

"We'll have to toughen up the girls from Spain and Florida," Jake says, his eyes trained on the ice.

"Women," corrects Aurora.

"Right, just like I said. GET HIM!" Jake shouts.

I'm enjoying the view, and I don't mean the game. Jake's cheeks are flushed, and there's a solidness to him that appeals to me. Sometimes when I look at the sturdy slope from his neck to his shoulder, I wondered how it would feel to rest my hand there.

Aurora catches me watching him. She winks.

Oops. I turn my attention to the rink. "It's probably a bad sign that most of the game has been played in front of our goal, huh?"

"That would be correct," Jake grumbles. "If the center could only—" He stands. "Breakaway, baby!" One of the Claiborne players is sprinting toward the opposing side. "SHOOT!"

The player shoots. And misses. And when the game ends, the score is 0-1.

——————

The following weekend, Aurora packs an overnight bag. She's headed to Boston for the evening, to see her father who's in the country on business. She has a few minutes until it's time to leave for the bus, and she spends them texting with someone.

"Who are you talking to?" I ask peevishly. I'm annoyed at having to spend a Friday night alone.

"It's my old boyfriend in Spain."

"Isn't it the middle of the night in Spain?"

"Si. He is in a club, and his friends have all hooked up and ditched him."

"You never told me about a boyfriend. Do you miss him?"

Aurora tucks her phone into her pocket. "No, not really. He's a great guy. Really great. But we are totally wrong for each other. One of the reasons that I chose Claiborne was to make the breakup happen."

"Aurora, seriously? I wouldn't have thought you'd ever done a cowardly thing."

My roommate inspects her fingernails. "I've done a few."

I'm floored. "Well, I'm glad you did. If you liked him more, I would have missed out."

She reaches over and squeezes my hand. "See, I don't understand why you can say nice things to me, but you won't tell Jake how you feel about him."

"Maybe I don't have anything to tell." That's a total lie, which is why Aurora rolls her eyes when I say it.

But Jake is too special to risk. If I make it awkward, he might disappear.

Aurora gets to her feet. "You two deserve each other." She picks up her bag. "I'll see you tomorrow."

"Have fun!"

Our room is too quiet once she leaves to meet her father. So I pull out my phone and call my own. I haven't seen Frederick all week.

"How you doing, kid?" he answers.

"Good. I just called to see what you were up to tonight."

"Tonight?" There's a pause. "Well, I assumed you'd be busy with your friends. So I planned to stay in. I think I'm fighting off a cold."

"Okay…"

"Can we get lunch tomorrow or Sunday?"

"Sure."

After moping around for a couple hours, I remember there's something I need from the bookstore. So I put on my coat and open the door.

Lucky for me, Jake is just coming down the stairs.

"I'll come with you," he says, when I explain my errand. "I just need to drop this in a mailbox." He holds up an envelope. "For the parents. My mom writes me these letters, and I never seem to reply."

"Can we speed walk?" I ask. "I think the bookstore closes at eight."

We walk together through the cool night. Jake chatters beside me. He's all fired up about the astronomy club, which gives me an excuse to admire him under the pretense of listening. "We're looking for unidentified planets," he says. "Amateurs find planets all the time. It doesn't matter that the telescope isn't powerful enough to see them."

"Really? Then how do you know they're there?"

"Well, gravity. Stars travel in smooth orbits, unless they have a planet around them. They wobble. The size of the wobble tells you something about the planet. So you can prove they're there, even if you can't actually see them."

"Cool." I love how animated his face becomes when he's talking about telescopes.

"Why are you going to the bookstore at eight on a Friday night, anyway?" he asks.

Ouch. I know my social life isn't exactly setting the world on fire. I don't need a reminder. "Why are *you* walking me to the bookstore on a Friday night?" I counter.

Jake shrugs. "It beats playing another level of Black Ops."

"Well, *there's* an endorsement," I say under my breath.

"What?" he asks, his eyes wide.

I shake my head. "Nothing. I left my copy of *Anna Karenina* under Frederick's couch in California. And the lecture is Monday. If they don't have one, I'm screwed."

"I thought you read it already."

"Didn't memorize it, though. But you're right, I should probably find something better to do with my Friday night." As hints go, it's awfully weak. But I can't tell Jake how hyper I feel just walking with him. Or that I've memorized the shape of his smile.

"I suppose you could download a digital copy," Jake suggests. "If they're sold out."

"True." *Sigh.*

On Main Street, we pass a bar called Mary's. Something makes me stop and take a closer look at a couple who's seating themselves at a high table near the front. Maybe it's an oblique glimpse of his leather jacket, or the set of his shoulders as he arranges himself on the stool.

It's my father. The same one who just told me he was spending a quiet night alone.

I stare. Opposite him sits a woman with shiny brown hair. They're already deep in conversation. As I watch, he puts his hand on the woman's arm, and then she laughs at something he's said.

"Rachel, what's the matter?"

I don't answer. Instead, I move to the other edge of the window, so I can see the woman's face. She's pretty, with smiling eyes. But the way he looks at her makes my head ache.

"I see my dad, that's all."

"Do I get to meet him?" Jake asks.

"No," I say more forcefully than I mean to. "He looks busy." And then I drag my eyes from the window, heading down the street again. My pace forces Jake to run to keep up with me. I stop in front of the bookstore, which is already dark. The sign says that they close at seven thirty.

"*Damn*," I swear. "Damn, damn, damn." But it's not really about the bookstore. My father lied to me so smoothly. It makes me want to howl.

I can hear my mother's voice whisper, *A man will say anything*.

"Rachel." Jake puts his hands on my shoulders. "She dies in the end."

I feel close to tears. "Who does?"

And then we're facing each other, close together, looking into each other's eyes. "*Anna Karenina*," he whispers. A smile flickers across his face. The moment yawns open, the outcome hinging on me. I feel him waiting for a tiny sign from me. A signal.

Or maybe he's not waiting at all, and it's all in my head.

Frederick's lie stings. His rejection makes it impossible to be sure that Jake's smile isn't mocking me.

"She dies in the end," I say slowly. And suddenly I just can't take the pressure or the disappointment. "That's not funny," I bite out, taking a half-step backward. Jake's hands slip off my shoulders.

"Well, wait… That's not what I meant!" he says, and then cringes. "*Shit*." There's a horrible silence, one I could have broken if I weren't so torn up inside.

Angry Rachel is back. "You'd better mail that letter to your parents." I point down the street toward the post office. As if it makes no difference to me what he does with his Friday night.

Jake tightens his grip on the envelope. "Yeah. I guess. You coming?"

Slowly I shake my head.

We have another stare-down, with Jake looking at me like he's trying to solve a problem. He waits, but I don't budge. I feel as closed down as the bookstore. And dark inside.

After one more tentative glance at me, Jake turns slowly around and heads down the street. By himself.

I watch him walk away, my misery complete. I'm very much alone now, at eight o'clock on a Friday night. Breathing in the chilly November air, I have no idea what to do with myself.

I will not go back and look in the window of Mary's again. That's too pathetic, even for me. So I cross the street. The bus from Boston has just disgorged its passengers onto the sidewalk, and they fan out in every direction, wheeling bags and suitcases behind them.

One figure has only a duffel bag over his shoulder, and an oddly familiar gait. It's such an improbable sighting that I almost don't bother calling out his name.

But, God, it really looks like him. "Haze!"

He turns around.

Chapter Sixteen

I RUN TO HIM, laughing. "My God! What are you doing here?"

"What do you think? I'm here to see you. Nothing else could get me onto a bus for thirty-six hours. It's a little birthday present I'm giving to myself."

"Oh! Tomorrow. Wow. But...why didn't you tell me you were coming?"

"Because you would have told me not to bother."

He has a point. "I just..." I smile up at him. "I can't believe it's really you." He's gotten a haircut. It makes him look older, more serious. "You look good."

"I was just thinking the same thing about you." He picks me up around the waist and spins me like a child. When my feet touch down again, he takes both of my hands. "What are you doing out here alone anyway? Your hands are cold."

I exhale. "I was just running an errand, and it didn't work out."

"So where to?" Haze asks.

Now there's a good question. I'm more than a little stunned to see him and don't know quite what to think. "Let's walk," I say, sounding too much like Frederick.

Damn him.

"Actually, there's somewhere I've been meaning to walk. But it's far."

"I have time," Haze says. "Hold my hand." He hitches his bag a little higher on his shoulder, and off we go.

———

"There are bells in that tower," I say as we pass the library. "Music students play songs twice a day, and they pick the strangest things. Last week I heard Queen. "We Will Rock You."

"Those crazy prep-school kids," Haze says, squeezing my hand. "I'm glad I found you," Haze says. "I was worried that you'd be out somewhere, not answering your phone."

"Not this time."

"It's beautiful here. All these old buildings."

"Sometimes I feel like I'm walking around in a storybook. Do you want to see the library? It's kind of cool."

"Libraries really aren't my thing. Where are we headed, anyway?"

"An address in the next town. My mother lived there when she was in high school. I want to see it."

He's quiet for a second. "She went to your school, right?"

"Only for senior year."

"And then?"

"She got into U Mass, but she took a gap year. But I was born before she could start college."

"So your dad lived here somewhere?"

"Somewhere."

"You don't know where?"

I shake my head.

We walk a while in silence before Haze asks me a question. "Have you found what you were looking for here?"

Have I? I still don't know what Frederick is thinking half the time, or why he's never been in my life. "I'm working on it," I say.

He doesn't call me on it.

It takes us forty-five minutes to find the house on Armory Street. And when we arrive there isn't much to see.

"Kind of needs a paint job," Haze observes.

"At least," I say. It's a sad old wooden house with a sagging porch. "It must have looked better in 1997." That would have been the year my mother graduated from Claiborne.

"I'm sure it did," Haze says softly. But we both have eyes. This isn't a nice neighborhood. There's a rusting boat in the yard across the street.

If I came to Claiborne seeking my mom, I haven't found her yet.

"Let's go back," I say.

———

By the time we make it back to campus, we're both freezing. "Are you hungry?" I ask. "I already ate. But I could get you something."

He squeezes my hand again. "No. And I really just came to see you."

When I look up, my old friend is watching me, his gaze so familiar that it makes me ache. "My building is over there."

He stops on the sidewalk. "Are you going to get in trouble if I stay over?"

"Well..." *God*, I really don't like breaking rules. But I know the odds of getting caught are negligible. "You're not allowed to be in my room after ten. But nobody ever checks. And my roommate is away tonight."

"Okay then."

The courtyard of Habernacker is lit by old-fashioned lanterns. Haze pulls out his phone. "Which room is yours?"

"That one." I point. Aurora's red curtains are visible in the window.

Haze points the phone at the building and takes a picture. "So I can remember where you are."

I look all the way up the facade of our entryway and see someone looking down, a figure silhouetted against a fifth-floor window. *Jake*. I'm about to raise a hand to wave when he turns away.

"Lead on," Haze says.

I lead him upstairs to my room, where Haze ducks in and looks around. "It's nice. Old-school."

"Literally. Students have been living here for ninety years."

He puts his duffel bag down on Aurora's chair and runs a hand through his hair. "After two days on that bus, I could really use a shower."

"Oh. Sure. Let me get you my stuff." From the bedroom, I fetch my towel and my caddy with soap and shampoo.

He grins. "Just like summer camp."

"Follow me." I go out into the hall and check the bathroom, which is empty. "Okay, you're all set. Lock the bathroom door, okay? And I'll leave the door to my room open."

I try reading one of Aurora's magazines while I wait for him, but it's no use. I'm excited to see him, but more than a little unsettled.

When the door opens again, he tiptoes in wearing my pink towel around his waist, his clothes slung over his tattooed arm. I laugh at the sight. "You should see yourself. The badass in the pink skirt."

He doesn't speak until he'd closed the door. "Somebody spotted me," he says, his voice dropping low. "A guy was giving me the stink-eye in the hallway."

"Oh."

"Seriously. This guy looked like he was about to go and call security."

"Did he have blond hair and black glasses?"

"Yeah. He did."

I feel a pang. "That's our neighbor. He's a good guy. I don't think he'd do that." *But I do owe him an apology.*

"They let guys live here?"

"We're on separate floors."

Haze goes into the bedroom and closes the door. He comes out wearing his jeans, but no shirt.

Neither of us says anything when he sits down next to me, but my heart gets a little skittish at the proximity of all that bare skin and muscle. I punch him playfully, connecting with the eagle tattoo on his biceps, then shake out my fist. "Ouch."

"You see something you like? It's a lot easier to get to the gym when you don't have any homework."

"How's the job?"

"It's okay. I'm working in the parking lot right now. They move you around all the time, so you don't get too bored. But you do anyway."

"Did you register for classes yet?" Haze is supposed to start community college sometime this year.

"Didn't get around to it," he says.

It's very weird to sit here on our S.L.O. with Haze.

"You're staring at me," he says. "Like you never saw me before."

"Maybe if you put on a shirt I wouldn't stare." It embarrasses me to say it. But it's here with us in the room—the question of what will happen between us now.

Haze picks up my hand from where it lies on the couch, and then he brings it up to his bare chest and holds it there. His eyes lock onto mine. Then he leans toward me, and I watch the approach of his mouth as if in slow motion.

When his lips connect with the corner of my mine, they're softer than I remembered. His kiss lingers there, while I feel my heartbeat in my throat.

"Mmm…" He sighs, and I get chills. Everywhere.

Nervous, I close my eyes and focus on the warmth in his hands, which are pulling me into his chest.

"Rae…" His lips move along my jaw to my ear. When I bury my face in his neck, he smells like Haze. He smells like home.

His big hand lifts my chin, and his mouth fits against mine. His kiss is slow, like he knows I need to warm up to the idea.

And I do. Soon enough I'm leaning in for more of that affection. As his kisses build, I bask in the steadiness of his arms and the warmth of his body. He pulls me into his lap, and we keep going.

Until someone knocks on the door.

I lurch backward as panic sets in. Maybe someone *did* report Haze's presence in my dorm room? My eyes fly to the clock. It's ten thirty. Way past the legal hour for a boy to visit.

The knock comes again, and Haze eases me off his lap. Then—having more experience breaking rules than I ever will—he stands up and slips stealthily into my bedroom.

I get up and run to the door, my heart in my mouth. "Who is it?"

"Jenna from downstairs."

Okay, calm down. At least it isn't the dean standing there. I open the door. "What's up?"

My curly-haired neighbor drops her voice. "Do you have a shot glass we could borrow?"

It takes my freaked-out brain a moment to process the question. "You mean, for alcohol?"

She gives me the side-eye. "You know another use for it?"

"Sorry," I say quickly, feeling like a giant dork. "I don't have one."

"Ah, well. We're playing quarters if you want to come downstairs."

"Thanks, but I'm, uh, really tired. Going to bed."

"Suit yourself." She turns away to look elsewhere for a shot glass.

I lock the door and breathe a sigh of relief.

When I go into my bedroom, I expected to find Haze laughing about that bit of drama. But he's stretched out on my bed looking exhausted.

"You look beat," I say, patting his knee. "You should get some sleep."

"I haven't stretched out in two days."

"Get comfortable," I urge him. "I'm going to get ready for bed."

I take my nightie into the bathroom in the hallway. I change and brush my teeth.

When I get back to my room, Haze has taken my advice. He's lying in my bed looking cozy. "Come here," he says, looking at me with heavily lidded eyes. "Let me hold you."

I'd assumed I'd sleep in Aurora's bed. But I'm not good at saying no. And besides, he looks so inviting lying there. I slide into the bed with him and put my head on his chest. Our bare feet tangle. He's stripped down to boxers, his body warm and hard under mine.

"This is why I came," he says thickly. "To hold you and make sure you're all right."

"I'm all right." *Mostly.*

"After my dad died, nothing was all right for a while. Wasn't sure I'd ever be okay. Didn't want you to feel that way."

My heart gives a happy squeeze, and I snuggle closer, while his arms hold me tightly.

"Goodnight, honey," he says. And then he falls asleep.

———

When morning comes, I can't wake up. Somehow Haze extracts himself from the bed without dumping me on the floor. And the empty bed becomes so gloriously roomy that I roll over and keep sleeping.

When Haze returns, he fits his warm body against my back. I'm barely conscious as he begins dropping kisses on my neck. My shoulder. My jaw.

Wakefulness arrives slowly as his hands began to skim down

my hip and around to my belly. His lips are soft and teasing on the tender skin just below my ear.

"Rae," he breathes, and I turn my face toward the sound. He kisses me, his tongue minty as it sweeps over mine. I break out in goosebumps as he nudges me to lie flat on the bed, then covers me with his body.

Those dark eyes look down at me so lovingly. Then they fall closed as he kisses me again.

A flash of heat washes through me as his mouth connects with mine. We kiss, and for a couple of minutes I let myself enjoy it. But then his hand wanders under my nightie, his fingers skimming my tummy. When they reach the elastic of my panties, Haze tugs them down.

The next kiss seems to deprive me of too much oxygen. He lowers his hips onto mine, and suddenly everything is *way* too serious. His erection pokes me in the belly, and I'm not having fun anymore.

"Haze." I turn my face away from his to get some air. "We have to stop."

"Why?" he asks, his hand skimming up my ribcage, then palming my breast. "Is there someone else?"

I shake my head. But I don't say more, because I'm almost as afraid of the conversation as I am of...what he wants from me.

His fingers slide down again, between my legs. Panicking now, I grab his wrist.

Haze's hand goes still, but he doesn't take it away. Leaning over me, he presses a small kiss onto my belly. "Rachel. Am I not good enough for you? Because I'm not a prep-school boy?"

My heart bangs away in my chest. "What? That's not fair."

"Isn't it?" His dark eyes flash. "Who are you saving it for? Who loves you more than me?"

We both know the answer to that one: *nobody*. But I still need a time-out. I remove his hand from my crotch.

He studies me for a moment. Then he begins dropping little kisses onto my neck. It's kind of shocking, really, how many nerve endings my neck has. The slide of his lips feels much, much better than really seems fair. He teases the corner of my mouth, and then we're kissing again.

But then Haze spreads out on top of me again. The view of his muscular shoulders hovering above me is both beautiful and frightening. His kisses pick up steam, and I'm no longer comfortable.

"Haze..." I try.

"Yeah," he whispers.

I'm about to suggest that we go and find some breakfast. But he sits up and fishes a square packet off the floor—a condom. Then he shucks off his boxers. He's on top of me even as I'm picking out the words I need to call everything to a halt.

"Not that," I say, catching his face in my hands.

He drops his head to give me one quick kiss. "I know you're nervous, but I'll be gentle."

"No," I say forcefully. "It's not a good idea." I shift uncomfortably, but I don't shove his hands off my body like I want to, because I don't want to freak out at my oldest friend.

"What better chance will there be for us than this?" His dark eyes beg me. "I would never hurt you."

I know he means that. And yet people get hurt all the time, whether you mean it to happen or not. So I take the condom out of his hand. But he only takes it back from me with his teeth, chuckling.

Once more, I grab it, and this time throw it across the room.

Haze chuckles down at me. "You don't have to be nervous."

"Listen," I plead. "My mother wouldn't want me taking chances." Not only is this true, but playing the dead-mother card is the best idea I have at the moment.

His face softens. "Jenny knew this would happen."

"What?"

"She wanted us to be together. She asked me to look after you."

"Not like *that*," I argue. There are so many things wrong with his statement it's hard to know where to start. In the first place, there's a zero percent chance that my mother wanted us to be a couple. She'd called Haze a "lost boy," and welcomed him to our dinner table.

If rolling over in graves was really a thing, she'd be doing that right now.

Haze strokes my cheek. "Jenny was not as straight an arrow as you think. Why do you think she liked me so much?"

"What?"

He brushes a lock of hair out of my eyes. "Your mom had a thing for bad boys."

"That's ridiculous." It's also beside the point. My mother did *not* want me to have sex. She said so many times. She was too afraid that I'd repeat her mistakes.

Haze kisses me again, but I've already lost the thread. I'm rigid beneath him as he begins trying to heat me up again. His mouth coasts down my neck and between my breasts, but I'm done here.

"Honey," he whispers against my skin. "Love me. It's okay."

"No, it isn't." I give him a push. "And if you think it is, then you don't know me at all."

He looks up quickly, his expression made purely of hurt. "That's not nice."

"But it's *true*. Haze, get up." I feel the inconvenient press of tears at the back of my throat.

Instead of moving, he only studies me with puppy-dog eyes.

"I think you need to leave." Even as I say it, I know it's true. I can't keep having this conversation. And he isn't going to let it go.

"Rae, you don't mean that."

I give his shoulders a push. "I do mean it." But he doesn't move.

I forget to breathe. Just as I'm feeling lightheaded, he finally swings off me. "I'm going to get dressed, and then we can talk about it."

But even with a little breathing room, panic continues to rise like a crescendo in my chest. I'm practically trembling by the time Haze finishes pulling his clothes on. He jams one of his feet into a shoe.

"Is there a coffee shop around here?" he asks.

I shake my head. "I need to be alone right now." My head is so scrambled that I'm not standing up for myself well enough. But I'm afraid and he doesn't seem to care. "You shouldn't have come," I tell him. *Not if you won't listen to me.*

His reaction is a predictable mix of hurt and horror. "How can you say that to me? I took a thirty-six-hour bus ride to see you."

My throat cracks. "I didn't ask you to do that." This is *exactly* what I'd been trying to avoid. My oldest friend loves me in a way that I can't return. And I only know one way to make it stop.

His eyes narrow. "No. But you asked me to be there all the times you needed a ride from school or the group home. But now that you're at the big fancy school, I'm no good anymore."

The tears come then. I can't hold them back anymore. "It's not like that."

"It's exactly like that. I'm good enough to play chauffeur, but not to be your guy."

"You are my *friend*," I sob.

"Then why are you throwing me out?"

"Because you won't *listen* to me."

"I've been listening to you since second grade. Don't throw me out, Rachel. That will be it for us."

I get up off the bed on shaky knees. I walk through to the front door of our suite and hold it open.

"Don't do this," he says, his voice gravel.

Studying my bare toes, I almost cave. But if he doesn't go, we are just going to end up horizontal on some other surface, and I can't have that. And he should really know better.

It's a standoff. He doesn't move, and I don't meet his eyes. And then I finally do. His face creases with grief, his eyes get red.

But he shoulders his duffel bag. He stalks past me out onto the landing, and then turns to face me. "Don't do this. I love you."

I loved you too, you ass. But I don't say that, or anything else. Because we'll just end up arguing again, and he wants something I'm not willing to give.

I close the door.

Then I go right over to the lumpy Sofa-like Object and throw myself onto it. Numb, I lie curled up there, teary and tired, until my phone rings. I squint at it, hoping it isn't Haze. It's Frederick. "Hello?"

"Rachel, did I just see that kid from Florida at the bus stop?"

My breath catches. "He was here." I will not let my voice break. "I asked him to leave."

There's a deep silence on his end. "Are you okay?"

I clear my throat. "Perfectly."

Silence. "You don't sound so good."

"I'm fine. How is your *cold?*" I ask, the question dripping with sarcasm.

He doesn't even bother replying to the question. "Rachel, I feel like I'm missing something important, here. Do you want to get brunch?"

"I just ate," I lie.

He sighs. "Okay. Call me if you need me."

———

Eventually Aurora comes home, dropping her bag into the bedroom. Then she walks over to the S.L.O. and bends over me. "You look *terrible*." She rolled the R's for emphasis.

"Thanks. I missed you too."

"Rachel, what's the matter? Have you been to brunch yet? There's only a half hour left."

"No."

"Get up, no? I hope the bagels aren't finished."

Grumbling, I pull on some clothes, rope my hair into a ponytail, and follow Aurora to the dining hall.

Jake is sitting alone at a table, a long-neglected tray beside him, and the crossword puzzle open in front of him. He barely looks up as we sit down. But to me, he says, "So. Did you get it done?"

I swallow. "Get what done?"

He raises his chin slowly, his blue eyes flashing from behind the lenses of his glasses. "Your *reading*."

I shake my head.

"What is the problem?" Aurora asks us.

"Not a thing," Jake says, tossing his newspaper onto the tray. "But you're not allowed to go out of town anymore." He lifts the tray and stands.

"Jake?" I call as he walks away.

He stops and looks over his shoulder. "Yeah?"

"I'm sorry I was an asshat last night."

He gives me the tiniest of nods, his face awash with hurt. Then he leaves.

"Explain, please." Aurora eyes me over the rim of her coffee cup.

"I had the worst night. Absolutely everything went wrong."

Aurora's eyes widen. "Did something…*happen* with Jake?"

I shake my head. "Only that I was rude to him. It wasn't until later that things really went bad."

"Tell me."

I feel teary immediately. "I don't think I can." Reliving the experience will not make it better.

"But you are upset. And there is a condom on the floor under my desk."

I press two fingers against my tear ducts. "My friend from Florida showed up. He had a lot of expectations, and I wasn't…willing."

"Ouch. You don't like him that way?"

"I did a little. I think. Honestly, there was so much happening that I never got a chance to figure that out. And he just showed up last night, and when push came to shove, I couldn't go through with it. We fought this morning and I kicked him out."

Aurora puts down her cup. "Back up a second. When is the first time you hooked up? Last night?"

I shake my head. "Right after my mom died, he…" This is so hard to talk about. "There was just a little hooking up."

"Wait…*right* after? And was it your idea? Because grief can make you do all kinds of things."

I shake my head. "I was just really numb after she died. He took care of me."

"By removing your clothing. When you were still in shock."

I open my mouth to defend him, but nothing comes out. Instead, two tears run down my face.

"Oh, sweetie," Aurora says, yanking a napkin out of the dispenser. "That is really fucked up."

"Everything about that time was effed up. Except…" The tears are running freely now. "Every awful thing that happened to me happened to him too. He was there all the time, and when she… He *closed her eyes*, Aurora."

I grab all the napkins off my tray and press them to my face. I'd forgotten that last detail. In fact, since coming to Claiborne, I've successfully blocked every memory from those awful days.

But now it all comes rushing back—the nurse who turned off the heart monitor that was shrieking its alarm. Haze's red-rimmed eyes as he leaned over my poor mother's body, easing her eyes closed for the final time. The terrible moment when I finally let go of her hand.

And now I'm coming unglued in the dining hall. Seriously unglued. Every sob is followed by another.

Aurora passes me every napkin in the bunch. Eventually, I pull myself together. I'd done so much crying in the past few hours that I will probably have swollen eyes for a week.

"Okay," my roommate says, passing me a glass of water. "So this guy was there for you at the end, and it was a really intense time."

I nod sloppily. Brunch is over, and we're the last two people in the room.

"But did you guys ever talk about it? Did he ever say, hey, I'd like to take our friendship in a new and exciting direction?"

I shake my head.

"But that's *wrong*, sweetie. Even if he didn't mean to take advantage of you. He did."

"He was the only one I had," I say in a shaky voice. "And I just threw him away."

"I have a question. Where was your father when this was all going down?"

Ugh. "That's a whole other story." And I'm so sick of keeping it to myself. "I told you I didn't live with him before. But what I should have added is that I'd never met him until my mother died."

Aurora's mouth falls open. "What? Why?"

"You'll have to ask Frederick. Because I haven't managed to."

My roommate's mouth is set in an angry line. "Rachel, you are surrounded by sombreros de culo. I want to *maim* them for you."

"Sombreros de culo... Asshats?" I smiled through my tears. "You are a very good friend. And now I think you're the only one I have. Since I threw my other one out this morning, after he rode a thousand miles on a bus to see me."

"He just showed up?"

"Today's his birthday," I mutter. "I threw my best friend out on his birthday."

"After he tried to sleep with you against your will."

I drop my forehead into my hands. "I could have handled it better. I shouldn't have let things go so far."

"I don't know, Rachel. Maybe men just don't do it for you."

I look up to find Aurora's eyes smiling at me, and I laugh for the first time in a day. "Very funny."

She drains her coffee. "In truth, I'm the worst example. I can't sit here and tell you that saying no is easy. I let many things happen with my boyfriend that I did not want."

"You did?"

She doesn't quite meet my eyes when she nods. "Absolutamente. And never once was I happy about it afterwards. I know your morning was all kinds of stinky. But I promise, you would feel even worse if you just let it happen."

"Was he...aggressive?" I feel a latent shiver for her.

"Not at *all*. But I said yes when I wanted to say no. Over and over again. And I felt terrible after! See? That's not how it goes for you now."

"You moved to another continent to say no?"

Aurora reaches over to squeeze my hand. "That's right. Don't do what I did." She looks toward the dining hall's exit door. "Jake saw this boy who visited you, didn't he?"

"I think so."

"The *look* he gave you. It was like the lasers in his video games. Deadly."

Chapter Seventeen

EVEN WHEN YOU'RE SAD, there's homework.

I reread *Anna Karenina* and then write the best paper of my life. I hope so, anyway. One day in the library I find a shelf full of old Claiborne Prep yearbooks. My mom's year—1997—slides off the shelf and into my willing hands.

In her senior picture, Mom is wearing a blouse with puffy sleeves and a big smile. I look so much like her that it takes my breath away.

I flip through every single page of that book looking for more photos of her. She's not in any of the sports team photos, but I spot her in the debate team group.

And—this is the one that surprises me most—she appears in a group photo of two dozen people labeled, "Jazz Band and Vocal Quartet." They're not holding instruments, though. And she never told me she was in a musical group. If she sang, she would have said so during one of our million discussions about my school choir.

I put the book back on the shelf, knowing I'll visit it again soon.

The weather turns colder, and Frederick is back in L.A. His

Instagram feed is full of photos with Ernie and the guys in a recording studio somewhere.

With Frederick's credit card, I buy myself two new sweaters and a winter coat. One of the sweaters is cashmere. Spending Frederick's money is something I do without much thought these days.

"Thanksgiving is coming," he tells me one chilly morning when I answer my phone. "I have an idea."

"What is it?" I've been eying the approach of the holidays with trepidation.

"Let's go to Boston. We'll stay in a hotel, eat turkey in a restaurant, and see a couple of movies."

"What do you usually do on Thanksgiving?" I ask.

"Eat in a restaurant and see a movie."

"Okay, then. Sure." I think about this for a second, and then blurt out another idea. "Aurora has no plans for Thanksgiving."

"Huh. I guess Thanksgiving doesn't play well in Spain. May I speak to her, please?"

I go into the bedroom and stand over my roommate, who is sorting her notes for biology class. "Frederick would like a word." I hold out the phone.

"Si, señor?" she says to him. "That is a very tempting offer. One moment, please." She covers the phone. "Do you want me to come?" she whispers. I nod vigorously. "I would love to." She gives the phone back to me.

"She's in!" Frederick says.

———

Boston is wonderfully distracting. Together, the three of us eat out, shopped for winter coats, and watch the Christmas decorations go up on Newbury Street.

As I watch Frederick and Aurora try on parkas in the Patagonia store, I wonder if he designed this weekend around my need for preoccupation.

Probably not, I decide. It's more likely that Frederick is simply a guy who knows how to have a good time, and is comfortable telling tradition to go suck it.

Either way, the first holiday without my mother is somehow endured. It helps to have Aurora there, a cheerful spirit unburdened by the ghosts of Thanksgivings past.

There is no one to remind me of the previous year, when Mom and I survived a tense holiday under the cloud of her relapse. We'd gone to Mary's house for dinner. Mary's little boy made place cards for the table. "Rachel" and "Jenny" had been scrawled in crayon.

My mother had asked what we could bring, but Mary replied that she had way too much food, and not to bother.

But my mother couldn't show up at someone's door with nothing, so we brought a bottle of white wine. My mother ate and drank almost nothing, ill as she was from chemo.

From the perspective of a year gone by, moments like that seem so obvious now. There were clues about how it would end.

I hadn't caught any of them.

On the Saturday night before we go back, Frederick decides we should dine at Oishii, a chic Japanese restaurant. He makes a call to California. "Henry, dude, sorry to bother you. Can you do me a favor? I need a reservation at this place. Seven o'clock would do it. Thanks."

"Can't you just use Open Table?" Aurora asks.

"Tried," Frederick says. "They're booked."

Aurora's eyebrows go up. "So you're 'dropping a name.'"

"That's when you use someone else's," my father argues. "In this case, it's my own. But Henry drops it for me."

"Doesn't it bother you," she asks, "that someone who made a reservation will be turned away?"

Frederick shakes his head. "Nah. These places always save a couple of slots for regulars who call at the last minute. It's *those* people who won't have the good fortune to pay a hundred bucks a head for sushi tonight. Poor bastards."

———

"Right this way, Mr. Ricks."

Henry doesn't even bother to confirm that the restaurant has a table. We walked in at seven and the maitre d' is ready for us. Our table is right in the center of the room.

"Good evening," the server greets us a moment later. "May I pour you a complimentary cup of my favorite sake to begin the evening?"

"I think a little bit wouldn't hurt us. Thank you very much."

The sake is poured into tiny ceramic cups. When the waiter retreats, Frederick lifts his cup. "To corrupting minors."

Aurora picks hers up. "To name droppers everywhere. Salud."

The first dish is a tiny taste of octopus and edamame salad drizzled with sesame.

"Oh," Frederick says. "That was so good, I might cry."

This is easily the finest restaurant I have ever been to. Each dish looks like a little work of art. There are tiny dumplings in tissue-thin wrappers, and sushi marching across shapely dishes.

Aurora is unfazed by the decadence. Not for the first time I wonder what sort of palace she calls home.

I'm enjoying myself, but I have that feeling again of looking in the window at my new life, and finding it difficult to believe.

We sample broiled eel and fatty tuna. But I draw the line at foie gras sushi, so Frederick and Aurora split my piece. I sip at my tiny glass of sake, but it has a peculiar piney taste that I can't seem to enjoy.

"So what do you do with yourself, Frederick, when you are not buying us nice dinners?" Aurora asks.

He leans back in his chair. "I sneak into the practice rooms in the music department at the college."

"They just let you in for free?" Aurora asks.

"Well." He chuckles. "I'm an alum. But also, the graduate student in charge of assigning practice rooms is a fan."

"I see." Aurora smirks.

"I get a lot of work done there," Frederick says. "Like a monk in my little cell. I'm still hoping to buy a house, but there aren't many on the market."

"You only need it for one year?" Aurora asks. "Why not rent?"

"I might rent," he admits. "But Rachel wants to go to Claiborne College, so it really isn't just one year."

"But I might not get in," I say quickly. *Let's not jinx me.*

"Of course you will." Frederick shrugs. As if getting into an Ivy League school was as easy as convincing this restaurant to take our last-minute reservation. "You can check the legacy box on your application. And I can make a strategic donation."

Or maybe it's the same as getting reservations after all.

"What will you do if you don't find a house?" Aurora asks.

I've been wondering the same thing for weeks. I keep expecting him to say, "Well, it's been fun. But I'd better head back to L.A. For good, now."

"There's this one house—an old one that's been on the market a while. I'd have to renovate it, because it's butt ugly." He digs his wallet out of his jacket and takes out a folded piece of paper. He smooths it out on the table. "It's the right size, but the windows are too small, see? And the kitchen is forty years old. I wasn't looking for a project, but if nothing else comes up…"

I find the paper fascinating—but not because of the house. In one corner of the sheet there's a picture of the listing agent. She's an attractive woman with dark brown hair. And I've seen her before—in the window of Mary's restaurant. *Norah Peters*, it reads. *Vice president, residential sales.*

My father is dating his real estate agent.

I tap the picture. "Is this your broker?"

He doesn't meet my eyes. "Yeah," he says. "Nice girl." Then he drains his beer.

Chapter Eighteen

ON THE EVENING of December first, it snows.

I sit on our window seat, watching it fall. Exams are looming, and I'm supposed to be reading a thick play by Chekhov. But I can't tear my eyes off the scene outside, where fat flakes fall past the courtyard lamps.

One of the first things my mother said after I received my scholarship to Claiborne was, "I want a picture of you in the snow." I can see her in my mind, too thin in her bathrobe, hands clasped together.

I could take a photo now, but who would I send it to?

Not Haze. I wonder if we'll ever speak again.

The next morning it's still snowing, and Aurora and I walk so slowly to brunch, kicking through the fluffy whiteness, that our hands are frozen by the time we arrive.

"Morning, ladies," Jake says when we set down our trays. He has a map spread out on the table in front of him. "Who wants to ski? I'm going right after brunch."

Aurora's face breaks into a smile. "Yay! We will teach Rachel."

I see Jake's eyes flick up from the map to meet mine. But they dive again just as quickly. He's been avoiding me since The Worst Weekend Ever. "The bus leaves from the Green every half hour," he says. On the matter of teaching me to ski, he says nothing.

"I will have to rent skis." Aurora actually gets up and moves around the table to sit next to Jake. "How many trails are open?" she asks, a hand on his sleeve.

"Let's check," he says, pulling out his phone. "If they're a hundred percent open, I'll bring my board. If the base isn't that deep yet, I'll ski."

"You can do both?" I ask, biting into my bagel.

He answers with a shrug, and without making eye contact. "I'm from Massachusetts."

"That's not very nerdy," I tease, trying again.

"When we were little, my dad used to let my brother and I blow off school on powder days," Jake says. "I once heard him tell the principal's office that we'd be out that day because we'd be performing an independent study of gravity. It is possible to be nerdy about anything." He finishes his coffee.

Aurora grabs his phone out of his hand. "Look, every trail is open. They got twelve inches. This is going to be great." She bounces in her seat next to Jake. "Rachel, you have to come."

I look across the table at the two of them. "I don't think so," I say slowly. "I have too much to do." Plus, I'm beginning to feel like the third wheel. If Jake and Aurora end up together, I'll just have to find a way to be okay with it.

———

When my phone rings that afternoon, it's Frederick. "We have to go for a walk in the snow now," he says.

"But I'm studying for finals."

"You can study after. Have you looked outside? Dress warm, and meet me by the statue of what's-his-name."

When I get outside, he's waiting for me. And that's beginning to seem almost normal.

Weird.

And this is our most beautiful walk yet. Big, fat snowflakes fall on my new coat and all over Frederick's hair. They coat the sides of trees and the shingled roofs.

"What are you and Aurora up to this weekend?" he asks. "Or is it all studying, all the time?"

"Well, today she went skiing."

"But you didn't go?" He pulls a pair of gloves from his pocket and puts them on.

"I'm from Orlando," I remind him. "I don't know how."

"Huh," he says, reaching down to scoop up some snow, forming a snowball. "But now you live in New Hampshire. Maybe you should learn."

I shake my head. "I don't have the gear. Also, I didn't want to be the one they were scraping up off the hill all afternoon." Looking clumsy in front of Aurora is one thing. But flopping around on my ass in front of Jake is quite another.

"We'll have to work on that," he says. "Maybe over Christmas break. I wanted to talk to you about the holidays, anyway."

"Okay."

"If it's all right with you, I'll give in to my mother and take you to Kansas City over Christmas."

"It's okay with me. Is it okay with you?"

"I'm not looking forward to it. Christmas isn't really my thing, even when nobody wants to kill me. The last few years, I always made sure to be on tour."

I laugh. "That's a lot of effort to avoid drinking eggnog with your parents."

Frederick grimaces. "Eggnog is a mean thing to do to a perfectly good shot of brandy. Drinks aren't supposed to be thick."

"Maybe Alice has calmed down by now."

"You hear from her?"

"She writes me letters. Last month I got a box of cookies."

"You didn't share?"

"You were out of town. Aurora and I ate them."

Frederick dusts the snow from his hair. "Your vacation is two and a half weeks. I'm playing a concert in California for New Year's…"

My heart leaps.

"…so you'll have a few extra days with Alice without me."

"Oh, okay." *Damn.* I could always *ask* him to take me along to the California gig, and he might say yes. On the other hand, if he wanted me there, he would invite me.

"You'll meet your grandfather. He's less excitable than Alice. Thank the lord."

"What can I bring them?" I ask suddenly.

"Don't worry about it," he says. "They don't need anything."

"It's Christmas. I'm going to bring gifts."

"Well. My father enjoys booze, which you can't buy. And baseball. My mother likes to find my flaws. Does that give you anything to go on?"

"I'll bring him a bottle of whiskey shaped like a baseball bat. And I'll bring her a magnifying glass."

"I guess you don't need my help," he says, swiping accumulated snow from the capstone of a stone wall. He makes a snowball, then hurls it at a nearby tree.

"You missed," I point out.

"See? You and Alice will get along great."

———

"So how does Christmas dinner work tonight?" Aurora asks the following weekend. We're sitting on the S.L.O, three in a row, each with a book we were supposed to be reading.

But tonight, nobody will study.

"Dinner is served at seven, in Bartleby," Jake says. "The meal seats the entire senior class at once. It's a big spectacle, with ice sculptures and a roasted pig with an apple in its mouth. You get the idea. And we're supposed to steal the plates."

"Wait, what about the plates?" I give up on my book.

"They bring out the fancy china, with the school crest in gold. And everybody swipes them."

"Hang on," I point at his tee shirt, which reads *Nerds SQRT16 Ever*. "Are you wearing that?"

Jake shakes his head.

"Oh boy," I say. "I feel a fashion crisis coming on."

"Sorry. I should have mentioned that everyone dresses up."

"Dear Jake, you are usually such a useful person." Aurora snaps her book shut, too. "But some events require *extra* warning. Please make a note of it."

"You have to leave now," I say, standing up. "Because we're going to try on everything we own."

Jake gets up, his eyes darting back and forth from me to Aurora. "Can I pick you up at six forty-five?"

"Hmm…" Aurora muses. "Which of us do you mean?"

Jake clears his throat. "It's traditional to bring two dates."

"That is an interesting tradition. One wonders how they managed for the two centuries before the school was co-ed."

"The guy also sneaks in a flask of champagne."

"Well, then," Aurora says. "We will both be ready."

———

I end up wearing one of Aurora's dresses, a dark green velvet affair that looks very Christmassy. It's a little low cut for my taste, and I have less to fill the bust line than the dress requires. But my winter wardrobe is still in its formative stages, and nothing I own will work.

Aurora wears a black dress, borrowing my slinkiest earrings.

Christmas Dinner Jake—in a coat and tie—arrives right on time, looking like a completely different person. He's left his glasses at home. "Wow," he says when he comes to our door.

"Is it too much?" I ask, putting my hand over the neckline of Aurora's dress. I feel exposed.

Aurora rolls her eyes. "Rachel, that was a compliment, not a warning. *Vamos*. Get your coat."

I don't quite understand the zeitgeist of Christmas Dinner until we step into Bartleby Hall. It's decked out for a medieval feast, with garlands and tables laden with ornamental foods, as if Henry the Eighth is expected for dinner. We pass a tower of shrimp laid out in front of an ice statue in the shape of a mermaid. With a thousand candles flickering on the beams overhead, the cavernous room becomes weirdly glamorous, in a sixteenth century sort of way.

Jake's two roommates, Sal and Arin, wave us over to a table. Jake removes a flask from his jacket pocket and sets it on the table, camouflaging it amid the pine boughs of the elaborate centerpiece. Then he pulls out two chairs for Aurora and me.

"Hi, Sal," I say, sitting down beside Jake. "Hi, Arin."

"Hi," they reply. It's the most they ever say to anyone.

A waiter props a tray beside our table and begins setting salads in front of everyone. Aurora puts her napkin in her lap. "This *is* fancy. What if we could dine this way every night? I hear there is entertainment."

I look down the long room. The tables at the other end are practically in the next zip code. "Both the a cappella groups get a set." I'd rehearsed three Christmassy songs with the Belle Choir.

"Of course they do," Jake says. He collects our coffee cups from each place setting and surreptitiously pours bubbly into each one.

The first group to sing is the Senior Songsters, and Jake mimes plugging his ears. Their three songs end just in time for the salad plates to be cleared.

I see my own singing group approaching. As a senior, I don't have to participate, since this fancy dinner is for us. But Jessica and Jessica are both up there, and I don't want to be a slacker.

So I get up to stand on the end of the horseshoe in the alto section. We all link arms. Jessica hums a note, and we begin.

Good King Wenceslas looked down

On the feast of Stephen
When the snow lay round about
Deep and crisp and even

As the harmony resonates in my chest, I'm basking in the perfection of the song, the candlelight, and the cozy half-circle of girls tethering me here. I look across to our table, where Jake's eyes are trained on my face. The warmth I find there is so distracting that I flub the words to the third verse.

I'm supposed to be rhyming "hither" with "thither." But my heart is singing a different tune. *Please keep looking at me like that.*

We sing each of our three songs in a different corner of the room, and then I take my seat just as the prime rib is being served.

"Sorry if that was painful for you," I say as Jake pulls out my chair for me. "I know you're not a fan of a cappella."

"I try to keep an open mind," he says, as Aurora smirks from across the table.

"This dinner is an excellent tradition," I announce. "Especially the champagne." Jake pours the last drop into my cup.

———

After the last course—chocolate mousse—the three of us go tripping back across the cold lawn in the dark, Aurora in the lead. I'm the tiniest bit tipsy and wearing heels. So naturally I stumble on a frozen clod of snow and nearly fall. But Jake catches my hand to steady me. "Thanks," I breathe.

Curiously, his warm fingers remain curled around mine until we reached the door of Habernacker.

I try not to feel ridiculously excited about it.

He lets go when we all reach the third floor. When Aurora opens the door, he follows us inside until we all collapse on the S.L.O., with me in the center.

"Oh! I forgot to steal my plate," I realize.

"Me too." Aurora sighs.

Jake reaches into his jacket and pulls out a plate.

"Well done, Mr. Jake!" Aurora laughs. "The party in the annex starts in fifteen minutes." She heaves herself off the squishy couch. "I have time to redo my makeup."

I watch her walk over to the stereo, where my phone is already ensconced, and turn on our Christmas playlist. Then she grabs her makeup bag off her desk and leaves the room.

When the door clicks shut, neither Jake nor I speak for a moment. The low chords of a Straight No Chaser song play through our little speakers.

Suddenly, it's awkward. We've been circling each other for a while now—since the night he was trying to be nice and I wrecked it.

"You're probably sick of a cappella by now," I say, just to find something to talk about.

But Jake turns slowly toward me and says something unexpected. "Rachel, I need to ask you a question."

My stomach does a little flip flop, and I turn to face those blue eyes I love so much. "What?" I whisper.

"Well..." He clears his throat. There is a very long pause, during which I hold my breath. "Will you come skiing some time?"

I exhale. "I guess so?" Another beat of silence passes. "That was your big question?" I ask, feeling like I've missed something.

His color deepens. "Well, no. I just..." His brow furrows, as if he's trying to explain some point of astronomy. I love his look of concentration. I've missed it.

Jake's blue eyes lock on mine, and I see how our own orbits might finally collide. This time, I will not send the moment winging back into space. Instead, I lean an almost imperceptible degree in his direction.

And that's all it takes.

Reaching up, Jake cups his hand to the side of my face. I'm still processing the sweet touch of his fingers when he leans in farther, his lips brushing the sensitive corner of my mouth. His eyes are tentative, seeking permission. My heart thuds with expectation.

And then—finally—Jake kisses me for real. We come together the way a well-timed drummer kicks into the chorus of a song—swiftly, and without hesitation.

We broke apart a moment later, eyeing each other while I try not to smile. "Can I do that again?" he asks, his voice rough. "That was my real question."

"Well, since you asked so nicely…"

Jake makes a low noise of approval, then draws me closer. I reach up for the back of his neck, my fingers grazing that golden patch of skin I've always wanted to touch. He kisses me again, his arm finding the velvet waist of my dress and encircling me.

My heart flutters, but not from fear. Warm lips tease mine gently apart. And when his tongue tangles with mine, I lose myself.

He tastes like champagne. Everything is wild and sweet, until the moment Aurora's voice rings out. "Ay, caramba!"

I feel an unwelcome rush of cool air between us as Jake retreats.

"I *did* say I was going into the bathroom, right? And not on a trip to Fiji?"

Neither of us says a word; we only look sheepishly at Aurora.

"Just to be clear, now I'm ducking into the bedroom for my coat, which only takes a second." She steps into the bedroom, and I hear the rustling of fabric. Then she peers dramatically around the door frame. "Good listening! Now I'm going to the party. Will I see you both there? Don't answer that. We'll speak later."

Jake laughs. "Sorry, Aurora."

"I've seen worse." She departs, the door closing behind her.

And now I'm self-conscious. Rising, I decide to fiddle with the music playlist. "Do you want to go to the party?"

"I'll go. But I'm not great at parties. It's all shouting over the music, drinking warm beer out of a plastic cup."

"Then let's not." My fingers shake as I adjust the volume. I go back over to the sofa and sit down.

"So." He clears his throat. "Where are you going for break?"

As he asks, he takes one of my hands in his, massaging my palm with his thumb.

His light touch is so distracting that I almost forget to answer. "Kansas City," I manage. "To meet my grandfather for the very first time."

"Um, what?" He squeezes my hand.

So I tell Jake the embarrassing highlights of my weird story—that I hadn't met Frederick until this past summer.

"Wow. I'm sorry," he says.

"Don't be."

"I guess I'm not that offended now that you wouldn't introduce me. If the normal waiting period is seventeen years."

My laugh begins with an unladylike snort. Ah, well. "With me it's just all soap opera, all the time. Believe it or not, a year ago I was really a boring person."

"I don't see how." He regards me with darting eyes. "You look beautiful tonight."

"It's Aurora's dress," I whisper.

But Jake doesn't seem to care. He slips his arms around my waist. Scooting closer, he slides his lips from my forehead, down my nose and onto my mouth. And we begin again.

———

"*Jesus Cristo!* Do I need to wear a bell?"

Jake and I startle apart.

"I've been gone, oh, an hour and a half. Just saying." Aurora kicks off her shoes and takes off her coat.

I feel my face begin to burn. My hair is tousled, and my lips are swollen from Jake's kisses.

"Your singing group pals were at the party. Jessica kept asking me, 'Where's Rachel?' I told her you were *beeesy*." Aurora giggles to herself. She looks fairly drunk.

"I really should be going." Jake stands up, gathering his

things. I follow him out of the room and into the echoing stairwell.

"Goodnight," I whisper. You never can tell who might hear you in the stairwell.

Jake looks at his shoes. "Can we study tomorrow?" His smile is lopsided.

I laugh. "I have to write an essay for Russian Lit. So we shouldn't study until after I study."

"Deal." His face gets very serious, and then he kisses me one more time. Then he runs up the stairs without looking back.

I go back inside to find Aurora sitting sideways on the couch, her hands pressed to her mouth. "At last!" she shouts. "Now you can both stop pining for each other."

"You're not mad?" After I say it, I realized it sounds vain. I don't mean to imply that I've won some sort of contest.

She rolls her eyes. "Jake is not my type. And you are not the only one who got kisses tonight."

I throw myself on the couch by her feet. "Really? Who is he?"

She shakes her head with a wicked grin. "I don't think I'll tell you. It was probably a one-time thing. Christmas Dinner is, I think, some kind of aphrodisiac. At the party, I saw people hooking up *everywhere*."

"Tonight was a good night." I giggle again, which I never do. But who knew a few kisses from Jake could make me crazy?

"No," Aurora argues. "Tonight was fabuloso."

COMMAND
PERFORMANCE

COMMAND PERFORMANCE: *presentation of an opera or concert at the request of royalty.*

Chapter Nineteen

SADLY, Jake and I both do more studying than kissing for the last week of the semester. I pull an all-nighter before my last exam, and he departs to meet his parents before my last test finishes.

I'm bleary by the time Frederick and I climb into the back seat of a hired car headed for the airport. I wake up halfway to Boston with my head on his shoulder.

"Sorry!" I sit up quickly.

He gives me a smile. "You look like you just played a three-week tour. In Asia."

I rub my eyes. "I'm too tired even to be nervous about this trip." We're flying to Kansas City tomorrow.

"Good. Because you have nothing to fear. It's me who's in the doghouse."

"Still?"

"I guess we'll find out."

"She can't stay mad forever."

"Alice? Yes she can. She's been pissed for twenty years that I didn't become a surgeon like my father."

I swivel to look at him. "Really? Why would she care about that?"

He tips his head back onto the seat and closes his eyes. "I don't know. Wasted potential. Blah blah blah."

What a startling idea. It had never occurred to me that Frederick would be anything but a musician. His choice seems obvious. Fated, even.

Outside the car, the sky has gone dark. Frederick's reading light reflects in the window. I have the sensation of floating through the night with him, as if we're the only two people in the world.

———

Another driver picks us up at the Kansas City airport. My father directs him off the highway and into a residential neighborhood. "It's that house, the one with the tree in the window."

We pulled up in front of a big old house with a gambrel roof, like an old-fashioned barn. There's a smattering of snow, and it crunches underfoot when I step out of the car.

"You grew up here?" I ask. Another piece of the puzzle.

"According to Alice, I never grew up at all," he answers.

As the front door swings open, I feel jumpy, like a nervous cat.

The first person I see is my grandfather, who looks a lot like Frederick. When he smiles, the corners of his mouth turn up just the same way. And when I come through the door, his smile goes wide.

"Rachel," Frederick says behind me, "meet Dr. Richards."

The older man gives me a polite bow. "At your service," he says. He's charming, and I appreciate that he doesn't run up and hug me. This is easier when everybody gives me a little space.

But then Alice comes bounding down a flight of stairs. "She's here!" she trills, her eyes shining. "I've been impossible all week, waiting for you to come. My friends wanted to put me on sedatives, let me tell you."

Frederick smirks. "I should have brought you some," he says. "With a ribbon around the bottle."

Alice ignores him. "Let me show you your room, honey," she says to me.

I'm given the guest room. Frederick is down the hall, in his old childhood room. Since my grandparents have their bedroom on the main floor, the two of us have the upstairs all to ourselves.

After I put my suitcase away, I hover in the doorway to my father's room. He sits on the bed, taking off his shoes.

"There's an AC/DC poster on your wall? Really?"

"They're in good company," he points out. There are posters of U2, the Who, and the Stones. "AC/DC was the first concert I ever went to. What was yours?"

My stomach dips, and I sit down on the bed next to him. He doesn't know what a loaded question he's just asked. I'm *never* telling him about my first concert.

He mistakes my silence. "You haven't been to concerts?" He sticks a fake knife in his heart. "That's terrible. It's what I lived for when I was your age. Still is. If I can go hear somebody play—watch some guy with a quirky banjo technique, or a great drummer—that's what makes me feel okay. Even if everything else is going to shit, I hear some live music, and I feel all right."

———

After a dinner of Alice's homemade lasagna, she chases everyone into the living room, where a Christmas tree stands eight feet tall. It's covered in tiny white lights.

"Rachel, you really rate," Frederick teases as Alice brings in dessert. "Usually I'm not allowed to eat in the living room."

"Frederick, any time you come home to Kansas City, I'll serve you high tea in here."

"*Easy*," he cautions. "I'm here now. And to hell with tea. I'm ready for a big piece of that pie."

"It looks really good," I agree, plopping down next to Frederick.

"Thank you!" Alice beams. "This is just what I wanted for

Christmas. All of us here together." She hands me a piece of pie. "Now look at this." She goes over to the mantel and opens a bag. She pulls out a stack of red velvet Christmas stockings. There are names appliquéd to each one. A minute later they hang in a row: FRANK and then ALICE and FREDERICK and RACHEL.

Mine is a brighter red than the other three, which have faded gently over the years.

"Wow," I say. "Thank you." My face feels hot. Alice is not going to let me ignore Christmas the way I'd brushed past the Thanksgiving holiday.

I wish Frederick and I were eating takeout food in L.A. right now, with no tree and no stockings. Somewhere in those boxes I'd put into storage from our Orlando house is another stocking with my name on it. And also one that says "Jenny."

She's not here to make cocoa for me on Christmas Eve, or to hide lip gloss in my stocking.

She's not here at all, and she never will be again.

I hate Christmas now. But Alice is trying so hard that I'm going to have to pretend.

"I pulled out some things to show you," Alice goes on, dragging a wooden chest across the rug. "I'll bet you've never seen baby pictures of Frederick."

My father rolls his eyes. "Time to break out the scotch, Dad?"

"Good a time as any." Grandpa Frank sets his empty pie plate down and crosses the room to a set of crystal decanters.

I kneel in front of the chest, which Alice opens. "Let's see…" She hands me an album. "Try this one. It's my Christmas book."

I open the cover and discover that Alice was a devoted scrapbooker well before it was cool. There are little snippets of wrapping paper, and programs from church services. "Christmas 1980," the first page announces. And there's a photo of two-year-old Frederick holding a wrapped gift and staring up at the camera. "Aw. What a chub you were."

"He was a chunky little thing until puberty," Frank says,

handing a glass of smoky brown liquid to Frederick. "Then he shot up a foot and the girls started swarming like moths."

Frederick takes a sip of his scotch and unfurls his father's newspaper. I flip the pages of the book, watching Frederick evolve from a toddler into a school boy. His smile is recognizable even from his kindergarten days. The first picture of him with a guitar is from 1989.

Alice roots through the chest. "I saved some other things," she says quietly. She draws out a silver baby rattle, tarnished with age. It chimes when I shake it. There are three die-cast metal cars, their paint chipped. "I thought a grandchild might use them some day," Alice says, her voice heavy.

I roll a tiny Camaro across my palm and say nothing. On the sofa, Frederick's newspaper is raised like a shield. When I put the toys back in the box, my eye is drawn to the words "Wildcats 1995" stamped in gold on the spine of a book. I pull out my father's high school yearbook.

Alice chuckles. "It was a bad-hair stage," she says. "You really do have to see that."

I bring the yearbook back to the sofa and open it up to the senior section. "Oh my *God*," I howl. Alice is right about the hair. Frederick had rock-band hair—big and long. Eddie Van Halen hair. "I wonder how much *People* would pay me for this?" I tease.

"I'll kill you dead," Frederick says from behind his paper fortress.

I nudge him with the book. "I'm saving this as blackmail. So stay on my good side." It's easier to ignore the tightness in my chest when I'm teasing him.

———

The week wears on, tugging at intervals between tension and Christmas cheer. Alice and Frederick are both unfailingly nice to me, but their discomfort with each other is palpable. My father begins to resemble a caged animal. He avoids Alice, pacing the living room while she cooks, or shutting the door to his old bedroom to make calls. Sometimes I hear the strains of his guitar from behind the door.

"Would it kill you to spend time with me?" my grandmother asks on Christmas Eve.

"Would it kill you to stop starting sentences like that?" he counters, ducking into the refrigerator to get a beer. Then he goes into the den to watch the football game with his father.

I'm teasing icing onto a gingerbread cookie with a toothpick when Frederick comes back to put his bottle in the recycling bin. "Hey." I stop him. "I made one for you."

He puts a hand on my hair. "You know it makes your grandmother real happy that you do this stuff with her." His voice is like gravel.

"Here," I say, lifting the cookie I'd set aside. "Check out his T-shirt." I place it in Frederick's hand.

He lets out a bark of laughter. "I never saw a gingerbread man wear an AC/DC shirt before. You got the lightning bolt and everything." Then he gives me a kiss on the head. "Thank you, kid. Would it be rude to eat it?"

I shake my head. "Do your worst."

"Frank?" Alice calls to my grandfather from the other room. "Cathy is here. Can you help me with the trays?"

I get up to see if they need help. A white van has pulled into the driveway, *Cathy's Catering* painted on its side.

I hold the door while Alice, my grandfather, and the caterer make trip after trip from the van into the kitchen.

Frederick stands munching cookies and watching. "Mom," he says. "How many people did you invite over tonight?"

"I have my open house every year," she replies. "If you ever came home, you'd remember. As it happens, I believe it will be very well-attended this time, seeing as there is a new guest of honor."

My stomach twists at this idea. I don't want to be the guest of honor.

My father studies me, then turns to his mother. "Maybe Rachel doesn't feel like being your show pony. Couldn't you keep it small?"

Alice's lips make a tight line. "She has the right to meet her extended family," she says. "If it happens to spotlight nearly two decades of your stupidity, there's really nothing I can do about that."

He takes another cookie and leaves the room.

I taste something bitter in my mouth. "I'd better go upstairs and change."

When I walk past Frederick's door, I hear only silence.

———

The first guest to arrive is Alice's sister Anita. "Oh! Let me look at you," she gasps. "Of course Frederick's child would be beautiful. That boy gets the best of everything."

"More than he deserves," Alice adds.

It's the beginning of a long night of compliments that I didn't know how to handle. I look between Alice to Anita. "Are you… twins?" I ask. The resemblance between them is striking. Anita's hair is more gray, but otherwise they're so similar.

My great-aunt laughs. "Bless you, Rachel. But there's a few miles more on this model." She taps her own chest.

Anita has four children, and three of them come to Alice's party. And those three children bring *their* children. Before an hour is through, I'm dizzy from trying to remember the names of my second cousins, who range in age from twenty down to six.

And everyone stares at me. The women are effusive, the children curious. The men circle the food. Meanwhile, my heart gallops at unusual speed. Every few minutes Alice makes a disparaging remark about Frederick's absence and then glances toward the stairs.

He finally wanders down when the house is full of people. And even though he's abandoned me here all evening, I'm still happy to see him. He looks sharp, in a nice shirt and a leather jacket.

"Freddy!" someone calls. It's Anita's son...Vic? I can't keep track.

Frederick is swarmed by well-wishers. It's clear to me that A) he wasn't kidding when he said he doesn't come around much and B) they love him anyway. One of his cousins fetches him a beer.

"Let's hear you, then," Anita says, pushing him toward the piano. "How about something Christmassy."

"Because I'm known for my holiday spirit," he says, winking at me.

"It wouldn't kill you," his mother adds.

Frederick throws a leg over the piano bench. "The scene of the crime," he says. "My mama got me piano lessons because she thought a little classical music might make me smarter. I think she regrets it now." He puts his hands on the keys and begins to play. The song is bouncy and familiar, but it takes me a minute to place it.

"Grandma got run over by a reindeer..." Frederick sings.

There's a huge guffaw at his choice of tunes. And Alice turns red.

I eat a few of the catered appetizers—tiny spinach turnovers and pigs in blankets. When I take my plate out to the kitchen, the back door opens.

"Ernie!" I haven't seen him since August, and I didn't know whether he was in Kansas City to see his folks too.

"Hey, kid!" He stomps the snow off his boots, smiling. He wears a knit cap over his bare head.

It's good to see a familiar face. I go over and hug his cold jacket. "It's kind of intense here," I whisper.

He claps an arm around me. "So I hear. I'm sorry, kid." He nods toward the music in the living room. "She's got him singing?"

"Under duress."

"No wonder he texted me."

In the living room, Ernie kisses Alice on the cheek and accepts a beer. I stand with them behind the piano bench.

"I've been wondering," Grandma Alice says to me, after Frederick finishes playing, "whether you might have any more family on your mother's side?"

"My mother had a little sister," I say carefully. "But we're not close."

Alice's eyes get wide. "You have an aunt? I feel terrible. I would have invited her to visit. We'll call her tomorrow."

I shake my head. "Maybe another time."

"Honey!" Alice throws a hand over her heart. "Family is everything. It's hard to appreciate when you're young and healthy. But it's so important—"

"Mom," Frederick warns. "Rachel doesn't have to see anyone she doesn't want to see."

Alice's eyes narrow. "Think about what you just said, Frederick." She stares him down. "How did that policy work out for your daughter?"

There is a horrible silence while Frederick works his jaw. "Wow," he says at last. "And you wonder why I don't come here more often." He puts his beer bottle down on the piano. And then he heads for the door. After another awkward moment, Ernie trails him.

"Where are you going?" Alice demands, running into the front hall after them.

"To hear some blues," Frederick calls over his shoulder.

"Let him go, Alice." Dr. Richards sighs.

"That's all he ever does!" Alice shouts. Everyone in the neighborhood hears the door slam.

Chapter Twenty

I FALL into bed that night, overwhelmed. I miss Jake and I'm desperate to talk to him. But we said we'd talk on Christmas, so I only have to wait one more day.

When I wake the next morning, it takes me a few minutes to remember that it's Christmas Day. I get up and comb my hair, putting on the slippers that Aurora gave me for Christmas. From my suitcase, I take the presents I'd brought for my grandparents and the big box I'd shipped here for Frederick.

I feel heavy today. Like everything is just too much effort. I wonder who's waking up in our old green house on Pomelo Court. There's someone else's tree in the corner of our too-small living room now.

The only way to get through the day is not to think about that.

When I leave my room, Frederick's door is open. I peek inside, but he's not there.

Downstairs, I find Alice fussing in the kitchen. "Good morning," I say.

Alice turns. "Good morning, sweetie! I was just going to bring your grandfather some coffee by the Christmas tree. Would you like some?"

"Sounds great."

"Why don't you wake your father? We'll have a little Christmas breakfast together." My face must give me away, because Alice's smile slides away. "He's not up there?"

I shake my head.

"Oh, Frederick." She turns away. "You wouldn't dare," she says to the coffee pot.

————

We stall, drinking coffee and eating a breakfast quiche that Alice got from the caterers. "I used to do all the cooking myself," she says. "But this year I was in the mood to work less and celebrate more."

I wonder how celebratory she's feeling now. I'm embarrassed for Frederick. And it dawns on me that we shouldn't be waiting around for him. It only makes his absence more glaring.

I lean down to my little stack of presents. "I think we need this," I say, handing a wrapped CD to Alice. It's a recording of the Belle Choir singing Christmas tunes. "They're some of my friends," I explain when she opens it. The disc was made last year, so I'm not on it.

"Thank you! Let's put it on." A moment later, a cappella voices warm the room with "Let it Snow" in three part harmony.

"Here's one for you," my grandmother says.

I open up a box to find a cashmere scarf and gloves. "Pretty!" I say. "I think I'll be wearing these until April."

"I figured." Alice smiles.

And so it goes, with my grandparents and I exchanging gifts that we've labored to choose, since we don't know each other well enough to make it easy. I feel the strain of all our mutual effort.

When my gift for Frederick is the last one unopened, and Grandpa Frank has already collected the discarded wrapping paper, the front door finally opens. I sneak a look at my watch. It's after eleven.

The three of us wait for him to appear in the living room. But as I watch, Frederick stumbles past, heading toward the stairs without a look in our direction. I hear a small thud and a curse, and then the sound of him ascending the stairs.

"Sweet Jesus," Dr. Richards says.

I can't even *look* at Alice. Instead, I get up slowly, pick up the gift I've brought for Frederick, and go to the bottom of the stairs. When I hear the shower running in the bathroom on the second floor, I climb the stairs slowly. I put the gift beside his empty bed and then go into my room to curl up on mine.

The only ray of sunshine is a voicemail message from Jake. "Hi Rachel. I've been trying to leave you alone, I know you're busy with family stuff. But I wanted to say Merry Christmas, and that I miss you. A whole lot. Pretty much all the time. Yeah. Okay. Bye."

I listen to it twice more before calling him back. "Hi," I say when he answers. "I liked your message."

"How are you doing?" he asks, sounding winded. "Sorry, I was splitting wood when the phone rang."

I would give anything to watch Jake split wood rather than sit in the tensest house in Kansas City. "I'm okay. My father has been an asshat."

"That sucks. To you?"

"To his mother. But I'm caught in the middle."

"So fly back, and I'll pick you up in Boston. Have you ever been to Vermont?"

My heart leaps at this offer, even though I can't accept. "That is super tempting, but I don't think I could do that to Grandma Alice."

"My own selfish desires aside," he pants, "I hope it gets better."

"Me too." Then I smile so wide that I'm glad he can't see me. "Jake, I *loved* your gift." On the morning he left Claiborne, I'd found it on my desk. From a nest of tissue paper I'd pulled his Christmas dinner plate, all shined up with a note. *Rachel—you should keep this. There's enough Claiborne paraphernalia in my family already. But put it somewhere I can see it, because it will remind me of the best night of the year.*

"Oh, good," he says. And then there's an awkward pause, because neither one of us is any good at taking a compliment. "I'm going to split another dozen logs now," he says. "It beats listening to Asshat brag about his conquests. But call me tomorrow and let me know how you're doing."

"I will. Bye, Jake."

After a while, I dare to peek into Frederick's room. I find him passed out in his underwear, his hair wet on the pillow.

I tiptoe back into the guest room and lay down again.

———

When I wake up, it's to the sound of shouting.

"All I wanted was a Christmas morning with my son and my grandchild!" Alice wails. "Is that really too much to ask?"

"That's all you want? That and a quart of my blood."

"What a role model you make."

"Rachel is a big girl, Alice. She knows my flaws, okay? But she's nicer about them."

"Does she have a choice?"

My chest quivers with unhappiness, and I feel positively ill. It's too hot in my room, and there isn't enough air. I walk out of the bedroom and speed down the stairs. Stepping into my shoes in the front hall, I go out into the cold, shutting the door behind me.

The stoop feels icy through the fabric of my jeans, but breathing cold air feels good. Still, my heart races like the drum line of a speed-metal track. When the door opens behind me, I whirl around.

It's Grandpa Frank. He sits down next to me. "Hi."

"Hi," I gasp.

"You don't look so good."

"Don't feel so good."

"What's the matter, exactly?"

"Can't breathe," I say.

"You're about thirty years too young for heart trouble." He takes my hand and puts two fingers on my wrist. "Rachel, are you having a panic attack?"

I turn to look at him. "How do I tell?"

He pats my hand. "Feelings of doom, shortness of breath. Maybe nausea."

"Sounds familiar."

"It's the most common thing in the world. It will pass. Some people have too many—it gets in the way of their lives. And they need to get help. But if you're just having one or two, say, on the most stressful Christmas ever, I predict you'll make a full recovery."

"Good to know." I try not to gasp.

"I prescribe...a walk around the block. But we'll need coats." He goes inside for them.

The walk helps. I follow my grandfather through the deserted neighborhood park, past chilly-looking playground equipment. "Frederick played Little League on these fields," he says, pointing.

"That's hard to picture."

My grandfather chuckles. "He was no good at it. He got cut from the team his second year."

"I'll bet he didn't mind."

"Not a bit," his father agrees.

"We do this too," I say. "Frederick and I go for walks."

"He's always liked walking," Dr. Richards says. "He told me once that he finishes a lot of song lyrics that way. Walking around, rearranging the words in his head."

"Why doesn't Frederick drive?" I ask suddenly.

"He didn't tell you the story?"

I get prickles on my neck. "There's a story?"

Grandpa Frank stops under a silver birch tree, where flaps of papery bark wave in the wind. "He used to drive. But when he was nineteen, he crashed his car into a tree. Scared him so badly he never drove again."

I don't know what to make of this story. It's hard to imagine Frederick afraid of anything. "Was anyone hurt?"

"He was alone, and most likely drunk. He cracked a couple of ribs against the steering column, that's all. But that was enough, I guess."

We walk on.

———

"He changed his ticket," Alice spits when we reenter the house. "He's leaving tonight."

My heart clenches. He wouldn't just *leave* me here. I run upstairs. His room is empty, the gift I'd left him is gone. There's no guitar. I throw myself on his bed and press my face into the crook of my arm.

Someone comes in and sits on the bed next to me. From the sound of the footsteps, it's Alice. "Rachel," she says.

I don't bother raising my wet face. Kind words from Alice won't cut it right now.

"Rachel, I'm so sorry he let you down like this. He doesn't know how to be anyone's father."

Seriously? He does a fair-to-middling job most of the time. I sit up quickly, anger coiling in my stomach. "Why do you push him away?"

Alice reels at the question. Her lips tremble. "He pushes himself away."

"My aunt Lisa…" I swallow. "We're not calling her."

"Okay," Alice whispers.

I can hardly spit out the reason. "She left me in the *home*. In Orlando. She left me there, and Frederick didn't."

"Oh." Alice's eyes begin to fill.

She reaches for my hand, but I jerk it away. "If you can't f-forgive him," I stutter, "then we can't come here." I consider

Jake's offer to pick me up in Boston. If Frederick can leave, so could I. "If *you* can't forgive him, I can't stay here. Because..." I choke on my tears. "Because I love him too. And you're making it so hard on me."

Alice pales. Then she gets up off the bed and leaves the room.

I wait until her footsteps retreat down the staircase before I put my face back down in my arms and cry. Because Frederick has finally done the thing I've been afraid he'd do.

He bailed on me.

———

My father doesn't even call me until the next morning at nine. I'm lying in bed, trying to decide whether it's worth getting up when my phone rings.

"Rachel," he says, his voice gruff in my ear. "I owe you an apology."

Or ten. Or a million. I'm not ready to accept even one. "Where are you?"

"Standing on the beach. It's still dark."

Why didn't you take me too?

"Rachel, what did you say to Alice?"

"Why?"

He chuckles. "Whatever you said, it was very effective. Either that, or zombies got her."

"What do you mean?"

"Last night she came over to Ernie's, and then drove me to the airport. She said she was sorry."

"Really?"

"I owe you big."

Then why don't you come back?

"I like the hat," he adds.

"Oh. Good." I'd noticed that he never wore one, even on the coldest days in New Hampshire. I'd found him a sort of wool

Stetson, it's cool-looking, but also warm. I'd been so eager to give it to him, and now it's hard to remember why.

"I'll call you tomorrow, okay?"

"Okay," I whisper, and hang up.

———

I'm reading an old biography of Eric Clapton that I found in Frederick's room, when my phone rings again. I don't recognize the number. "Hello?"

"Hi Rachel. It's Ernie."

"Hi." I hope he won't apologize too. I've had enough awkward conversations to last years.

"You busy?"

I smile. "No. Why?"

"Are you up for a little adventure?"

"Um, sure? What kind?"

"Frederick left you a present in his closet. Open it and bring it outside with you. I'm on my way over."

"That's very mysterious, Ernie."

"You'll see," he says. "I'll be there in ten."

I go into Frederick's room and open the closet door. Sure enough, there's a big box, wrapped in Christmas paper and tied with a fancy ribbon, but no card. I kneel down in the closet doorway and pull the ribbon off, then tear the paper.

Inside the box I find a pair of waterproof gloves, a fleece neck gaiter and a pair of surprisingly bulky goggles. Also, I find a pair of North Face snow pants just like Aurora's. At the bottom of the box there's a note in Frederick's handwriting.

Come with me to Snow Creek this week. Even girls from Orlando can handle a Missouri "mountain." We'll have you skiing the wilds of New Hampshire in no time. — Dad

Stung, I flick the card aside. Then I pick up the box and run downstairs, shoving my feet into my boots. When I open the front door, I see a Buick pull up in front of the house, exhaust wisping from its tailpipe.

I run down the walk, fling open the passenger door and jump inside. "You've got to be kidding me."

Ernie's hand pauses on the way to the gearshift. "Why?" He's wearing black snow pants, a bright orange parka, and the same look of gentle surprise I often see on his face.

"He sent *you* to take me skiing. And you said, 'Sure, dude, I've got it.'"

Ernie hesitates. "I like skiing."

"That's not the point!" The pitch of my voice approaches hysteria. "He sent you to babysit me, to clean up his mess. Why do you put up with his shit?"

And why do I?

Ernie doesn't say anything. He just waits.

"*Damn* him," I swear. "I can just hear him now. 'Too bad I put that note in the box. But I'll just get Ernie to cover for me. I'll tell Henry to pay him rehearsal scale for the afternoon.'"

The low burble of Ernie's chuckle fills the car. "You're funny when you're pissed."

"Then I'm having a really funny week." I smack my hands on the dashboard. My eyes have begun to burn.

"It's complicated, Rachel," Ernie says, turning the key to shut off the engine. "Frederick and I have been covering for each other for a long time."

"Really?" I press. "How come you wrote so many songs with him, but it's *his* name on the front of the albums? You're his enabler." I can hear myself going too far, taking it out on Ernie. But yesterday I'd *defended* Frederick. Now I feel like pounding my own head against the dashboard.

"Can we go skiing now?" he asks quietly. "Just go get your coat. This will be really fun."

"Turn, turn, turn!" Ernie calls as I accelerate toward the tree line.

Just before it's too late, I force my weight onto my right leg and roll my feet. Miraculously, I turn.

But then my skis cross. And I fall. *Again.*

Two little kids, probably about five years old, zip past the spot where I lay in the snow.

Ernie arrives with a spray of powder. "That was pretty good. You turned three times before you fell."

"Score." I sigh.

"Let's do a couple more runs," he says. "Then we'll go into the lodge and order one of everything."

"It's a deal," I agree. "But Frederick is buying."

Ernie tips his chin toward the impossibly blue sky and laughs.

"I'm sorry," I tell Ernie thirty minutes later as we dip our fries in barbecue sauce.

"For what?"

I give him a miserable look. "For losing my shit in the car. The song-writing stuff is none of my business."

He dips another fry. "You know, not everybody wants to be the frontman."

"I guess."

"I mean it. Have you ever wondered why he's so lonely?"

"What?" My eyes cut to his big brown ones.

"He hasn't made a good friend in a decade," Ernie says, sipping his Coke. "If you're Frederick, you have to always wonder what people want from you. Women want their picture in *US Weekly*, or they want his money. Fans want a picture, so they can post the best Facebook status ever. There's almost nobody he can trust."

I play with the straw in my drink. "Then how come he isn't here with us right now? You and I are very trustworthy."

"Rachel," Ernie says with a chuckle, rubbing his bald head. "Are you considering law school? I think you have a future in the courtroom."

A few days later, Alice returns to her job at the university library. That leaves me with the quiet companionship of Grandpa Frank. He teaches at the med school, so he's still on break.

"I've been given a list of things to buy at the grocery store," he says the first morning we're alone.

"I'll help," I offer.

"We might need to wander around the bookstore first." He nods. "They make a nice hot chocolate there too."

I already love this man. "I'll get my coat."

At the store, I buy a book that's on the syllabus for the music theory course I'm taking next semester, and we install ourselves at a cafe table. Across from me, my grandfather turns pages in *The Economist*, and breaks off pieces from a cookie he bought to share. It's the size of a dinner plate.

Sipping my latte, I open my book to the introduction. A fresh page, a fresh beginning, a new class. A cup of coffee and my grandfather's silence. These things make it possible to set aside the heartaches of the past week. For a while, I lose myself in an explanation of how the human ear converts sound waves into music.

Then I read about an experiment so wonderfully nerdy in its execution that I need to remember to tell Jake about it later. A 1950s composer made several recordings of a song, each on a different musical instrument. Then, splicing like crazy, he shaved off the *beginning of each note*—the attack of the hammer hitting the piano string, the first breath of a flute's sound, the buzzing start of a guitar's pluck—and something odd happened. Listeners, robbed of the violent front portion of each note, could no longer distinguish which instrument was playing. Even professional musicians who listened to his tapes could not guess correctly.

I put down the book, straining to believe that the familiar twang of a guitar note, with its beginning nipped off, could be rendered unrecognizable. I'm willing to bet cash money that my years of listening to Frederick's guitar meant that I could identify his sound no matter what.

Frederick calls me every morning now, but I don't answer. I don't feel like fighting with him, but I'm not ready to forgive and forget.

Still, each morning he leaves me a voice mail. His messages don't mention Christmas or Alice's wrath. Instead, he tells me little pieces of news—that he'd tried my favorite pizza topping combination—onions and olives, and that Henry has a new girlfriend.

He talks to me more in these messages than he usually does. I listen carefully to each one. But my bitter heart doesn't let me call back.

"And make sure Grandpa Frank takes you to Woodyard Bar-B-Que for the burnt ends," he'd said at the end of his latest message, making no mention of why he wouldn't be taking me there himself. "See you in a couple weeks," he always says before hanging up.

Our relationship is like an experiment gone awry. Maybe my father and I will never be able to hear each other properly, because so much of our beginning was spliced off and thrown away.

CONTRARY MOTION

CONTRARY MOTION: *Melody and harmony lines moving in opposite directions—one climbing the pitch scale, one descending.*

Chapter Twenty-One

JUST BEFORE NEW YEAR'S, I finish filling out five college applications. I charge the application fees to Frederick's credit card. Since we're still not speaking, it's his only way of learning which colleges I'm applying to.

Claiborne College is my "reach" school. And—grudgingly—I check the box indicating I had a Claiborne College parent, and I fill in his name.

Frank and Alice drive me to the airport in Kansas City. After quite a few hugs, they send me off to Boston.

And Jake. I'm so excited to see Jake. The kiss I get from him when I finally reach Habernacker lets me know that he feels the same.

Way back when Jake was still just a name on an email account, he warned me that New Hampshire winters were no joke. Turns out he's right about that. I spend the entire month of January shivering. The tile floor in our ancient dormitory bathroom is so cold it hurts my feet. The window seat in our room becomes uninhabitable due to the drafts that blow through the old-fashioned leaded glass windows.

"This is what minus-twenty feels like," Jake says one morning when we leave the dining hall together after breakfast.

I take a deep breath. "The inside of my nose is freezing."

"At least you don't have to walk a mile to the college," he says, rewrapping the scarf around his neck, leaving only the top half of his face showing. Jake is taking two science courses and an advanced calculus course at Claiborne College this semester, because he's already taken everything that CPrep has to offer.

With a track record like that, there's no way he won't get accepted to the college this spring. But he hates it when I say so, because he's superstitious.

I stand on my toes to give him a quick kiss on the bridge of his nose. "I'll see you in English?"

He nods. "Now run before you freeze."

I trot off to the first class of the day. Sitting down in the music department's lecture hall, the only thing I'm willing to shed are my gloves. The old radiators under the windows clank to life, but the lecture hall is still cold.

My phone buzzes with a text, and I reach for it with stiffened fingers. It's from my father.

Hi Rachel. Meet this imbecile for coffee?

"Imbecile" is a good addition to the canon, and I wonder how long it took Frederick to think of that one.

I've been getting these clever, begging texts for a while now. He's managed to use "dejected" and "disaster," this week too.

I don't reply to any of them, even though the word "inept" begs to be used right about now.

When he'd hightailed it to California, I'd given myself a well-deserved break from all things Frederick. But now that he's back in Claiborne, I've begun to feel ridiculous. Frederick is the one who had acted childishly—who couldn't even get through a few days with his parents without blowing up.

Ignoring him while he was a few thousand miles away was one thing. But if I snub him after he's traveled so far to be near me, that makes *me* into an immature beast, doesn't it? It's the equivalent of slamming my bedroom door and pouting.

By now, an entire month has passed since we'd spoken. He

stopped leaving chatty voicemails about two weeks ago. But at least once a day his name lights up as an Incoming Call. And his texts have begun to weaken my resolve.

Even worse, ignoring him makes me increasingly insecure. How long will he hang around before he gives up on me entirely?

From the front of the room, the professor opens his lecture with a discussion of key signatures.

"Now, an accidental is a note in the piece that *departs* from the stated key signature. But there's nothing accidental about an accidental, in spite of its name. The use of accidentals adds color and depth to the music, effectively allowing the composer an expanded color palate from which to paint."

Shrugging off my coat, I begin to take notes. Thank God for school and its many distractions.

———

The following Thursday, expecting a call from Jake, I answer my phone without checking the caller. "Hello?"

"Hi, Rachel." Frederick's words are rough and warm in my ear.

I close my eyes.

Into my silence he asks, "Is my long lost-daughter there?"

Seriously? "Frederick, you did *not* just say that."

He snorts. "It's just gallows humor. I'm in town," he says, as if I don't already know that. "And it's a gorgeous day outside. Come out, we'll get a cup of coffee."

I waiver. Refusing to see him is confrontational. And good girls avoid that like the plague. And I have no midday class, so there's really no reason I can't go.

"I'm just about to meet…" I almost say Jake's name, but something holds me back. "I'm having lunch with Aurora. How about one thirty? I'll meet you in front of the Inn."

"I'll be there," he says.

He comes outside at the appointed time, wearing the hat I

gave him for Christmas. He gives me a quick squeeze around the shoulders. "You've been busy?"

"Sure," I say, grumpily. "New classes." *New boyfriend*. I'm still not sure he deserves the inside scoop on my life. So I ask him a question instead. "What have you been up to?"

"A few new songs. I keep busy." We walk down Main Street together, toward the pale winter sun. "What classes are you taking this semester?"

We're back to safe topics, just like in Orlando. "An English class that's doing Chaucer. Spanish again. Art history. Music theory." I just slip that one in at the end, wondering if he'll notice.

"*Really.*" He gives me a sideways glance. "I didn't know that was an interest of yours."

"I'll let you know," I downplay it. "I like music, but I'm wondering if it's one of those things that gets less beautiful the more you know about it. Like astronomy." I like stars just fine, but unlike Jake, I don't need to know that they're gaseous balls undergoing nuclear fusion.

"Music theory is a great class," Frederick says. "I liked knowing there was a reason that some things sound good together and others don't—that the listener always wants a dissonant chord to resolve to a consonant one."

"But doesn't that make everything seem too simple? Like we're all so predictable?"

"People *are* predictable," he argues. "I don't mind knowing why."

We walk in silence for a moment. "How was your New Year's concert?"

"Good."

I wait for him to say more, but he doesn't. And I'm sick of feeling like the cool parts of his life are off limits to me. "You never tell me a single thing about your job. Why is that?"

"Fine." He chuckles. "We played a ninety-minute set for six thousand people, mostly music I wrote ten years ago, because that's what they came to hear. People clapped. And Henry deposited ninety thousand dollars into my account."

"Just another day at the office," I mutter.

"Exactly. What I do for a living is the most egotistical thing in the world. It's like...professional masturbation."

Now it's my turn to snort. "There's a phrase for *US Weekly*."

"No kidding. I don't talk about it because..." He pauses so long that I wonder if he'll finish. "Your mom became a nurse, right? For sick *children*. Christ. How can anyone compete with that?"

I make a choking sound, because he sounds just like Alice now.

"Can we go in there?" He points at a store.

I've been too busy trying to keep my head from exploding to notice where we're going. "Why?"

"There's something I want to show you."

I follow through the store to a display rack. "Wool long underwear? Sounds itchy."

"That's what I thought too," he says. "But it's merino. Feel this. A friend of mine convinced me to try them. Let's get you one pair, and I guarantee you'll be back for more."

"We'll see." I wonder which friend of Frederick's discusses underwear with him.

"By the time winter is over, we'll have this cold weather thing figured out," he says. "What do you think of this?" He hands me a giant furry hat.

"It's great. For someone else." I replace it on the rack.

The February sun pours down on us when we leave the store. Its warmth begins to thaw out my heart. We take an outside table at the coffee shop. "It's a heat wave," I announce, tipping my face back to feel the sun. "I'm photosynthesizing."

Sipping a cappuccino, I let myself bask in Frederick's attention. He begins to talk about music theory. And for once my little-kid idea of hanging out with him becomes true.

"You really can't learn the circle of fifths on a piano," he says, waving his hands for emphasis. "A keyboard is set up to play major scales easily. But on a guitar, you can *feel* the intervals. It's like looking right at music's DNA. I'll show you sometime."

"That would be nice." I still harbor a secret fantasy that Frederick will teach me to play the guitar. Someday I'll work up the courage to ask.

"It will be the only homework I can ever help you with. The Chaucer you'll have to figure out on your own."

I swirl the foam around in my paper cup. In my peripheral vision, I notice a woman watching us. Actually, two of them. They've stopped on the outskirts of the coffee shop crowd.

At first I think they're gawking fans. That still happens sometimes, even in Claiborne. But then I recognized the woman I saw through the window of Mary's restaurant, and on the real estate listing sheet. And she's staring at us, disbelief on her face.

Why?

I feel something go slightly wrong in my gut. Very deliberately, I put my hand on my father's sleeve. I leaned in, my face closer to his. "When did you start playing the guitar?"

His smile is at close range. "In middle school," he says. "I bought a Les Paul Junior with my carwash money."

Of course I know that already. I'd read about it years ago. When I glance quickly toward the woman again, she's still there, her face transfixed, as if she cannot look away.

"Oh, shit," my father says. Now he sees her too.

"What's the problem?" I ask, trying to keep my voice casual. Frederick looks like he wants to leap out of his chair.

At the edge of my vision, the two women put on a burst of speed. They pass the cafe and walk up the street.

My father lets out a strangled breath. "It's...just a misunderstanding heading my way. Perfectly avoidable, of course. My usual good work on display."

"She's your girlfriend?"

He turns to me, his eyes narrowing, and he pauses longer than the question requires. I can see him trying to decide whether or not I'd caused confusion intentionally. "Yeah."

"And she doesn't know you have a daughter?" Even as I say it, my heart contracts with surprise.

He closes his eyes for a brief moment. "Right. But she's about to learn."

"Seriously? I didn't know I was still unacknowledged. *Wow*." My voice squeaks on the last word.

"That's not fair." His face flushes red, startling me. "I really like this woman. And it's been hard to find a way to tell her that I'm a founding member of Assholes Anonymous." He stands up. "But that's what I'll be doing now."

I look up at him, still shocked. "So…nice of you to drop by."

He scoops his hat off the table, a look of defeat on his face. "Right. I'm going to go now, and apologize to Norah for being an ass. And then later I'll call you and do the same. It's what I do. Stay warm." And he strides away from our table.

I turn to watch him go. The woman has stopped halfway down Main Street. She and her friend watch Frederick approach.

Standing up, I turn my back on all of them. Tossing my coffee cup into a trash barrel, I walk back toward campus.

Chapter Twenty-Two

I HOLD the book in my hands, but I can't concentrate on Chaucer's poetry. Instead, I keep replaying my combustible hour with Frederick. For weeks I've felt guilty about not seeing him, and he probably hadn't even cared. He'd been too busy shacking up with his girlfriend.

When I went to meet Frederick today, I'd carried my report card along in my coat pocket. I'd meant to show him that I'd received two As and two A-minuses last semester.

I'm eighteen and a half years old, and still desperate for my father's approval.

Still pathetic.

On the sofa next to me, Jake groans. "Help me out here," he says. "'*He thakked her about the lendes weel?'* Am I supposed to know what that means?"

"I think he pinched her on the backside."

Jake rolls his eyes. "This Old English is killing me. It makes even fun things dull." One of his hands snakes over to give me a quick pinch on the rear.

I shrug off Jake's arm and squirm farther into the corner of the couch. I turn the page and try to read on.

"What did I do?"

"Nothing." I sigh. "I'm mad at my father."

"Okay. I asked you how that went, and you said 'fine.' But it wasn't?"

"It was…just typical Frederick. He doesn't think about other people."

Jake closes his book. "What did he do now?"

"He has this girlfriend…" I stop, because it probably won't make sense to Jake. *She doesn't know about me.* Said aloud, the complaint will only sound self-centered. "He didn't tell me about her," I say instead. Which was also true.

"Why, is she, like, twenty-one?"

"No, he just…" I shake my head.

"It sounds like… Isn't it better for both of you if he's happy here?"

I look up sharply. "It sounds like you don't know a thing about it."

"But I would if you told me," he says softly.

"Yeah," I whisper. "I know."

Then I feel even worse. I raise my stupid book and hide behind it. Jake and I are both reading *The Miller's Tale* in preparation for tomorrow's English class, which we have together this semester. But I'm not in the mood for the carpenter, his cheating wife, and the musician who cuckolded him. It's slow-going.

"Do I ever get to meet him?" Jake asks after a time.

"Who, Frederick? *No.*"

"So…that wasn't the right time to ask that question, was it?"

"Bingo."

He puts his book down. "I didn't mean it like I want to be his groupie. I just like you, is all. If my parents lived in town, I'd show you off immediately. 'This is Rachel. She likes me even though I don't understand Chaucer.'"

I close my book too, still feeling brittle. "I have rehearsal in fifteen minutes."

Aurora's voice comes out of the bedroom. "Jake, you're not

getting any of the good stuff tonight, honey. Better luck tomorrow."

Jake lifts his book with a sigh.

———

The temperature has dropped along with the sun, so I run all the way to rehearsal. The chill stings my face, but it feels good to move, to shake off the day's disappointments. I'll soon be warm, anyway. The Belle Choir practices in an overheated classroom.

I'm only one minute late, and the others are still unwinding their scarves and shucking off their jackets.

"Let's go, people!" Jessica calls. "We have only four rehearsals left before the jam. And Rachel and Daria still don't have solos. Lots to do here!"

I take my place on the alto side of the horseshoe formation.

"Actually, I'm taking 'Blackbird,'" Daria says.

"Oh, good." Jessica makes a note on her clipboard. "That leaves Rachel." Jessica fixes me with a stare. Lately I'm getting a weird vibe from her, as if I've done something wrong.

"Well," I begin. "I can take whatever solo you want me to. But I had an idea for something new—if you don't think it's too weird."

"Weird can be interesting," Daria pipes up.

"It's not the song that's weird," I say quickly. "In fact, it makes a great vocal piece. The only weird thing is that my father wrote it."

"Well, that's kind of cool," somebody says.

"Is he coming to hear us?" Daria asks.

I can't even look at Daria, because I really have no idea. I still haven't mentioned the Belle Choir to Frederick, let alone the concert.

"But how can we write a new arrangement in two weeks?" Jessica asks.

"Don't have to," I say, taking the music out of my back pocket.

"I did it already. It was really easy, honestly. It's like this song wanted to be a cappella."

This earns me another frown from Jessica. But then she says, "Let's warm up, run through what we have, and then we'll look at it just before we break."

We begin by singing some arpeggios, rising a half step from one to the other. Standing in my spot—third from the right—with warm voices vibrating around me, I finally begin to feel better.

The first song we rehearse is "Fly Me to the Moon," which is Other Jessica's solo. I let my voice dip and soar with the others. Often during rehearsal, my mother comes to me, unbidden. I can picture Mom looking down on the half-circle of shining heads, listening to me blend my voice with the others. Standing there, concentrating on the notes, it's possible to be sad and happy at the same time.

We'd never fought about choir. Even though Mom disapproved of my interest in Frederick, she never saw choir as the same threat. It was orderly, it was beautiful. It would look good on college applications. The school chorus had always been my middle place, where I could please everyone at once. I could hone my voice, dreaming of the day my father would hear me, and please my mother at the same time.

For ten years I'd imagined Frederick turning up to hear me sing, and in my daydreams, the fated performance was always magical, with Frederick hooting from the back row.

Now the chance to realize this weird little dream has presented itself, I'm terrified. Furthermore, if I expect him to attend, I'll have to tell him about the jam soon.

Damn him.

————

When I get back after rehearsal, Jake is still lying on the couch, his computer on his stomach. I'm still a little stunned that such an attractive guy is waiting for me and not someone else. And after I've been such a grump.

"Hi!" I get a rush of pleasure just walking into a room where Jake is.

"Hi."

"What are you doing?" I ask, hoping to sound conciliatory.

"My fun homework. I'm writing an algorithm to parse text in a string."

"Oh, baby." I drop my coat on the desk chair and sit on the edge of the S.L.O. next to him. "I'm sorry I snapped at you. I was stressed out, and I took it out on you, and I'm basically a horrible person."

He clicks his laptop shut. "Let's hear it for rehearsal! You always come back from there happy." He reaches around me to put the computer on the table, then he grabs the end of my scarf and begins to unwrap me. He kisses the skin he's just exposed on my neck.

I close my eyes at the pleasant shiver it sends down my spine.

"Aurora just left, by the way," he says. "She was meeting someone."

"Really?" I swivel to face him. "How do you know?" Aurora has gone missing a couple of nights this semester. When I've asked, "Who is he?" my roommate refuses to divulge her secret. Even when I complain that it isn't fair—that she knows *everything* about me—she won't budge.

"It's a new and fragile thing," she explained. "I'll tell you when I can." And then she'd given me a devious smile before flouncing out of our room.

"Well." Jake's eyes dance. "She answered her phone, and then I swear she said 'rehearsal is over?' So the mystery lover is either in a singing group or a play."

"Or a comedy group, or an orchestra or quartet. That doesn't give us much to go on."

"True," he says, grinning. "But since she's not here, and we are..." He leans back onto the arm of the sofa, pulling me with him. I brace my arms on either side of his head and look down into his smile, which quickly fades. I always know when Jake is going to kiss me, because his expression is solemn, as if he's about to do something serious.

He begins slowly, with a silent question, his lips fitting softly against mine, testing my willingness. In answer, I wrap my arms around his neck and lean in. He's suspiciously minty, as if he'd been chewing gum in preparation for my return.

This is a new thing in my life—all this affection. As Jake's kisses deepen, we're having a wordless discussion about how much we care.

I care a lot tonight, it seems.

Jake pulls me farther down until I'm lying on top of him. I run a hand across his jaw, examining the pleasant roughness of his whiskers under my palms. We kiss, and the heat of his mouth spreads through my chest. Every point of connection between us stirs me. And there are a lot of them. He puts his hands on my hips and holds me in place.

I feel it everywhere.

Jake's fingers slide underneath my shirt, skimming my ribcage. I can hear the lingering shimmer of a cappella music in my head, the vibrating voices still serenading me as our mouths join again and again.

At some point we roll sideways, and I end up propped against the back of the couch, my head lying on Jake's bent arm. His kiss travels along my cheekbone and across my brow. He smooths the hair away from my face.

Everything is beautiful until his hand slides down, over my jeans and between my legs. First comes the shock at how good this feels, even through two layers of clothing, my body thrumming beneath his touch.

But as my heart rate accelerates, that thrum turns on me. Tension begins to rise up through my gut and into my chest. We're very alone, and anything could happen.

I try to calm down, to go on kissing him, but it's no good. With a gasp, I shove him back, scrambling into a sitting position.

Jake looks up at me, his glasses askew. He doesn't say a word.

I straighten out my shirt, covering myself, then put my head into my shaking hands. "I'm sorry."

Jake rights himself slowly, leaning back on the couch. "Are you okay?"

"Yeah," I grunt. Unfortunately, there have been several of these incidents. I can never explain it to him, because I don't really understand it myself. Fooling around with Jake is always fabulous, right up until the moment it isn't anymore.

He looks at his watch. "I should really get going, anyway."

"You're mad," I say.

"I'm not."

"Just say it! You are," I hear an edge of hysteria in my voice.

"No." His voice is low and quiet. "Mad is when somebody did something wrong. This is…confused." He takes a slow breath. "It's like playing the fifth level of 'Real Enemyz,' when you think you're going along great, and then the serpent comes out of nowhere and bites your head off. The screen goes black, and it's game over." He adjusts his glasses. "It does not, however, dull my enthusiasm for the game."

"You may have taken the analogy too far."

"Let a guy cool off a minute."

I watch, at a loss, as he shoves his laptop into his backpack and stands up. My heart grows heavy as he goes for the door. Before he opens it, he turns around.

"Rachel." His eyes don't quite meet mine. "Am I the one you want to be with?"

What? "Of course you are!" I straighten up, indignant.

His hand is on the doorknob. "You know, I've had it bad for you since, like, the second email. And I still do. But there are these invisible tripwires. And I'm always stepping on them. If you told me where they are…" He opens the door. "That might help. I'll see you tomorrow."

Chapter Twenty-Three

WINTER HOLDS on with both hands and both feet, just to prove that it can. I learn—the hard way—how to avoid black ice on the sidewalks. Midterms loom, and I see Frederick exactly once, for brunch. We're both on our best behavior.

"I'm basically hiding in New Hampshire these days," he says. "The record label is pushing me to work with younger song-writers for the new album. And they all want to make me sound like Ed Sheeran."

"Why?" I ask, spreading jam on my toast.

"Demographics," he grumbles. "My fan base is starting to go gray, but the kids are the ones who spend the most money on music. So they want to make me sound younger."

"Huh." I consider this. "Sheeran drops the odd curse word into his lyrics."

"Fuck, is that what it takes?" His grin is wry. "I can fucking do that."

I smile in spite of myself. "We'll have to work on your York-shire accent."

Frederick doesn't mention his girlfriend at all. And I'm curious whether he straightened things out with her. But it's really none of my business. And for once, he volunteered something about his work. That seems like progress.

"So what's up with you these days?" he asks.

That should have made for the perfect opening to mention my upcoming Belle Choir concert, which is only a week away. "Not much," I say instead.

And—proving myself to be the biggest chicken that ever lived —I don't call him again until the day of the jam.

"Hi Rachel," he answers his phone. "What's shakin'?"

"Where are you?" I ask, almost hoping he'll say, "At Logan airport, waiting on a flight." It would serve me right.

"I'm in Norah's car. Just taking care of a little appointment."

So they *are* still together.

"Well..." I swallow. "Sorry for the short notice. But I want to invite you to something. I'm in an a cappella singing group. And the concert is tonight."

"*Reeeeally.*" He chuckles. "I guess you'd better tell me where and when."

———

Seven hours later, I follow the Belle Choir onstage, regretting all my life choices. This had seemed like a clever way to reveal my favorite hobby. But now it feels gimmicky and desperate.

And it's too late to change my mind. I have no choice but to stand on this stage and deliver my solo—*his own song*—knowing he's out there listening with a songwriter's ear.

I take my place with the altos, putting one arm on Daria's shoulder and one on Other Jessica's. We all watch Jessica in the opposite corner. Our pitch hums a note, which I drop by a fourth and bank in my brain. When Jessica raises her hands, we launch together into Bonnie Raitt's "Something to Talk About."

The singing makes me feel better. It's easy to blend with the others and forget myself. And for a while, the performance is nearly as therapeutic as rehearsal. Between songs I sneak looks into the audience. I can see Aurora and Jake in the front row, where the stage lights reach them. But the rest of the auditorium is too dark to pick out faces.

He's out there somewhere.

Probably.

As my moment in the spotlight creeps closer, stage fright grips me with her iron claws.

I used to sing in choral competitions all over the state of Florida. I had stomachaches every time we competed, leading my mother to wonder aloud whether choir was meant to be a blood sport.

I have a stomachache right now.

Daria steps forward to sing "Blackbird," which is one of my favorites. The alto part is bold and dissonant, and it soothes me to concentrate on singing it. It's such a beautiful lyric about waiting for the right moment in life.

I've waited plenty, but now all that waiting seems like a mistake.

And Jessica scheduled my solo for dead last. With each passing song—and there are fourteen—my anxiety mounts.

When the time finally comes, Daria gives me a gentle shove on the back, and I step into the center of the horseshoe. Time moves too fast, and I don't feel ready as Jessica sweeps her hands in a circle. The others launch into the bass line of "Stop Motion," by Freddy Ricks and Ernie Hathaway.

I force myself to exhale. Jake is looking right at me, his face wide open and smiling. I take a deep breath and sing the first verse.

You would build her up just to tear her down
You expect gratitude for the crumbs you throw around

I've changed the key of my arrangement, raising the pitch to the very center of my vocal range. And because I've practiced this song a hundred times, my voice doesn't shake.

You need another fan, an acolyte
She's the one who bears witness to the man at his height

The first thousand times I'd listened to this song, I'd heard it as Frederick had intended—an observation of an imbalanced love affair. But then I realized that from my mouth the lyrics take on an entirely different meaning.

You'd have her click that shutter only when you have the time

All the hours in between she's your woman on ice

If you don't look now, she's gonna come undone

I hit the high note with all the force and passion that I'd hoped to bring to it.

'Cause she can't live her life…

…as a stop motion flick

It's a forceful criticism. But he wrote those words, not me.

After the first chorus, I'm able to let the song take over. The other women's voices curl around me like a blanket. This is their finale too, and I feel the swell of their effort pouring forth from behind me. I'm lucky just to be a part of it.

The song seems to end too soon. It's followed by a swell of applause. I step back into formation and everyone takes a bow together. The audience stands up to cheer, and I see Jake put his fingers to his lips and whistle.

Then the horseshoe breaks apart, and everyone is in motion. Jake reaches me first, his hug lifting me off the ground. "That was awesome," he crows. "No wonder they put you last. You smoked them."

"Thank you," I say, my eyes darting around over his shoulder. I find Aurora next. She's stopped to give Jessica a congratulatory hug, which was awfully nice of her. Then my roommate hustles over to give me a squeeze.

But not Frederick. I don't see him anywhere.

There are plenty of parents in the crowd. A few of them stop me with praise. "What a solo!" Daria's dad says.

"We were lucky to snag her," his daughter is nice enough to add.

But I still don't spot Frederick. With the house lights on, I can now see all the way to the back of the auditorium. But his big frame isn't waiting in any of the chairs, or leaning against the back wall.

"Maybe he's out front?" Aurora suggests.

Maybe he didn't come. "Let me get my stuff and I'll meet you outside."

"We can wait some more," Jake offers.

I shake my head. "I'll be right out."

I fetch my bag from the wings and then hop down, the last one to leave the stage. There are only a few stragglers left in the auditorium and none of them is Frederick.

But as I walk up the aisle, a woman steps out in front of me. "Rachel?" After a beat, I recognize her as Frederick's girlfriend. "I'm Norah. Frederick will be just another minute."

"He was here?" I blurt.

"For the whole thing. You were amazing."

I can't stop myself from asking, "Did he hate it?"

"No," Norah says with a strange smile. "He liked it so much that he had to mop himself up off the floor after your song."

"What?"

"You didn't hear it from me."

And then Frederick appears in the aisle, walking toward us both, with red eyes and an embarrassed grin on his face. "Look at that. Both my girls in one place." He crushes me to his leather jacket. "I'm sorry to disappear. But I wasn't prepared for that. *Christ*, girl. You absolutely killed it."

"Thank you," I whisper, my heart nearly failing.

"Can we take you out for, I don't know, ice cream?" Frederick asks.

"You almost said, 'a beer,' didn't you?"

"Yeah. I don't know any other musicians who are too young to drink."

I flick my eyes to Norah. I'm still surfing on a killer wave of adrenaline. I don't think I can sit down with Frederick's girlfriend tonight. "Well, I have a quiz tomorrow," I hedge. "And my friends are waiting. Can we go this weekend instead?"

"Of course," Frederick agrees. "We can do dinner."

We walk outside. Norah hangs back, probably so that I can say goodbye to my father. "Thank you for coming." I feel Jake and Aurora watching me from the corner. I'd imagined introducing Jake to Frederick tonight, but now I feel too depleted.

"I wouldn't have missed it."

"Dad?"

His face changes with a soft kind of surprise. I've never called him that before. "Yeah?"

"I'm sorry."

He puts his hands in his pockets. "Music is supposed to be moving. Mission accomplished."

"Yes, but…" *I chose it to make you feel guilty.*

"But nothing. I didn't know you could sing like that. I've been kicking myself for nine months over all the things I stole from you. It never occurred to me that being my child might give you anything you could use."

I stare up at him. *Seriously*? He's the only man alive who could find some way to flatter himself in the face of my lyrical indictment.

"Uh, well… Then will you teach me how to play the guitar?" There, I've finally asked.

"Heck, yeah!" he says, hugging me again. "I love that idea. We'll start next week."

I let him hold me for as long as I dare, and then I run off to join my friends.

Chapter Twenty-Four

"OKAY, now *stretch* that third finger onto the low E string."

I stretch. Or at least, I try.

Frederick and I are sitting on Norah's sofa, in her cute little house on Maple Street.

"I've finally left the Inn," Frederick had told me over the phone. "I'm staying with Norah."

"Well, that's one way to solve your real estate woes." There's a joke in there somewhere about what a *full-service* brokerage Norah works for. I hadn't gone there.

When I'd knocked on the old wooden door today, it was Norah who answered. "Hi," she'd said. "I'm on my way out to show a condo, but make yourself at home. There's soda in the fridge."

"Thanks." Norah's house is little and pretty, with a carved wooden mantelpiece and stained glass. "I like your windows," I'd offered, looking for something to say.

"They're original to the house," she'd said. "I love antiques."

Then Frederick came out of the kitchen, and Norah laid a hand on his chest. "I'll see you for dinner?"

"Absolutely." He gave her a kiss, and I looked away.

Now it's just Frederick and I, and I'm learning that my fingers on Frederick's guitar are almost as awkward as those first few moments in Norah's house.

"Who invented this thing? Why are their six strings, when I only have five fingers?"

"Aliens, duh. Now switch back to D7," my father coaches. "Yes! Now try for G again…"

Unable to quickly cram my fingers into position, I flub the G chord. "Damn."

"You'll get it. Just takes some practice."

But I don't believe him. I'd had this foolish idea that Frederick's daughter wouldn't have trouble playing her first G chord. And yet here I am, smashing my fingers together on the frets. Then I strum softly.

"That's right, except…" Frederick reaches down and strums again, hard. And the chord echoes throughout the room. "Got to hear you, whether it's right or wrong. If you're going to make a mistake, make it loud."

"Okay." I check my fancy watch. I always wear my birthday present on the days I'm going to see him. "I have Spanish in half an hour."

"All right." He takes the guitar into his own lap and strums it absently. "There's two things I want to talk to you about, though. Do you have just a couple more minutes?"

"Sure."

"The first one is easy. I'm playing a music festival in Quebec next weekend. Do you want to come?"

"Sure I do." *Yes, yes!* I'm flailing inside. *Finally.*

"There will be some boring parts. I'll have to make nice with some industry people. But you can watch the concert, and there's a party after."

"Okay. Done. What's the other thing?"

"Well, that one's a little more complicated." He stops playing. "There's going to be a baby."

"What?" Did he just say *baby?*

"Norah and I are going to have a baby. In October."

I feel suddenly dizzy. "I thought you just met her."

He strokes his chin. "It depends on your point of view. We've been together since the fall. But also, Rachel, we're old. After you turn forty, it's like dog years."

My throat is tight. Congratulations are probably expected of me. "So...I guess you're staying in Claiborne, then."

"That's the plan. Is that okay with you?"

Does it really matter what I think? "Sure." I almost choke on the word. "Sorry, I've got to run." I grab my backpack. Thank God for Spanish class. I can't wait to get out of there. "Did you tell Grandma Alice?"

"No." He's quiet. "I will. Soon."

He catches my hand as I pass him. "Good work today." He taps the guitar.

"Thanks," I say, breaking for the door. "See you next week." I run up Maple Street, toward school, taking gulps of the cool March air.

————

That night I knock on Jake's door, feeling low.

He opens up, wearing jeans and a look of surprise, but nothing else. "Hi," he says. "Come in?"

Once inside, I have to work hard to keep my eyes from lingering on all the bare skin of his chest. I glance around his space. "Sal and Arin actually left the room?"

"I know, right?" He cups the back of my neck, one thumb stroking my shoulder. "How was your guitar lesson?"

I'd come upstairs intending to tell him, in excruciating detail, about Frederick's awful announcement. But that's not what happens. Instead, I move quickly, pasting myself to Jake as tightly as a bumper sticker. Then I kiss him. Hard.

SARINA BOWEN

Jake makes a noise of surprise, which sounds something like "*armf.*"

But he recovers speedily, taking the kiss deeper, then steering me down onto his bed. All his velvety skin draws me in. I close my eyes and let my fingers enjoy the solid warmth of him. I love the way we fit together, wrapped around one another, legs entwined. We kiss as though planet Earth has only a few precious minutes left, and we're trying to make the best of them.

Under my hands, Jake's heart beats quickly. His body is warm and tight, his mouth worshipful. I pull him even closer, extinguishing all the empty space between us. He gives a low, happy growl that lights me up, shoving aside all the ragged worries of the day.

Everything is great until he rolls on top of me, his body fitted against mine like a jigsaw puzzle piece. That's when the little frightened voice in my head says: *now what?*

My breathing stutters. I try to ignore my fear, to shove it back into its drawer. But soon my pulse is ragged and I just need air.

I push Jake off, gasping for oxygen.

For a moment, his eyes are wide and startled. But then he raises himself on one elbow, studying me. "Rachel," he whispers. "Are you okay?"

I nod like a bobblehead. But it's a lie. My heart is going a thousand miles an hour. And I'm mortified. A half hour ago I'd knocked on his door. He'd asked me a question. I hadn't even answered him. Instead, I'd *launched* myself at him.

Then, when he was really into it, I pushed him off. Like a psycho.

And Frederick is having a *baby.*

"I think we shouldn't do this anymore," Jake says, his voice low. "Not for a while."

I sit up, instantly afraid. "Not do *what?*"

"Not do *this,*" he says, pointing at the two of us, sprawled on the bed. "This is stressing you out. That's no good. I don't want to be the thing that freaks you out all the time."

242

My eyes got the message faster than my brain. Two tears ran down my face even as the truth hits. He's breaking up with me.

"Oh boy. I'm not trying to make you upset, I'm trying for the opposite. To take the pressure off. You're just so…" He frowns.

"Just so *what*?" I demand.

"Hard to *read*. Everything is great, and then all of a sudden it's not. And I'm like an ogre you have to escape from."

I try to stop the tears from coming by looking up at the ceiling. "A man will do anything to get away from a woman who's crying," my mother had once told me.

"Rachel, can I ask you something?"

"*What?*" I gasp.

"Did something scary happen to you before? Because… It's like you panic."

"I do panic," I mumble. "But it's nobody's fault."

"So you weren't ever…" Jake's eyes travel to the floor, and he doesn't finish the question. He can't bring himself to say "raped" or "attacked" or some other ugly word.

"No," I whisper. But I'm faced with an unwelcome realization. It isn't Jake's enthusiasm that frightens me. It's *mine*. That zing I feel when he touches me is a dangerous thing. My mother proved it when she was only nineteen years old.

I can't repeat her mistakes. It would be so easy to do anything —*everything* with Jake.

Jake's face is flushed. "I hate scaring you. It makes me feel like Asshat."

"You're not an asshat," I say, my voice cracking. Jake isn't the problem. I am.

"What is it, then? I keep asking, but you don't say."

"I'm not afraid of you." I barely get the sentence out, because my throat is closing up.

"If you're not afraid of me, then maybe I just don't do it for you. Is that it? Or, do you have religious objections?" He throws his hands in the air. "Something is the matter, but you don't…" He swallows. "You don't love me enough to tell me what it is."

"That's not…" I clench my teeth. *Fair? True?* I can't think. All I know is that I'm so embarrassed I've begun to sweat. I jump to my feet, and so he stands up too. He moves close, as if to hug me, but I spin around and leave his room, flying down two flights of stairs and back into my own.

Aurora isn't home, and so there's nobody to hear me cry.

Chapter Twenty-Five

INSTEAD OF STUDYING, I sit in the back of the bus, watching Vermont go by.

"You can bring Aurora to the concert," my father offered yesterday. "There'll be two beds in your hotel room."

"I think she's busy," I'd told him, although it isn't true. I'd wanted to go to a concert with him so badly, for so long. I wanted this trip to be mine alone.

Only it isn't. I should have known better.

Norah has come along too, and it's her first concert and her first time meeting the band. Naturally, they're enthralled with her. Even before we'd boarded the bus, Ernie, Henry, and the rest circled Norah with the same curiosity they'd shown me, but with none of the strained awkwardness.

Across the aisle from me, Norah spreads a document on the bus's back table, then pulls a calculator from her bag. "Sorry, I don't usually geek out during happy hour," she says. "But I owe someone a response by five o'clock."

Ernie plops down next to me. "Don't apologize! We're fascinated. Freddy's girlfriends don't usually come with calculators."

"Freddy's girlfriends don't usually come with *brains*," the keyboardist puts in from one row up.

My father makes an irritated noise.

Henry hovers in the aisle. "What can I get everybody to drink? Norah, a beer?"

"Seltzer?" she asks. When Henry goes away, she drops her voice. "I might as well wear a sandwich board that says 'pregnant girlfriend.'"

"Well, gosh," I hear myself say. "There's never been a pregnant girlfriend around musicians before."

Frederick's laugh is a bark. "Good one, kid."

Norah's eyes flash in my direction. But I just look away.

———

Four hours later, we pull up at the hotel, and everyone gets off except for Henry. "The rez is in your name," he tells Frederick.

"Where's Henry going?" I ask.

"We're a little late for our load-in," Frederick says, without bothering to explain what that means.

"Bonjour," the doorman calls. I'm about to discover how disconcerting it is to ride a few hours north and find that everyone speaks French.

"Good afternoon," my father says to the woman at the desk. "Reservations for Ricks."

"Oui," she says, typing furiously into her terminal. While everyone watches, she frowns into the screen.

I see Norah duck into a door marked *Femmes*. And when she returns a couple of minutes later, the people behind the desk seem no closer to handing out keys. A manager has swooped in to assist the desk agent, and Norah puts an elbow on the counter to listen to their rapid French.

"Excusez-moi," Norah breaks in after a minute. "Le nom est R-I-C-K-S, ne Riche."

"Ah, merci!" the manager exclaims.

A minute later, six room reservations are located.

"I guess they're not fans of yours, honey," Norah says over her shoulder, while the band gapes at her.

"Gawd," Ernie says. "Freddy's gone upscale. First a smart kid, and now a girlfriend who speaks French. I fear for my own job security."

"Trust me," Norah says. "This is a rare use of my expensive education. I'm useful in Germany too."

"Really? I didn't know you spoke German," my father says.

It's Everyone-be-Gaga-Over-Norah Day.

———

I'm given the hotel room adjoining Frederick and Norah's. Even after I close the pass-through door to change my clothes, I can hear muffled voices from the other side.

Frederick sings to himself, warming up. Then he breaks off to say, "Damn, you look sexy in that. How am I going to keep my mitts off you?"

"Just keep two hands on the guitar, cowboy."

I go into the bathroom and turn the water on full blast.

Eventually my father knocks on the connecting door. "Rachel, Henry says the opening act is half done. Let's head over." The venue is just across the street.

I open the door. "Coming."

He puts something in my hand, two little plastic balls with tubes in them.

"What is this?"

"Earplugs. You need to wear them if you're hanging around me."

"Really?"

"Don't want to damage your hearing. I wear them too."

Norah holds an identical pair. "We can look like aliens together."

"Also, you need these." He gives us each a lanyard with a pass on it.

"Thanks," I say as casually as possible. It says, *BAND*. Tomorrow, it will go right into my keepsake drawer.

We cross the street, where Henry stands tapping his foot outside the back door of the theater. "Let's go," he says, leading us inside and then through the bowels of the building. We sail through a green room. The last door has *STAGE* printed on it. Then suddenly I'm standing in the wings of an enormous theater, with a roaring crowd filling every seat.

While techies swap the opening act's equipment for Frederick's, Henry paces like a jaguar at the zoo. "Are you ladies staying here, or do you want seats?" he asks Norah and me.

"I'll stay here. If that's allowed," I say.

"Me too," Norah agrees.

"Somebody bring Norah a chair," Frederick says, tuning his guitar one more time.

Henry brings two. "Three minutes," he calls.

A young man crawls around onstage, taping down Frederick's guitar cord. The PA system plays a Springsteen tune. When I peek around the curtain's edge, I can see the crowd. There are so many people, the rows seemed to stretch back forever. Yet Frederick referred to this place as a small venue.

I watch my father, who looks entirely calm. He hands his guitar to Henry, who walks out on stage to put it on the stand. Frederick puts his hands on Norah's shoulders, his thumbs on the bare skin of her neck.

Norah looks giddy. "What am I supposed to say to you? Break a leg? Merde? Good luck?"

He slips an arm around her waist. "I already have the good luck."

I turn away while he kisses her neck.

In the theater and onstage, the lights dim.

A warm hand lands on my shoulder, and it belongs to Ernie. Then Frederick says, "Let's do this thing," and Henry barks something into the earpiece he wears.

The PA system rings with an announcement. "Let's hear it for

Freddy Ricks!"

My father passes by me, the stage lights reddening his hair as he steps onto the stage. The audience roars when they see him, his confident walk bringing him center stage. The ferocity of their cheering startles me. It's like a tsunami of love crashing over him.

He tosses the guitar strap over his head and waves to the crowd. Ernie and the others take their positions behind him. My father sets his hands against his instrument and begins to play the introduction to "Watching in the Rain."

I've been waiting a long time for this moment. From the wings I can only see his profile. Between verses, he looks in our direction and smiles.

At Norah, probably.

But as he keeps singing, I forget everything else. I become a student of the look on his face during "No More Paradise," eyes closed, squeezing out the high notes.

I love watching him work. And it really is *work*. There's sweat pouring off his face in rivulets. His fingers never stop moving on the guitar, and the songs just keep coming. I can see the crowd swaying before him, deep inside the sound.

I wish I knew what that feels like—to do a thing so well that thousands stand before you, drinking it in. It's magical.

When he finally says goodnight to the crowd, they clap and stamp their feet until he goes back onstage for an encore. Now that it's almost over, I remember to take out my phone and snap a blurry picture of my view from the wings.

Finally the curtain falls after his final encore. And after that, things aren't as fun anymore.

There's a party onstage, and I don't quite know what to do with myself. Frederick is surrounded by well-wishers, and I don't feel like introducing myself to strangers. I'm exhausted from the experience, and don't want idle chatter.

A boy in a green *STAFF* T-shirt brings me a beer. He tries to talk to me in a thick French accent. Usually, I find beer repulsive. But this one has the benefit of being ice cold. I drink it and listen to the boy tell me about his job in the theater. I understand about a third of what he says.

When I finish my beer, he brings me another.

"You want to zee zeh catwalk?" STAFF asks me.

"Sure."

Backstage, we have to abandon our drinks at the bottom of the ladder and climb. The theater looks even grander from the fly space than it does from the stage, a great oval under shimmering lights. My perspective on the partygoers shifts to the tops of their heads. My father is surrounded by what looks like a great flowering of people. At the center of the blossom are Frederick and Norah, in her vibrant red top, his arm around her. Music people ring him in layers according to some hierarchy I can't understand.

STAFF says, "I have to take a *pisse*. You must come with me down from here."

Descending the ladder makes me feel woozy. I wander the outskirts of the little mob onstage until STAFF brings me another beer. "Salud," he says, and we clink our plastic cups together.

Time passes, and I have only STAFF and beer for company. But the more I drink, the less it matters.

"Oh… Rachel! Yikes. I think it's time to go back."

I squint upward, and it's Norah's face that swims into view. I'm still holding a beer, but its predecessors have already done their work. I am half leaning on STAFF, who is whispering something in my ear. I'm not sure what.

"Rachel, come with me."

I shake my head. "You're not my mother." One of the benefits of having a dead mother (and there aren't many) is that any time I invoke her name, people always back off.

Except for Norah.

"That's true, I'm not. Would you like me to fetch your father instead?"

Well played, Norah.

Unsteadily, I consider my options. Norah is not going to let it drop, and now that I feel so sloppy, it's no longer half so appealing to have my father seek me out. "No."

"Then come with me. Actually—stay here for just one second while I tell him we're leaving. Don't move from this spot."

I watch Norah dart away. The sudden motion makes me feel more than a little nauseous. When Norah returns, I let myself be led away. Outside I gulp cold air, and Norah helps the situation immensely by not trying to talk to me. The hotel is only across the street, and I soon find myself in an overly bright elevator, the floor moving unevenly beneath my feet.

"I don't feel good," I say.

When the elevator stops on our floor, Norah scrambles toward our rooms. She flicks her key card against a door and sweeps it open for me.

I press my lips together and move as quickly as I can. But Norah's room is the reverse of my own, and it's confusing enough to delay my voyage toward the toilet. At the last second, Norah puts a wastebasket under my face, and I vomit into it.

"Shot scored," Norah remarks.

"Oh, hell," I groan.

"Been there," Norah says with a sigh. "Come on. Let's go to your room."

When I cross through the adjoining doors and sit down on my own bed, I feel the slightest bit better. I hear Norah go into the bathroom and dump out the basket. She fills it with water from the bathtub and then dumps it again.

"Where're your PJs?" she calls.

I wobble toward my bag. I can't let Norah do everything. Although it takes forever to change, since any quick movement makes me want to throw up. "I think it might happen again," I say in a small voice.

"The wastebasket is right here," Norah says. "Or you could always try the toilet."

"Oh," I moan. My stomach feels foamy and hot. I stand up and

SARINA BOWEN

take myself into the bathroom just in time to puke again. I wipe my mouth with toilet paper and flush twice.

"All right." Norah sighs. "You're going to be fine. It's not the most memorable ending to your first concert, but everybody does it at some point."

"It's not," I say. It's bitter medicine to be cared for by Norah.

"It's not what?"

"My first concert."

"My bad." Norah is giving me a wide berth, but I don't take it.

"I was thirteen. He played Orlando." I open my eyes to find Norah watching me, curiosity written all over her face. I close my eyes again. "I spent all my money on a scalped ticket."

"Oh Rachel," Norah whispers.

Unfortunately, that's only part of the story. First, I'd begged my mother to get tickets. The concert had been in June. "For my birthday," I'd bargained. "My *only* present."

"Well, that's just pathetic," my mother had said. "It doesn't make sense for us to pay for tickets to his concert."

"Then ask for them," I pleaded. There was a P.O. box number on the checks. My mother always said she didn't know where he was, but I knew it was just an excuse.

"You know I'm not going to do that," she'd said. She wouldn't even speak his name, let alone ask him for a favor.

I'd expected my mother to cave in and buy me a ticket. But she didn't. For my birthday, I received a pretty dress from Abercrombie and an iTunes gift card.

"You went to the concert by yourself?" Norah asks me now. Her voice is cautious.

I burp before answering her. "I was grounded for a month afterward."

And it hadn't even been worth it. I was high up in the second balcony, and Frederick was a tiny Lego minifigure below. Every fantasy I'd ever had about meeting him was shattered that night. Somehow, I'd expected that he would notice I was there, or someone would spot me and alert him.

I was only thirteen. That night, I'd felt lost in the crowd of thousands. The cheering mob, concert T-shirts I couldn't afford, and a long bus ride home afterwards just added to my misery. And the funk had lasted for months, souring my interest in everything.

Norah's voice cuts through the fog in my head. "Rachel, did you ever tell your father about that?"

"No." My voice sounds like gravel. "And neither will you."

———

I throw up only once more, after which there's a lull in my misery. Then my head begins to ache. I lay alone in the dark. The doors between our rooms are left ajar, and I can hear Norah turning the pages of her book.

I must have fallen asleep, because when I register my father's voice, he and Norah are arguing in the dark.

"Why didn't you come and get me?" he asks.

"There was no need. It's not a big deal."

"Like hell it isn't! There are creepy guys who work these things. If she wants to come along on junkets, this can't happen. I have to be able to turn my back for a couple of hours without hiring a nanny."

The sound of his voice comes closer, and I flinch.

"You wait a minute," Norah's whisper is a hiss. "Calm down first. There's something you don't understand. Not all of us are used to sitting at the cool kids' table," she says. "This is all pretty hard to take. And I have a question."

I stop breathing. I'd been stupid to confide in Norah. But the temptation to shock her had been too strong.

"What?"

"Have you ever had a serious argument with Rachel? Has she ever challenged you in any real way?"

He's quiet at first. "I suppose it doesn't count that we don't like the same things on pizza."

"What did she say when you told her I was pregnant?"

"She said… 'Wow, really?' And 'I guess this means you're staying in Claiborne.'"

"I rest my case."

"And now I'm totally lost."

"Look, Frederick. What she meant was, 'How could you, asshole?' I know you think the world of Rachel, and you should. But getting along perfectly—that's not a sign of her good nature, that's fear."

"Well, that's heavy. Thanks for that."

"She has to test you, Frederick. She knows you've got her back when she's got straight A's at Claiborne. But she has no idea how you'd deal with her if she needed bailing out of jail."

"And you got all this just from watching her puke?"

"Insecurity and I are very old friends. We go way back."

He laughs, but it has a nervous quality. "So instead of yelling at her, oh great one, what would you have me do?"

"You still get to say your piece. But you say it tomorrow, calmly, and when she's sober enough to hear you. Right now you can check her breathing, be nice, and tell her the worst is over."

"How much did she drink, anyway? Should I be worried?"

"It was just your average teenage puke. No records were broken."

The edge of my bed depresses a minute later. "Rachel." He puts a hand on my shoulder.

"Hmmm?" I do my best impression of a sleeping drunk. Not like it's hard.

"I hear you tossed your cookies."

I turn my face away.

The mattress wiggles as he lies down on the bed next to me. One hand skims over my hair. "Rachel, I love you anyway."

My eyes burn. It's the first time I've ever heard those words from him. I blink into the darkness, trying to hold still. And he stays a while beside me, which is all I've ever wanted from him.

After I begin to doze, I feel him rise and tiptoe away. I hear him slide the door barely closed, as if trying to shut it without the loud click. But a minute later I feel the breeze of my door fanning open again in the pitch dark. The pain in my head has ramped up, and there's an evil taste in my mouth. But I feel too poorly to get up and fix it.

"Oh, honey," I hear Frederick say. "I'm getting a tattoo. You know what it's going to say? Three words. 'Listen to Norah.'"

"Can I choose the location?" There's the sound of soft laughter, and then a rumpled silence which implies kissing.

I've almost fallen asleep again when I hear him speak one more time. "Marry me, Norah."

My eyes snap open again.

But Norah's answer surprises me. "One of these days I'm going to say 'yes,' and then you'll have to go through with it."

"Try me," he says.

Chapter Twenty-Six

SPRING FINALLY SHOWS signs of arriving in Claiborne. It's still cool, but the snow is gone. There are little buds on the trees, and the air smells muddy and green.

But I'm completely depressed.

I'm annoyed with Frederick and lonely for Jake. Aurora is preoccupied, and midterms loom.

It's a Thursday afternoon, and I usually spend those with my father. "Guitar today?" he asks me on the phone. "I could bring it over to your place."

At least he's noticed how uncomfortable I am at Norah's house. But I feel too troubled to sit and struggle with the guitar. "I would rather walk. It's nice out."

So we meet in front of the library and head west.

"What's the matter?" my father asks after only about ten paces.

Perhaps my poker face needs work. But what to say? Of all the things on my mind, most of them have to do with him. Except for one.

"Spit it out already," he prompts.

"Well… There's a boyfriend." Or there *was*, anyway.

"And he's a problem? Wait, is it that guy from Florida?"

"*No.*" I shake my head. "You haven't met him. He's great, and he likes me a lot."

Frederick waits.

"And I like him a lot too." We turn left to angle toward the pond.

"I'm still waiting for the 'but,'" my father says. "So far this is a happy tune. Nobody is singing the blues."

"Right." And that's as far as I get. I'm too chicken to go on.

"So, is this conversation about sex?"

I feel my cheeks get hot. "It might be."

"Well, hallelujah! My area of expertise."

I laugh for the first time all week.

"Seriously, I'm on very solid ground here. Also, I don't embarrass."

"*Okayyy…*" We continue walking. "Well, it's just not something I do. It's a deal I had with my mom."

"And when was this deal struck?"

"At birth." My whole life, she'd made it clear that she blamed herself for her own setbacks. *If I'd had you at thirty instead of twenty, I'd probably be a doctor right now. But you're smarter than I am,* she'd always add. Translation: *Don't even think about it.*

"I see." He's silent for a moment. "Do you think she expected you to carry it to your grave?"

"No." I snort. "But she wanted me to graduate from college more than anything."

"I'm sure that's true. But I'm also sure that you will." We reach the pond and turn onto the grass. "Rachel, it's great that you take this seriously, and God knows you don't want to get pregnant. But telling yourself that sex just isn't part of your life is a doomed strategy. It's part of being human; you can't just turn off the urge. When you try to steamroll nature, that's when the stupid shit happens."

I grimace. "I guess you do know a thing or two about this."

"Yes ma'am, I do. The trick is to know your heart ahead of

time. Don't let a guy do your thinking for you. He will go until you say stop."

That sounds depressingly familiar.

"Now, abstaining, that's very effective birth control. But you have to be upfront about it. Tell him when he can hear you, which is when you both still have clothes on. If he's a good guy, he'll understand. He might not even mind. There's a lot of fun two people can have in a bed without doing the deed."

I'm glad I don't have to look him in the eye. He wasn't kidding about not getting embarrassed. "Because..." I clear my throat. "Every method of birth control still leaves a risk."

"Sure, but it's risky just crossing the street, right? And a smart girl like you—if she wants to—can figure out how to protect herself. If I were you..." He thinks for a second. "At this fancy school, I'm sure they give out the Pill like candy. If that's where things are going with this boy, make an appointment and go get them. But then you keep that information to yourself. Make him wear one every time. And he won't mind, because he'll think it's the only thing standing between him and the world's most awkward conversation."

"Isn't that dishonest?"

He shakes his head. "That way if you forget one, you don't have to worry."

My head spins. "Okay—*winner!* This is our weirdest conversation ever." Although my birth must have turned him into a birth-control connoisseur.

He stops. "Rachel, it isn't even close to our weirdest conversation. It wouldn't even make the top ten." He leans down to palm a stone. "The winner is the one about why I couldn't even send you a birthday card for seventeen years."

But we never actually have that conversation.

Aloud I say, "I thought you didn't embarrass?"

He tosses the stone into the pond. "There's a difference between simple embarrassment and deep shame."

We walk back the long way, past the college football field.

"Can I ask you something?" I ask.

"Anything."

"Did you mean to have a baby with Norah?"

He whistles. "I'm not going to lie, Rachel. The short answer is no."

I hold my breath. That's just what I'd guessed.

"But now I'm really excited about it," he says. "It broke us up for a little while, though."

"I see."

"Well, you probably can't see, honestly. Because there's a lot more to the story. Before I met Norah she was trying to have a baby, all by herself."

"Really?"

"It's a little weird, telling you her troubles. But I don't think she'd mind. She went to doctors who deal with that sort of thing, and it wasn't working."

"And then…it suddenly did?"

"Yeah. And it freaked both of us out. But I got over it. The trouble was that she didn't."

"What do you mean?"

"Well, she felt so damned guilty. The thesaurus is full of words for women who end up pregnant by accident. Knocked up… You've heard them all."

"Did you know that the Spanish word for 'pregnant' is embarazada? Embarrassed."

"I didn't. But what do you call a man who sleeps around?"

"A player."

"That's right. So there's Norah, who had always organized her life the way you do—college degree, graduate school. A smart lady. And she has to tell her boyfriend—who has a shitty track record with relationships—that she's pregnant. So just to prove that I wasn't on the hook, she vanished. She cut me off. That got my attention, because I'd gotten used to having a sane, intelligent woman sitting across the table every night. That's when I figured out that being a player wasn't fun anymore. I had to beg her to let me settle down."

"That seems backwards."

"It does to you, because your life isn't a wreck. But when you're me, backwards is forwards. Every good thing that's ever happened to me was an accident. Think about it. I became a singer because I was too lazy to do real work. My first record deal happened because the producer showed up at the wrong club on the wrong night. And then there's you, another accident. And your poor mom dying gave you back to me. Then Norah thought she was too old to get pregnant, so now I get to have an even bigger family."

It is, hands down, the longest speech Frederick has ever given me. "You're, like, a double negative. Everything wrong goes right."

"Eventually, anyway. And what's the trouble with double negatives?"

"They're confusing."

"Absofuckinglutely. There were plenty of tears over Norah's pregnancy, and that's between two people with good jobs, and enough money, who love each other. So if you want to avoid a lot of heartache, keep doing things your way. Have a plan."

Chapter Twenty-Seven

TWO DAYS LATER, I come home from class to find a paper bag leaning against our door. "Rachel" is penned on the outside. I open it to find a big box of condoms inside—a variety pack. There's a note. *Rachel—These expire four years from now. So no hurry. Dad.*

"Oh my God!" I yelp, blushing in the empty stairwell. Then I go inside to find a good hiding place for them.

Since our confrontation on his bed, Jake and I haven't shared more than polite conversation. And today I'd spied him in the dining hall, surrounded by a laughing cluster of junior-year girls.

I'd felt it like a kick to my gut.

"Where's Jake?" Aurora asks from the window seat, as if reading my mind. She glances around our messy room, as if she might have misplaced him. "I haven't seen him in a while."

"I guess he's busy," I say, trying to keep the pain out of my voice.

Aurora eyes me over the top edge of her computer screen. "Too busy for you? Never."

I'd been meaning to plunge into my Spanish homework. But my mind is too cluttered right now. "I'm going to clean up a little bit. I can't think."

"*Digame*, Rachel. What's the problem with Jake?"

"I don't want to talk about it." I begin stacking the papers on my desk, where things have gotten out of hand.

"That boy loves you. It can't be all that bad. Tell me."

"I'll tell you," I snap. "Just as soon as you introduce me to your secret boyfriend."

Aurora gives me a look of anguish. Then she puts her eyes back onto her computer screen, and doesn't say another word to me.

Feeling guilty, I go into our bedroom and begin to clean up, hoping it will clear my head. I ferry a big stack of last semester's notes into the recycling bin. I stack up Aurora's magazines, where they've slid all over the floor of our bedroom. It feels good to do something productive.

Missing Jake makes me crabby. I don't like thinking of myself as someone who needs a boy's attention. "The trouble with so many women," my mother used to say, "is that they think they need a man to define them. But the man, on the other hand, he wants only one thing."

Dropping another armload of old paper into the bin, I get stuck on a very uncharitable thought. My mother had a lot of things to say about men. But no man ever set foot over the threshold of our house, unless he was there to fix an appliance or read our water meter.

Why was that? Fear? It's like Frederick giving up driving after hitting a single tree.

And no matter what Mom might say, right this second I'd give anything to be able to call her up and pour out my heart. Anything.

Tidying up my dresser gives me something to do with my hands. I banish all the hair bands and brushes into the top drawer. I change the sheets on my bed, knotting all of my dirty laundry inside them.

Plugging in the old vacuum we'd bought at the second-hand

store, I attack the dust bunnies in the corners of our bedroom. The place is starting to look better. Using an old T-shirt, I even dust the things on my bureau. My mother's jewelry box is there, with a dust-free rectangle underneath it. I set it down on the bed while I work.

The jewelry box is the last thing I wipe clean. Opening the top, I set the tray of my mother's jewelry aside and turn my attention to the pictures underneath. There I am on Santa's knee, smiling. I'd been six or seven. My mother told me that when I was littler, we'd wait in the line to see Santa, only to have me chicken out at the last minute.

Mom had loved that story. "One year we waited in line *twice*, because you swore you were ready to talk to him. But no dice."

I drop that photo on the bed and look at the next one. It's a picture of me onstage at my last spring concert. I haven't seen this picture before and didn't know my mother had taken it.

That night was only a month before she died.

I dig deeper into the pile. There are several school pictures— those hideously posed shots against a gray mottled background. And a picture of me and Haze smiling from behind one of my birthday cakes. I count thirteen candles on it. That would have been two years after Haze's father killed himself.

I study Haze's smile in the photograph, and decide that it isn't marked by disaster. Maybe a year or so from now I'll feel lighter too.

In the bottom of the box is a glossy yellow envelope. I lift it out. It's sealed with a brittle adhesive that gives way when I put my fingernail under the edge. Inside I find a stack of photographs, all the same size, probably the same batch.

The very first one takes my breath away.

Looking out at me from the photo are young versions of Mom and Frederick. He has his arm around her, his free hand on her knee. My mother looks sideways at him and laughs. They're wearing shorts and sneakers, and sitting on the porch of a little house somewhere. But it isn't the smooth faces or the too long hair that surprise me. It's the look on my mother's face. She wears a smile so loving, so unguarded that it shocks me.

I'd never seen her look that way at anyone.

In the next photo, Frederick has a beard. He's seated, shirtless, in a chair with a guitar, and my mother stands behind him, her hands on his shoulders. The casual curve of her fingers on his bare skin gives me a shiver. Here is the very thing I've never been able to picture—the two of them together. The uncensored joy on my mother's face is astonishing to me.

I don't even know I'm crying until Aurora comes running. "What's happened?" She sits down on the bed. "Oh! This is your mother."

Aurora takes the stack from my hands and flips through them slowly. "Where is this?" she holds up a photo. Frederick stands on a pathway, his guitar across his body. There are orange and yellow autumn leaves behind him. In the next picture, Mom is there too.

They're kissing.

I wipe my eyes with the heels of my hands. "I have no idea. I've never seen these pictures before. She lied to me."

Aurora looks startled. "She lied? About the pictures?"

I nod. I'd asked my mother many times whether there were pictures of him. When I got a little older, of course, I stopped asking and started Googling.

"Sweetie, she didn't want to remember this. It's not that hard to understand."

"Yes it is!" I gasp. The next picture is of the two of them, bent over a map. His fingers have swept the hair off her neck. My mother's hand covers his.

They were so *happy*.

The true lie, I realize, is not that the pictures exist, but rather what they show. Every time my mother mentioned him, it was as if he'd been inflicted on her, like a disease. But it wasn't true. My mother had *loved* him.

It wasn't all just a shady accident, a tawdry mistake.

"She was just so unlucky." Aurora sighs, setting a picture down on the bed. It shows Frederick carrying her, piggyback, through a meadow somewhere. "How old was she when she died?"

"Thirty-eight."

Aurora wipes her eyes. "She could have fallen in love again, no?"

I really don't know. My idea of her is undergoing a rapid shift. The mom I knew had measured risk and reward with an eyedropper. She believed in delayed gratification. But it obviously hadn't always been so. And it was *me* who'd changed her from the happy girl in the photos to the tired woman working double shifts in hospital scrubs.

The next picture makes me squint. But then I let out a little shriek of surprise. "Dios!" Aurora gasps. "Your mother played the drums?"

There she is, onstage, sticks poised over a drum kit. Her hair is pulled up into a knot on top of her head.

The bass drum has a decal on its face: WILD CITY BLUES.

"Wild City," Aurora says. "Just like the song."

I am speechless. There's really no other way to handle my surprise. The photo shows Frederick at the microphone, and a bass guitar is propped against the amp stack.

My whole life I'd been trying to understand my missing father. And the whole time I hadn't had the first clue about my mom.

"Who took all these pictures?" Aurora asks. "Who is this?" She holds up the final picture, which had three subjects instead of two. Three heads lie together in the grass, and one man's arm reaches up above them to take their self-portrait.

I hadn't even thought to wonder who took them. "That's Ernie," I say slowly. "When he still had hair." I pick up the envelope and turn it over. "Hathaway" is scrawled at one end.

"What a blessing that this Ernie took them, and now they are yours."

I'm not so sure. They make my head spin.

The next few days are rough.

For most of the year, Claiborne Prep has been my Hogwarts—a separate place in my life where things mostly go well. But now my grief has followed me all the way to New Hampshire. I'm just plain sad. Sorrow hangs over me like a cloud.

I still get out of bed every morning and go to class. But once I get there, I can't concentrate. I've taken to Googling my mother now, instead of my father. Searching for "Wild City" had always led me nowhere. But searching for "Wild City Blues" leads me to an old set list from a Kansas City club.

The song titles on it are unfamiliar, or else covers. But the singer was Fred Richards, the bassist Ernie Hathaway, and the drummer Jenny Kaye.

My mother had a stage name.

Meanwhile, classes go on. I sit in the back of the English lecture hall, reeling. I'm puzzling over my mother's life instead of the complexities of Middle English.

Two rows up, Jake takes fervent notes. But I'm thinking about the little green house we'd shared in Florida, of doing homework on my bed while Mom bumps around in the kitchen making dinner.

I spent so much time longing for this—the prep-school experience, living on a pretty New England campus. But now the loss of my mother is all I can think about. I want to go backward in time, to slide off the bed in our little house and wander into the kitchen, to watch the planes of my mother's face as she seasons two chicken breasts and sets them in the oven to bake.

If I could just see her *one* last time, maybe I could understand everything that happened. But she's gone. All my chances are used up.

The whiteboard at the front of the lecture hall becomes misty.

There are still ten minutes left of the class, but I swing my bag onto my shoulder and slip out. Usually I have lunch with Aurora after this class, but I don't feel like talking to anyone.

Walking back to Habernacker, the flagstone pathways are slicked from a spring shower, and the air is cool and moist. But in my mind, I'm back in my mother's hospital room. For the first time in months, I let those memories come. The first few days in the hospital, she was still mostly conscious. Whenever the doctor came in to talk to us, I would try hard to absorb the things he said about new antibiotics and bringing down her fever. But Mom never seemed to listen. Her eyes never left my face.

I think she knew.

There was nothing to do but wait and hope, and hold Haze's hand. Every few hours, he would drag me down to the cafeteria and beg me to eat something. His presence was a real comfort. And now even that link to my old life has been shattered by misunderstanding and regret.

I climb the stairs to my room. In my desk, I find a clean sheet of paper and an envelope. Even if my mother and I are never going to have another conversation, there's one I can have before it's too late.

It takes me a long time to come up with the right words.

> Dear Haze,
> I know it's been months, but I'm still upset about fighting with you. I've wanted to say so for a long time, but I couldn't figure out how. I still can't. You made me feel so <u>caught</u>. Because I couldn't be what you wanted me to be.
> I loved you as a friend. But you pushed me into more when I wasn't ready. If there was a better way for me to get that across, I missed it. And for that I'm sorry.
> But I won't ever forget that you helped me survive last year. I love you, Haze. Even if it's not the way you hoped.

Rachel

It's a small thing, but I feel better for saying it. I put his name on the envelope, and write out his address from memory. Then I go off to buy a stamp.

Chapter Twenty-Eight

A FEW DAYS LATER, when the weather decides to take one more crack at being chilly, I watch my father approach the intersection where we've agreed to meet.

I'd almost made an excuse to blow him off, because I'm still feeling so blue. He'll probably be able to read it off my face, and I don't feel like explaining. But I haven't seen him in a while, and if I blow him off, he'd probably just call me again tomorrow.

In my back pocket, I've stashed one of the photographs I'd found of Frederick and my mother. But I haven't figured out what question I want to ask yet.

My mother spent seventeen years not talking about what happened. Hopefully it won't take me the same length of time to ask.

As he reaches the corner, he gives me a little wave. Yet he's missed the light, and traffic begins to stream between us. I rub my hands together against the cold and wait.

"Hey!"

I turn and smile at the sound of Jake's voice, the way a flower turns toward the sun. Instinctually.

"I was just missing you," he says. "*Terribly*. And you appeared." He takes my cold hands into his.

I open my mouth to say something, but Jake is quicker. He leans in and kisses me on the lips. It's been over two weeks since our awful talk, and there's a whole lot of yearning in that kiss. The only thing keeping me from absolutely melting onto Jake is the fact that my father is probably watching from across the street.

I hear the traffic slow. I take a half step backward, but too late.

"Hands off, buster," my father's voice says.

Jake startles and pulls away.

"Dad!" I gasp.

"But isn't that my line? Did I not deliver it well?"

I feel my face redden. Across from me, Jake looks beaten. Interrupted again.

The timing is awful, but it has to be done. "Well, Frederick, this is Jake. Jake, meet my father."

Finally.

They shake hands. There's a silence while I wonder what I should say next.

"So, we walk?" Frederick prompts.

"Where are you headed?" I ask Jake.

"The gym."

"Walk with us," Frederick says. He turns toward the main part of campus.

Jake raises his eyebrows at me, and I give him a tiny nod.

"Sure," he says.

"What do you think, Rachel?" Frederick asks. "The pond? The hill?"

"Your pick."

"There's one more option," Jake says, his eyes on me. "Do you want to climb the bell tower?" He points up at the white spire rising over the library building.

"You can do that?" I ask.

"Only if you happen to have a key," Jake says. "Which you might, say, if you took it off your asshat brother's keyring while he was passed out over the holidays."

Frederick laughs. *"Excellent.* Let's go break a few rules. That's all I ever did in school."

"During reunion week," Jake explains as we cross the quad, "there's a tower tour. But other times it's off limits." Jake stops. "Rach, is this okay? I know you don't like to break rules."

He's right, of course. But I think I've been looking at the whole good girl thing wrong. I need to trust my gut more and worry less. "Let's do it."

They both smile at me, and we head for the library.

Jake leads us through the library stacks, up to level six. We reach a metal door marked "Maintenance Only."

Jake spins around to flash us a little smile. Then he turns the handle and looks inside for a moment. The coast clear, he walks in.

I follow him into a poorly lit room, containing a few cleaning supplies and a pile of dusty fluorescent lightbulb sleeves. An arrow-shaped sign on the wall reads: *To Tower.* We follow a passageway until it ends at an old wooden door.

"Well, now we find out if the key works, or if I've brought you here for nothing." Jake takes a set of keys out of his pocket and chooses a big flat brass one. He fits it into the lock and jiggles it. The door clicks open.

"Score," Frederick says. "Now we climb?"

"That's right," Jake says, leading the way.

I follow, my legs beginning to burn after the second flight. It's cold in the stairwell, but soon I'm sweating. Frederick pokes me on the backside when I stop in front of him for a breather. I whip around to see him wink at me. Somebody's having fun.

After each set of ten steps, I turn left and see ten more. The stairs are a steep, metal affair, the railing a piece of old pipe. The light gets brighter with each flight, and soon I can see why. The four clock faces on the tower are made of thick, translucent glass. Each one must be eight feet across. I pass first one and then another clock face, their shapely black arms rising toward noon.

The stairs go on in spite of my burning thighs and the stitch in my side. Just when I think I can't take any more, the steps finally break through a plank ceiling and into a little wooden room. Jake stands, winded, against the wall. He wears a shy, triumphant smile.

"Cool," I say, and his smile widens. "Coming, old man?"

Frederick emerges, grasping his chest in mock exhaustion. And then he looks up. "Wow."

Above us hang dozens of giant old bells, all different sizes. Some are as big as me. But at the top, on the end, a few are only the size of a toaster. On one wall in front of us is a set of levers, arranged like the pattern of an organ keyboard. Nearby there's a music stand and an ancient wooden stool. Frederick bends over the levers for a closer look.

"If you ring a bell, we're totally busted," Jake says.

"Gotcha," my father replies. He counts the levers. "Two and a half octaves. This thing looks *old*."

"Some of the bells are from the 1860s. But I think those levers aren't quite so old. The people who play this are part of the Carillon Guild. They hold auditions every spring. It's very competitive."

On the adjacent wall is a single door. Jake slides back the metal bar securing it and swings it inward. An ancient metal hook chained to the wall holds it open for us.

I follow Jake outside, where I'm greeted with a sweeping view of the Connecticut River valley to the west, and the mountains of Vermont beyond. "This is amazing." The students on the sidewalk below are miniaturized.

"Great view," my father agrees, stepping outside. "What am I looking at? Are those the Green Mountains?"

"Yeah. And that's Smarts Mountain up there." Jake points to the north.

The three of us move slowly around the tower walkway, stopping to take in the different viewpoints. From up here, Claiborne's brick buildings look like pretty little toys.

It's breezy, and the cold stings my face. I rub my hands

together again, wishing I hadn't left my gloves at home. "That's Mount Ascutney," Jake points toward the south. He reaches around me from behind, taking my hands in his and rubbing my cold fingers. He does this almost absently, as if we've never fought, as if everything is still okay. I lean back against him, fighting a lump in my throat.

I catch Frederick watching us, and he winks. The wind whips through again, and Frederick brings the hood of his sweater up over his head and holds it there.

"I guess we should go in," Jake says. He walks toward the corner of the tower, and I follow him. But just as we're about to reach the door, there's a slam.

Jake scoots over to the door and pushes the handle. It doesn't move. When he looks at me, the fear in his face is undisguised.

"Oh my God," I say.

Frederick snorts. "No way."

Jake stares at the door. "There wasn't even a lock on it," he says. "What the hell?" He lets go of the handle and presses on the door itself. "Goddamn it." He kicks the bottom of the door in frustration.

I don't even know what to say. But just as I'm beginning to panic, the door opens suddenly from within, and a narrow face peers out. "I was just having a little fun with you," it says.

Jake pushes the door open and jumps over the threshold. "Did you have to do that?"

Inside, the narrow-faced person is revealed to be a skinny guy with a curly black mop of hair. Whereas Jake styles himself as a nerd, this guy is the real deal. His Adam's apple bobs nervously as he stares at the three of us. "Sorry," he says. "You're not supposed to be up here, anyway."

Jake takes a deep breath. "True. But I think you took a year off my life just now."

Frederick laughs. "Good prank, kid. You had us."

The guy squints at Frederick. "Do I know you? You look familiar."

"I get that a lot," my father says.

The skinny kid checks his watch. "Whoops, I have one minute." He opens a folder on the music stand and sits down on the stool.

It's 11:59. I'd forgotten that the carillon is played every day at noon.

"If we stay to watch, will there be any retribution?" Frederick asks.

The kid shakes his head. "Nah. I'm over it. But the whole concert lasts about five minutes."

The sheet music reads, "Simple Gifts." At twelve o'clock, he begins pressing levers, and the folk tune rings out at a deafening volume from the bells overhead. I look up to see the bells tipping one at a time, pulled by metal cords that rise from the backs of the levers. Even when the skinny kid stops pressing levers, the bells' ringing tone hangs in the air.

Frederick stares up at the mechanism. "The time delay must mess with you," he says.

"You learn to anticipate yourself," the kid answers. Then, when the reverb stops, he begins playing a second song from memory.

Jake and I turn to each other. "That's…" I can't put my finger on it.

"Duran Duran!" Frederick snorts. "'Hungry Like the Wolf.'"

"I like to play it at lunchtime," the kid says as he bangs out the chorus.

———

Jake drops a ten-dollar bill on the dining hall entry desk. "We have a guest," he tells the nice old lady who staffs it.

"You didn't have to do that," Frederick argues, but Jake is already headed for the line.

"Don't go for the burrito," I warn. "It doesn't taste like L.A."

Frederick leans over me. "Jake is good people," he whispers.

I look up at him, and his eyes are smiling. "I know."

"Why've you been hiding him?"

"I'm not even sure."

———

"Scoot in," I say to my father as he slides onto the banquette bench. Jake sits down across from us, his tray piled with two sandwiches, chips, and a salad.

"This is pretty good," my father says after taking a bite of his clam chowder. "You should see the slop they used to serve us in high school."

"I'll bet it didn't cost thirty large a year, though," Jake says. The dining hall glasses are small, so he has three of them full of milk, lined up like soldiers at the front of his tray.

"Good point. I'm not sure Rachel's getting her money's worth."

"She gets it back in library books."

And now I feel self-conscious.

"Thanks for the bell-tower tour. That was pretty cool," my father says.

"Oh, no problem."

Then Frederick puts down his spoon with a chuckle. "When that door was shut…" He breaks off and laughs. "You should have seen your face."

I can see Jake's cheeks beginning to color. He takes a sip of milk, but then a laugh threatens, and he has to put his hand in front of his mouth.

My father rocks back against the ancient wooden bench and roars.

Jake almost chokes, and then laughs harder. And that gets me going. I wonder what Jake would have done if that door had been truly locked? I giggle until tears begin to prick my eyes.

The three of us are still shaking when Aurora stops in front of our table. "Oh my God," she says. "What did I miss? And where was my invitation?" She puts her tray down next to Jake's.

Frederick pulls it across to our side of the table, and wipes his eyes. "You come here, missy. I haven't seen you for a while."

Aurora walks over to the end of the banquette, where I sit. She steps over my back. "Lean in, Freddy."

"Oh, I forgot to get coffee," Aurora says after she's begun eating.

"I'll get it." I hop up. "Anyone else?"

When I come back with four mugs, two in each hand, Aurora is hysterical too.

"Can you imagine our 911 call?" Frederick asks with a smirk.

I sit close to my father, listening to the low sound of his voice, and Aurora's laugh. I take in Jake's bashful grin.

How had Hannah once put it? She'd said she hoped I would soon have my feet back under me. Today it was possible to think I might get there.

Jake has to leave first, so he can walk all the way to the college for a chemistry lecture. Frederick shakes his hand across the table. "Pleasure to meet you, Jake. Let's do it again."

When Jake stands up to bus his tray, I follow him with my own. Placing it on the conveyor belt, I turn to him. "Thank you," I say. "That was really fun. I'm sorry..." I take a deep breath. "I'm sorry I didn't introduce you to Frederick before. That was stupid of me."

He gives me a little shrug that might mean anything. It might say, *Hey, no problem*, or it might say, *You're an idiot*. I'm still trying to decide when Jake leans close to my ear.

"I love you, Rachel," he whispers. And then he turns and walks out of the dining hall.

When I sit down again in front of Frederick and Aurora, I have trouble following their conversation. Jake's words are like a gem I clutch in my hand. I can't really hold it up to the light and examine it until I'm alone.

"It's on Choate Street," Frederick is saying.

"What is?" I ask. He's trying to explain something.

"This house that's for sale. I want you to come and see it."

"Oh, okay," I say, shaking off my distraction. "I'll see it this weekend."

"Don't you have Spanish now?" Aurora asks.

"Yes. I should go."

Frederick pushes his tray toward the edge of the table and slides out of the seat. "Nice place you've got here," he says.

"Come back any time!" Aurora grins.

I walk my father out. "Guitar next week?" he asks.

"Absolutely."

"Good." He ruffles my hair and walks away smiling.

Chapter Twenty-Nine

THE NEXT EVENING, I sit alone on the window seat in our room, watching the sky turn pink over Claiborne. My phone buzzes, and I have to turn away from the sunset to get it. I hope it's Jake. I've been thinking of him all day.

But the message is not from him.

When I open it, I see a single photograph. The glove compartment of Haze's old car is framed in the shot. The compartment stands open, with something resting inside—the envelope I'd mailed him, containing my apology.

"Oh, Haze," I whisper, touching the screen. I look back up to the sky, but the color has already deepened to gray. I get up and go into my bedroom.

My mother's photographs lay on the dresser, and I pick them up. I've studied them many times already, memorizing the details. At first, they were shocking. Young and in love, the Jenny in the photographs looks like an entirely different person.

Now the two women are blending together in my memory. In fact, I'm probably ruining my ability to recall my mother as I'd known her. But I don't care. I prefer to think of her as someone open to love, and not bitter.

Mom had been very clear that she didn't want a repeat of her own heartbreak for me. "Finish college, be your own person," she'd said. "That's what smart girls do. It's the stupid ones who are busy trying to catch a guy."

But now I know that's risky too. I've just spent most of a year trying very hard not to let anyone know how much I care. And here I sit alone, while upstairs someone who loves me waits.

So I text Jake, asking him to come over.

He replies immediately, saying he'll be right down.

While I wait, I tidy up my room again and light one of Aurora's candles. My father's advice to me was to know my heart ahead of time, and to tell Jake my fears. That sounds like a nice lyric for a song. With a little work, we could probably get it to rhyme.

Hell, it's probably easier to write a platinum single than to look Jake in the eye and tell him all the things that scare me.

But here he is already, knocking on our door.

"It's open," I holler.

A moment later Jake peeks around the bedroom door, his eyes shiny in the candlelight. He walks in. "It's nice in here." He sits down on the bed next to me and puts a hand on my lower back. Even that simple gesture fills me with happiness. I've missed him so much.

Turning, I wrap both arms around him. "I've been thinking about you all afternoon." He feels warm and solid against me.

With one finger, he stretches the neckline of my top aside and kisses my shoulder. "That's me on a good day. Hopefully I won't flunk this term."

Jake is not the scary thing, I remind myself. Very deliberately, I take his face in both hands and kiss him, picking up where we'd left off on the street corner yesterday morning. He makes a little noise in the back of his throat, and the sound of it sends shivers down my spine.

His kisses are sweet and slow. But this is not what I'd called him downstairs to do. And if I let it happen, we'll probably end up taking yet another trip to Awkwardville.

I force myself to pull back. "Jake," I say, my heart skittering. "I absolutely can't get pregnant."

With cheeks flushed pink, he raises his hands like a perp on a cop show. "Uh, okay?"

That sure didn't come out as smoothly as it could have. "I mean, I know we haven't…" I clear my throat. "But you probably want to. And that's why I panic. Because nobody ever lied to me. I was the pregnancy that messed up my mother's college education. And then her social life. And now I'm messing up Frederick's, and I think I cost him a million dollars this year alone…" I look up at Jake, whose mouth is hanging open.

He closes it and reaches for me, folding me into a hug. "Just slow down there for a second, so I can follow you," he says, rubbing my back.

"Okay." He smells like clean T-shirts and soap. I've missed this so much.

"First of all, I'm really glad you messed up your mother's life and Frederick's, if that's really even true," he says.

"Oh, it is," I mumble into the cotton at his collarbone.

His arms tighten around me. "Either way, I get it," he says.

"You do?"

"Yeah. I wish you'd just said that before. That you feel all this extra pressure not to…"

"Repeat history," I supply.

He gives me a squeeze. "So we won't."

"We won't what?" I lift my head to look at him.

The pink spots on his cheekbones deepen. "That's what you'll have to tell *me*. You give me the rules, and I'll follow them."

"Well… There would have to be two, um, methods. In case one of them fails." I put my chin on Jake's shoulder so I don't have to look him in the eye.

"Perfectly rational," he whispers.

"And I haven't taken care of things on my end. Because…it's not easy. You have to go to the doctor, where there are tables and *stirrups*. And put on a paper gown, probably. And then you have to tell the doctor to his face that you want birth control. I'll probably bring along a copy of my transcript to prove I'm actually a good girl."

I feel Jake's chest begin to shake. "I've never been so glad to be a guy."

"I'm pretty glad you're a guy."

"No, really," he says. "They even have self-serve check-out at the pharmacy. I'll bet those were invented by a dude who wanted to buy condoms without facing down the checkout girl."

I giggle into his neck. "You can just order them on the internet. Really, how is that fair?"

"I get it." He cups my face and gives me a quick kiss.

Feeling a rush of gratitude, I kiss him again. And then again and again. I'm so happy to be back in his arms that I kiss him as if I want to eat him for dinner.

Until Jake pulls back and stares me down. "You forgot something important."

"I did?"

He nods. "What are the rules right *now?*"

"Oh. We just can't have actual sex." Funny how easy it is to say it now.

"I heard that part. But I don't want any more misunderstandings. So what else is off the table?"

It's a fair question. "I guess nothing, really." And then, to prove the point, I reach for the buttons on his flannel shirt. He looks down, watching my fingers with a look of disbelief. Under the flannel I find the *Talk Nerdy to Me* tee. "You were wearing this on the day I met you."

His smile is shy. "It draws the babes like flies."

Very gently, I remove his big black glasses, turning them over in my hands. "Jake, why do you try so hard to look nerdy?" I put the glasses on the bedside table. "I mean—some people come by it more naturally. But you have to work pretty hard at it." Without waiting for an answer, I gather his T-shirt and raise it over his head. Dropping it to the floor, I put my hands on his bare chest. "I mean it as a serious question."

He looks down at my hands, as if trying to figure out where they'd come from. "Well, the nerd thing made me something that Asshat was not. But also…" He breaks off, reaching for me. He presses a kiss to my cheekbone so tenderly that a chill runs up my spine. "Also," he whispers, "if the pretty girl on the third floor doesn't want to touch me, then at least I'll have a good reason why."

Now *there's* a little stab to my heart. I pull Jake's handsome face toward me, kissing him in a way that I hope lets him know exactly how much I appreciate him. And when he gives a happy sigh, I feel it all the way to my toes.

Then, with all the wariness of a man diffusing a bomb, Jake lifts my top over my head, and fumbles with the back of my bra. But that isn't going to get him anywhere, because the clasp is in front.

"And you say you're so good with technology," I whisper, flicking it apart with my own hand.

His face registers surprise, but he isn't too bashful to push the straps off my shoulders. "God, I love your body."

I never do know how to take a compliment. So I go for his belt instead. Jake's reaction is a sharp intake of air. High on my own bravery, I plunge onward, unzipping his jeans. He pulls back, surprise on his face. But then he stands up and shucks them off. His boxer shorts have little terrier dogs on them.

I stand too. Gingerly, I skim the front of his boxers, causing Jake to take a deep, shuddering breath. I touch my lips to his ear. "The girl on the third floor would like to touch you," I whisper. "If she could get out of her own way."

He closes his eyes. Then he runs his hands down my shoulders, his kisses soft. A single finger slips across my belly underneath the waistband of my jeans, and his touch sends a charge of electricity through me.

But Jake takes his hand away. "This is where I always get into trouble," he says quietly.

Sad, but true. So I slide my zipper down myself, dropping my jeans to the floor. Reverently, Jake skims my hips with warm hands. When he pulls my body against his, my heart begins to pound.

Breathe, I order myself.

I must have tensed up, because Jake puts his chin on my shoulder, bringing his arms around me in a protective hug. "Rachel," he whispers, easing me down to sit beside him on the bed. "Just rest here with me for a while."

What an excellent idea.

We lay down together, and I put my head on his chest, willing myself to relax. The candlelight dances on the wall, and Jake's thumb strokes my shoulder absently. My thoughts quiet as I listen to the sound of his heart. "Jake? Why did you say that I made you feel like Asshat?"

His chest rises and falls with a sigh. "He hits his girlfriends."

I raise my head quickly. "Seriously?"

"Yeah." He eases my head back down onto his chest, smoothing my hair away from my face. "Well, I think he does. He was even arrested once. Later, the girl changed her story."

"But you think he did it?"

"I think...if he *didn't* do it, he should really stop the smack talk. The way he brags when he's drunk is truly disgusting. And this is a small town. Let's just say I'm not the only person who thinks he's capable of it. The football coach is always having to step in to make excuses for him."

Yikes. "Jake?"

"Yeah?"

"You're not like that. Not even a little." I snuggle closer to him, and he kisses the top of my head.

At close range, I admire his smooth skin, the curve of his chest, and the brawny arm that reaches across his body to rest on my back. He's beautiful and strong, and I'm lucky to know him.

"You know." I clear my throat. "I never had a boyfriend before you."

He tilts his chin to look down at me. "Really? How is that even possible?"

"I may have out-nerded you at my old school."

"See?" He runs a hand over my hair. "I knew you were special."

"Did you have a girlfriend last year?"

"Yeah, for two years. She graduated last year. And—get this." He chuckles. "She dumped me at the after-prom party. Total disaster. Claiborne has this event where the seniors are shut in together until dawn, to keep everyone from going out to get hammered. So this genius dumps me right as we're literally locked into the same room for six hours."

"Ouch!"

"I know! I wish I hadn't rented the stupid tux. Did your old school make a big deal about prom?"

"Yeah." My throat tightens. "I couldn't go last year."

Jake rolls so he can see my face. "Why not?"

My vision clouds, the candlelight becoming shiny. "That's the night my mother died."

"Oh, Jesus," Jake whispers, pulling me in. "I'm sorry," he says.

He has me in such a tight embrace I have trouble wiggling an arm free so that I can wipe my eyes. "I don't want to be that anymore," I say, my voice shaky.

"What do you mean?"

"I don't want to be the girl with all the issues. A downer. Tonight especially."

He kisses me on the eyebrow and loosens his grip. "You know that's not how I think of you."

"It isn't?"

He shakes his head. "I think of you as the hot girl who sings." His hand caresses my stomach. "Even when you have your clothes on." His smile becomes shy. "Let's just say you're never... a *downer*."

Even though I can still feel the sting of tears on my face, I laugh. There's something so *honest* about Jake. He isn't one to flatter, but his compliments always ring with sincerity.

His smile comes closer, and his lips find mine.

We come together, and I lose myself in his hungry kiss. My pulse kicks up a notch—but in a good way. As our kisses linger and deepen, I feel myself getting drunk on Jake. In the past, that feeling always freaked me out. But now it doesn't, because we'd already had the conversation that will prevent a nasty hangover.

And his kisses… Wow. We're skin against skin, and it's glorious.

Running my fingers down Jake's torso, I find a little trail of curly hair which begins at his belly button and thickens on the way into his boxer shorts.

I follow it.

His body is unfamiliar territory, and I had only a vague idea of how to touch him. But if the giant groan he lets out is any indication, then I'm doing all right.

But then he grabs my hand. "Hang on," he pants. "I have to think about English 125 for a minute."

"What?" He hates that class.

"Chaucer in verse. It's the most boring thing I can think of right now. I don't want this to end immediately." He exhales slowly. "Which one was the tale about patience?"

I've been holding my breath, but now I let it out in a whoosh. "'The Franklin's Tale,'" I sputter. I bury my face in his neck to avoid laughing in his face.

He nuzzles me. "I ruined the mood. Didn't I?"

"No!" I wrap my arms tightly around him. "You're perfect. Perfect, and you have no idea." In fact, my laughter unhooks the last pinch of anxiety from my heart. I reach for Jake again, and he pulls me into a kiss that goes on and on.

I forget to be afraid. I stop thinking, and let myself just feel.

———

Eventually the candle flickers and dies. We rest together, his body curled around mine. Jake drowses, but I don't feel like sleeping. Whenever I shift position, his hand finds a new place to rest, on the curve of my hip or on the back of my leg. I drink it all in.

But I must have fallen asleep, because I'm next conscious of someone bumping and tripping nearby in the pitch dark.

"Jesus Cristo," Aurora's voice says, sounding thick. There's another shuffle, and then a crack. "Mierda!"

As I blink in the dark, Jake's hand closes around mine. I hold my breath until Aurora makes her way out of the room again. The outer door opens as my roommate presumably heads to the bathroom.

"Does she usually come home ripping drunk at one thirty?" Jake whispers.

"Never."

His hand trails up the side of my hip. "Do you need me to sneak out? If you'll be embarrassed, I'll go."

"Don't," I whisper. *Please.*

He kisses my neck. "Hand me my boxers, then. Quick, before she comes back."

"Good idea." I slide off the bed. I hand Jake his underwear and grab a nightie out of my dresser drawer. I fling the nightie over my head just as the outside door opens again. I hop back into the bed as quietly as possible.

Humming to herself, Aurora stumbles into the bedroom. She drops her toiletry caddy noisily on the floor and paws at her bed. Then she begins *singing*. The words are slurred Spanish, but the tune is unmistakably Gloria Gaynor's "I Will Survive."

It's quite a performance.

I feel a giggle rising in my chest, but I hold it in. At least I try, until Jake also begins shaking with barely suppressed laughter. I have to clamp a hand over my mouth.

Aurora's song breaks off as she struggles with her bed covers. Then the room is quiet, except for the tremors of choked-back laughter rippling through two people in one small bed.

Behind me, Jake snorts, forcing me to roll my face into the pillow to suppress the giggles.

"SHHHH!" Aurora hisses from her end of the room. "*Silencio!*"

But that only makes it funnier. We clutch each other, trying to laugh noiselessly.

"Maybe you two had—" Aurora belches. "—a nice night. But mine was horrible. Now, go to sleep." Her voice rolls toward the wall.

Jake takes a deep breath. "Goodnight, Aurora," he whispers.

"Night," she answers. And in spite of the fact that Jake and I are still shaking in the dark, my roommate soon begins to snore.

When my spasms of laughter finally subside, I put my head on Jake's chest. "Goodnight," I whisper.

He strokes my hair. "Goodnight, my love."

I lie there for a while, wondering if it's possible to die of happiness. Instead, I fall asleep.

Chapter Thirty

THREE DAYS LATER, I meet Frederick in front of a big house on Choate Street. As I approach, he unlocks the door. "Seriously, the key is in the mailbox?" I ask.

"Apparently there's not a lot of crime in this town. Norah told me to go ahead and show you the place. It's vacant."

I step inside to see a gorgeous curving staircase in front of me. "Wow. Fancy."

"I really like it," he says. "I want to buy it, but Norah said I had to show it to you first before I make an offer."

"She did?"

"Yeah. She said 'It's great that you love this house, but give your people a minute to get used to the idea.'"

"Doesn't she like it?"

"She likes it fine. But she already owns a house, and thinks I'm being extravagant. The thing is, we're going to need some more space." He walks me through a grand living room and into a dining room at the rear. "Look out the window," he says. "That little building in back is currently an art studio."

"Interesting. With some ugly black foam, you could sound-proof it."

"Exactly. My man cave."

I turn around. "What a kitchen." In addition to miles of gleaming countertops, there are barstools and even a little fireplace.

"Isn't it great? The previous owners must have spent a bundle on renovations. They made it into a really nice family space."

In my mind, I populate this room with Norah and a baby. There will be a high chair at the kitchen table, and Frederick will wave at them through the window on his way to his backyard hideout.

The perfect little family, at home in their new mansion.

"Come upstairs," he says.

At the top of the curved staircase is a hallway that leads to four bedrooms. "Here's the nursery." Frederick walks along the shiny wood floor and points into a little room. "It's connected to the master suite."

As I peek into the empty rooms, I can picture how this will work. Frederick will stand over the crib in that cozy room in this gracious house. He's setting himself up for a do-over. If he's a good father to his second baby, then he can move on and declare himself cured. He can resign from Assholes Anonymous.

I feel a pain in my chest.

"Rachel, come here a minute," he calls. "See, most of the bedrooms are together. But once you go through this door, there's one more."

I follow him through a narrow little hallway until we're standing in a very pretty room with dormers and window seats. Out the windows, I can see buds on the backyard trees.

"Okay, it's over the garage, which is probably a bit cold in the winter," he says. "But it's very private, with its own bathroom too. And it's kind of pretty. It made me think of a girl's room. If I buy this house, I want you to have it. I know you'll be in a college dormitory for much of the year. But over summer and winter vacation you'll need a place to roost."

I turn around, taking it all in. There are built-in bookcases under the window seats.

"Look." He beckons. "There's a second staircase too, that goes down to the mudroom. What do you think?"

It's the bedroom of a girl's dreams. When I was little, I'd always wanted a fancy room like this.

I walk over to perch on one of the window seats. The room is too nice for someone who only needs it during vacations. It would be a waste, really. At that realization, a brittle piece of my heart chooses to splinter and break.

"Don't you like it?" Frederick asks.

"Of course I like it," I whisper. "But..." My eyes fill up with tears, and a sob escapes from my chest, unbidden.

"Rachel, what's the matter?" Frederick wears a panicky, what-have-I-done face.

"It's just... WHY? Why now?"

At first I think he doesn't understand the question. But then I see him swallow hard. "By 'why now' I suppose you mean why not a long time ago?"

I can only nod. The tears have begun to stream down my face.

"Oh, honey." He turns around in a complete circle and puts his hands on top of his head. "The reason you can never have an answer to that question is because I don't have one to give."

"But what were you *thinking* all that time?" I gasp. "And don't say it was a long time ago, or that you don't remember." I slip a photo out of my back pocket and hold it up. It's the one with my mother at the drums.

Frederick flinches as if he's been slapped. He sits down on the wood floor in the center of the empty room. "Have I ever said one unkind word about your mother?"

I shake my head.

"We were young and stupid. I was stupider than she was, trust me. But it takes two people to have a baby."

I sit lean back on the window seat, putting a little more distance between me and Frederick's story.

"We were great together, actually. She was smart and funny. But she was also full of opinions about my career. And I was a twenty-one-year-old jackass who didn't want anyone's help." He stops, swallowing hard. The sun angles in the window to put a spotlight on his shoulders. "Music was the only thing I'd ever been good at. And when the producers finally started showing up with offers, they didn't want Wild City Blues. They said blues weren't hip enough. They wanted the solo stuff I'd been recording on the side. They gave me a contract and I..." He takes a deep breath and sighs. "I signed it."

"She didn't want you to?"

He stares at a patch of the polished floor. "She thought if we went on tour, it would work out for both of us. But I wasn't willing to wait."

I tried to imagine how that would feel for my mother. But since I'd never known her as musician, I can't picture that dream.

"We fought about it," my father says, his voice dropping low.

"Is that how it ended?" I can't get those happy images out of my head—my mother and Frederick with love on their faces.

"Almost. I did something awful just to prove she didn't own me. I..." His confession seems to lose steam. "I didn't come home one night after a gig. And then she retaliated in a way that was designed to hurt me too. That's how it ended."

I try to decode this last bit of information, and find it impossible. "She *cheated*? With who?" It's hard enough to imagine my mother taking off her clothes for Frederick. But for a stranger?

He looks up at me and shakes his head. "She was really upset with me. And probably afraid. I think she already knew she was pregnant. But I was clueless. And then I went on tour, leaving her behind. The tour went really well, and I basically never came back to Claiborne."

He stares at the pretty slanted ceiling, as if the story is written up there. "She didn't even tell me about you until after you were born. She sprung it on me just as I was about to go to L.A."

"What did you do?"

"I went to L.A. I told her I had to do it for my career. I didn't want to be forced into coming back." He leans back on his hands and looks up into the dust motes floating on the sunshine. "I didn't know any babies, Rachel. I didn't have a clue what they needed. Your mother, on the other hand, was the most competent person I'd ever met. I didn't think you needed me."

"But you sent us money."

"Well, she didn't ask right away, because she was smart and she knew there was no point. I get that now. So it happens that she asked right after my first album. But I didn't see her timing as good common sense. I felt manipulated."

"But you paid."

"I did. And it made me feel very benevolent. The rising star pays off his little people. I doubled it at some point too. She didn't even ask me to. Every month I mailed a check, and every month she cashed it. And those months, they turned into years really fast. If you have a child you've never met, every year it gets a little easier to tell yourself that the kid is better off without you."

"But it wasn't true!"

He nods. "See, but she was very nice about helping me to perpetuate the myth—that I fulfilled my obligation with those checks. She never wrote me a letter, never sent me pictures. I sent the money, and she was willing to leave me in perfect ignorance. The problem was I never got a whiff of what I was missing, either."

"She did that because of *pride*," I sob.

"No kidding, you think?" His eyes are shining now. "When I lie awake at night, it's *her* I feel bad for. You—I've got years to make it up to you. But I can't imagine her final months. If I'd been in the picture even a little bit, I could have put her mind at ease."

He wipes his eyes with his fingers. "There was only one time when I almost did the right thing. It was five or six years ago."

Frederick doesn't look me in the eye, and I feel a pit in my stomach. Maybe I don't want to hear what he's about to say.

"It was the only time she asked me for something. I got a note in my P.O. box, asking for two tickets to an Orlando concert."

My heart begins to ricochet.

Two tears track onto his famous cheekbones. "I took two tickets, and I put them in an envelope on my desk." He wipes his face on the sleeve of his shirt. "And then I started to talk myself out of it."

I press my hands to my mouth, trying not to choke on my tears.

"I knew I couldn't just send them and not see you. So I told myself that it was all too complicated—it was a big tour, all big venues, lots of industry people. I had to stay sharp..." His voice breaks. "I didn't send them. I'm so sorry."

I fold over and cry, because if he'd sent them it would have made all the difference in the world. And my mom! I had begged for those tickets, and she had said no. But then she'd swallowed her pride and asked anyway. And she'd been rebuffed.

He gets up off the floor and comes over to where I'm sitting. He pulls my damp face to his shirt. "I'm so sorry, honey. It was a terrible thing."

"I'm still so *angry*," I choke out. Finally, I've said so. I've said it with snot running out of my nose. But I've said it out loud.

"I know," he says. "I know you are. And I can take it. I'm not going anywhere." I cry, and he holds on tight.

CODA

CODA: (Italian "tail") *An ending section which brings the composition to a close.*

Chapter Thirty-One

"I REALLY DON'T SEE why they do this on April Fool's Day," Jake grumbles. "That's just mean."

We sit on the S.L.O. together, my legs across his lap. It's college acceptance day, and we've agreed to look at the Claiborne College website at the same time. Jake is all stressed out.

"Can I look at yours for you? Would that make it easier?"

Wordlessly, he passes me his laptop. The password is already typed in. He's just reluctant to peek.

But I'm dying to find out if he's gotten in. He wants it so badly. I press the button.

Six seconds later the screen lights up in green. CONGRATU-LATIONS JAKE WILLIS! WELCOME TO THE FRESHMAN CLASS.

I must have squealed, because his face breaks with disbelief. Then he grabs me by the hips and into his lap, so he can see too. "Damn. This better not be an April Fool's joke." His grin is enormous.

"Congratulations," I say, hugging him.

"Now we have to look at yours."

Right. "If you say so. Can't we just bask in the glow of your victory for a while?"

Jake swaps our laptops, putting one on the coffee table and lifting the other one. "Go on."

I follow the link from the email and tap in my user name, all the while telling myself it will be okay if I'm rejected. Jake wants it more. His parents are professors there. And I've already been accepted to a good school in California.

But, God, *please*.

My fingers shake as I click the button on the screen.

It turns green, and Jake lets out a whoop of joy.

"Wow," I breathe. "I'm in."

"You so are!" He wraps his arms around me and kisses me.

I lean in, but my brain is going a hundred miles an hour. "Can't believe it," I murmur against his lips. Next year just got even better. Jake and I will be together.

"Mmm," he agrees, his tongue stroking mine. Then he pulls back. "If you're staying in Claiborne for the summer," Jake says, "I can drive up to see you." Jake is working another season at the clam shack on Cape Cod.

"That sounds like fun. But if you're working at the beach, it should be me who visits you. Except I don't have a car. Maybe I can borrow one."

"Awesome," he says, kissing me again.

The door bangs open and Aurora walks in. "Sorry," she mumbles.

Jake and I break apart. "Hi, Aurora," he says with laughing eyes. Lately, we are never alone.

"We both got into Claiborne," I say by way of explanation. "Just now."

"Congratulations," she says, her voice softer. Aurora isn't applying to colleges this year. Her dad thinks she needs a PG year at Claiborne to shore up her résumé. "You must be so happy."

"Yeah." I squint at her. She isn't happy, and hasn't been for a little while.

"You should come to the beach this summer with Rachel," Jake says, trying to include her.

She sits heavily on the window seat. Lately, she's spent a lot of time there, staring out the window and drowning in her teacup.

"Aurora," Jake tries again. "Did you hear the question? Don't make me come over there."

"Sorry," she says, looking our way. "I'm just distracted."

"We noticed," I say, watching her. "Don't you want to tell us what's wrong?"

Aurora shakes her head. She's been silent and sad for more than a week. We'd guessed that she'd had a breakup, but she didn't want to talk about it.

"Okay." Jake sighs. "But we're going to drag you off for dinner in a little while, okay? Friends don't let friends miss pasta-bar night."

Aurora smiles. "I'm sorry to be so little fun. I'm happy for you both, though. And I'm glad you'll be in the same town as me next year."

"That's right," he says, running a hand over my bare knees. He tilts his head back on the sofa and closes his eyes. I slip my fingers between the sofa and Jake's back, rubbing the bare skin under his T-shirt.

One unfortunate result of the sudden end of Aurora's secret romance is a loss of privacy for us. Aurora is home all the time now, barely leaving, even for classes. Jake is a good friend to Aurora, but these days he looks at me the way a hungry man eyes a buffet table.

Together, Jake and I poke around on the Claiborne College website. Ten minutes later, Aurora gets up to go to the bathroom. As soon as the door closes, Jake slides the computer to the floor and climbs on top of me. The kisses I receive are thermonuclear.

"You know she's coming right back." I laugh.

"Shh…precious nanoseconds wasted," he says, kissing me again. "How about we go discuss our college courses in your bed?"

"Sounds like a plan," Aurora says, reentering the room.

I'm not cavalier enough about the whole fooling-around thing to make such an obvious retreat. I gave Jake a gentle push. "Come on, now. Back into a vertical position."

"I'm always in a vertical position," he says, sighing.

My phone bleats with Frederick's ring tone.

"Hi Rachel," he rumbles into my ear when I answer.

Even now—after almost a year—he's able to startle me simply by saying my name. "What's up?"

"There's another concert next weekend. This one's in Massachusetts. Bring Aurora this time."

"Cool. Can Jake come too? We're celebrating! Both of us got yesses from Claiborne College."

"Nice. I knew you would, though."

"But *I* didn't know. Can Jake come along?"

"Well... Let me ask if there's room in our reservation."

"He could bunk with Henry," I suggest.

Frederick laughs into my ear. "No he can't, because that will cost me in other ways. I'll get Henry to add a hotel room. But nobody gets drunk this time."

"We'll stick to drugs only."

"You can drop that comedy course you're taking now," Frederick says.

"Back atcha, old man." I hear him laughing when I disconnect.

———

Some arrangement for Jake is made, and on the day of the concert, Jake and I meet up with the band at Wheelock's. We walk in to find that Henry has taken over a large area in back. I wave to Ernie, who's brought along his girlfriend. They're perched on sofas, munching appetizers with the other musicians. My father and Norah are conferring in a corner.

Darcy the waitress sidles up to me. "What can I bring you, sweetie?"

"A Diet Coke? Thanks."

"Is this your boyfriend? What a cutie." She rubs Jake's biceps, and he looks startled. "What would you like to drink?"

"A Coke would be fine, thanks."

"Coming right up."

I watch Darcy make the rounds. She's in her element, refreshing drinks and petting musicians with her shiny fingernails. And I'm not the only one who finds it a little weird. Across the room, Norah's eyes flicker with irritation.

My father comes over to join us, putting an arm around my shoulder. "If it's still okay with you, I'm going to buy that house on Choate Street."

We lock eyes for a beat. Melting down in that empty house isn't something I'll forget anytime soon. But you don't get to choose the big moments in your life. "You should buy it," I say. "Good plan."

"Thank you," he says, and we both know we're talking about more than a real estate purchase. He kisses the top of my head. "Now I only need to convince Norah."

"She doesn't want the house?"

Before he can answer, she comes over, offering her hand to Jake. "Hi, I'm Norah."

"It's nice to meet you," he says. Today his T-shirt reads, *Darwin is my Homeboy*.

"She *says* she likes the house," Frederick complains. "But she's taking forever to negotiate the purchase."

"Chill out, will you? The house is overpriced," Norah says. "They'll agree to the lower number. They're just waiting a few minutes to save face."

"Tell them I'll pay it."

"No!" she says.

A cheer rises up from the booth in the corner. "Go Norah. Go Norah," Henry chants. "I get all excited when somebody else bosses Freddy around."

My father checks his watch. "But we're supposed to *leave*."

"That house has been for sale for six months. It's not going anywhere." At that, her phone rings. She checks the caller's name and winks at Frederick. "Hello? Hi, Debbie... Oh, you don't say!" Norah gives Frederick the thumbs up. "That's really good news. I'll tell him."

"I can't believe you pulled that off," Frederick mutters.

"You want it signed today? Well, I believe the client is at Wheelock's for a few more minutes before he leaves town for the weekend. I can meet you there."

When she hangs up, Frederick picks Norah up and kisses her. "How much money did you just save me?" he asks her.

"A couple of semesters at Claiborne College," she says. "Now unhand me, so I can at least pretend to be a professional." She straightens out her shirt. Norah is just starting to show, and I've been sneaking looks at her rounder belly. "Debbie wants you to sign an offer sheet. It's just one page."

Two minutes later, an older woman with a poof of gray hair teeters into the restaurant on impractical heels. I see Norah's face close up as she approaches. "Afternoon, Debbie." They are obviously not friends.

"Norah." Debbie nods, handing her a page.

"Thank you." Norah reads it quickly. "Subject to inspection... good. Okay." She hands the page to Frederick.

Debbie beams up at my father. "It's a pleasure to do business with you, Mr. Ricks."

"The pleasure is all mine, Debbie," my father says, and Norah rolls her eyes.

Frederick takes his autograph sharpie from his pocket. "Turn around, Jake." My father presses the sheet of paper against Jake's back and signs.

Debbie gives him another megawatt smile. "Norah, we'll get a contract to you early next week." She starts to turn away, but her smile shifts. "Why, Norah! You're pregnant! Did you get married and I missed it?"

There is a dramatic silence, as if the needle had been yanked from a vinyl record. The only sound is my father sucking in his breath.

"*Jesus*, Debbie!" Heads swing around to locate Norah's defender, and I'm startled to note that it's Darcy, her serving tray cocked against her hip. She glares at the realtor. "Who *says* things like that? This isn't 1957." With outrage on her face, Darcy hands me two Cokes. "*Besides*. What an attractive and talented child that's going to be." Darcy pats Frederick on the chest and stomps back toward the kitchen.

Debbie looks slowly from Norah to Frederick and then back again. After turning three subsequent shades of purple, she carries the signed paper out of the restaurant.

It's still quiet when Frederick puts his hands on Norah's shoulders. "God, I'm so sorry. That's not what you signed up for."

She sighs. "Actually, that's exactly what I signed up for."

Her answer makes me flinch. Nineteen years ago, my mother must have heard that much and worse. Mom never had a ring on her finger, or a man at her side.

Maybe if she'd lived longer, she would have gotten over her anger. I sure hope so.

When Darcy next emerges from the kitchen, it's to a standing ovation. But she brushes aside the praise with, "It just had to be said."

"Okay, she's growing on me," Norah whispers to me after Darcy walks away.

"I hear you," I reply. Today I feel the same way about Norah. Almost.

She plays with the straw in her seltzer water. "You know, Frederick, I don't have enough furniture for this house. It's going to be awfully bare for a while."

He shrugs. "I have furniture."

My eyebrows go up, and Norah catches it. "Not so much?" she asks me.

"What little there is takes the style of Early American Bachelor."

"Oh dear," Norah says.

Frederick looks from Norah to me. "Tough crowd here for a Saturday," he says. Then he drains his beer.

Henry waves his hands in the air. "Let's go people. Time to saddle up!"

Unfortunately, Aurora has not appeared yet. I run outside to look down Main Street. There's a chartered bus waiting there, and its door swings open. "Hola, Rachel," says the driver.

"Carlos!" I cry. "I didn't know you were coming."

"Vamos a Massachusetts?"

"Momentito." But where is Aurora?

One by one, everyone comes out of the bar and boards the bus. But I pace the sidewalk, staring at my phone. When it finally it rings, I answer immediately. "Aurora, where are you?"

"Can I bring a date?"

"Well…" I'm annoyed by the last-minute question. But if there's already a hotel room for Jake, they can double up. "Sure. But only if you can both be here in three minutes." I realize I sound a bit curt. "I can't wait to meet him," I add.

"Right. You're going to be surprised."

"Whatever, Aurora. Get over here! It's time to go."

I run to the back of the bus to tell Frederick. But he and Jake are in the middle of a discussion.

"The problem with Beane's analytical model is not that it failed, but that it was too widely adopted," Jake says. "The effect was diluted by every successive adoptee."

My father looks perplexed.

"What are you talking about?" I have to ask.

"Baseball. I'm pretty sure," Frederick answers.

"Sorry to interrupt, but can Aurora bring her boyfriend? She just called."

My father's face is curious. "A boyfriend?"

"He can room with Jake, right? Carry on." I scoot to the front of the bus to wait for Aurora.

But when she finally climbs onto the bus, I am indeed surprised. Because the person holding her hand is Jessica.

"Sorry we're late," Aurora says. Her smile is nervous.

I try mightily to control my reaction. "I'm glad you made it."

"Dios mio, Rachel! Your face." Aurora flushes.

"I'll give you two a minute," Jessica says, sliding into the seat behind Carlos.

He closes the door, and the bus pulls away from the curb. A cheer rises up from the back, and I hear the sound of a popping cork.

"I said you'd be surprised." Aurora looks pained.

"Just give me a few seconds to get used to the idea." I take a deep breath and let it out. "Okay. All set."

My roommate still looks worried. "I'm so sorry I didn't tell you. I didn't know how."

Unaccountably, I feel myself tearing up. "Seems like something I should have figured out by myself." What kind of a self-centered jerk misses that?

"No, sweetie. I worked to keep it from you. But it was exhausting, and it made Jessica mad." Her lips quiver. "I was afraid you wouldn't want a roommate who liked girls."

I just shake my head. "I don't care, Aurora. It's only a problem if you won't be my roommate anymore."

"No! If I come to Claiborne College in a year, we'll share again. I can't wait." Aurora reaches out, hugging me tightly.

When I walk to the back of the bus a minute later, my father hands me a thimble-sized cup of champagne. Jake is already holding one. "Note the portion size," he says.

"Dad!"

Frederick chuckles. "Why don't you take a couple of these to Aurora and her boyfriend."

I look from Frederick to Jake. "Did either of you see that coming?"

They exchange a knowing glance.

"You've had a lot on your mind," Jake says loyally.

"Does anyone have anything else they want to tell me?" I ask, downing my little swallow of champagne.

"Here." Frederick hands me two more cups. "And they're not for you."

"Will I ever live that night down?" I ask.

He shrugs. "You've only done one stupid thing to my ten, okay? I have to hang on tight to this one."

I carry the two little cups to my friends. "Cheers!" I say, passing them to Aurora and Jessica. "I'm glad you're both here."

"Thank you," Jessica says. At least I don't have to wonder anymore about Jessica's frosty attitude toward me. Hopefully that will change now.

"I'll get Jake. We'll sit with you guys," I offer.

On my way back to the rear of the bus, Norah grabs my hand. When I stop, she tosses her chin over her shoulder toward Jake, and then she gives me a thumbs up. "He's adorable."

I smile at her. "I think so too."

Taking Jake's hand, I ask him to come and sit up front with me.

"Sure," he says.

"Hey, Rachel?" my father asks.

"Yeah?"

"You know that melody I made you try out last week?"

"Yeah." I let go of Jake's hand so I can hold on to the hand rail as the bus swings around a curve. "Why?"

My father's hands pass idly over the strings of his acoustic guitar. I'm used to that sound now. I hear it all the time. "I want to record it as a duet. Just fooling around, you know? If I find a sound booth somewhere at the college, will you sing it with me?"

"Sure? Can we talk about this later?"

He laughs. "Fine. Go."

So I do.

Chapter Thirty-Two

THE SOUND CHECK for Frederick's concert takes forever. But we don't care. My friends and I pass the time on a slouchy old couch we've found backstage.

"It's just like home," Aurora points out. I'm getting used to the sight of my roommate and Jessica together. Even better, Aurora isn't moping anymore.

I perch on the arm of the sofa while the three others take the seats. "Maybe our S.L.O. isn't big enough anymore."

Jake reaches up for my hips, sliding me into his lap. "Sure it is. See?"

"Spoken like a man who doesn't want to help us carry another one up the stairs."

Henry skids to a stop in front of our sofa, an envelope in his hands. "Seats or wings?" he asks. "I've got third row, left side."

"Seats, please," I answer. This night is going to be different than my last concert, in every possible way.

Henry counts out four tickets and hands them to me. "Oh, and here." He passes me two hotel-key folders.

I stare at them in my hand.

"Problem?" Henry asks.

"Well... Rooming got trickier." Does it really make sense to put Jake and Jessica in a room together? What is the point of that?

Henry snorts. "This is one of those times, Rachel, when you just have to ask yourself, 'What would Freddy do?' Solve the problem that way. I do it all the time." He walks away, whistling to himself.

It's perfectly good advice. So I solve the problem by giving one room to Aurora and Jessica, and taking a bubble bath with Jake in the other one. And the decision is very popular with everyone concerned.

Before the show, everyone eats dinner together in the dimly lit hotel bar, passing around plates of seafood and pasta. While Jake holds my hand under the table, Jessica quizzes the drummer about percussion instruments, and Ernie and his girlfriend tell a long story about locking their keys in her car at the airport.

"You should have driven the convertible," I point out.

Only Frederick is missing, because he never eats before shows. When Ernie's girlfriend gets up to go get ready for the concert, I move around the table to sit next to Ernie.

He pulls out a chair for me. "How are you doing, kid? Did you do any skiing since I saw you last?"

"Nope," I say. "But I'm going to get the chance next year." Skiing with Jake is only one of the things I'm looking forward to.

"So I heard." Ernie is sipping Diet Coke too, because none of them drink before a show. "I also heard you sang "Stop Motion" again. Freddy says you brought down the house."

"He's biased." But it's nice to think of my father bragging about it to Ernie, just like any parent. I lean forward in my chair. "There's a pack of pictures you took. I found them last month. There aren't many pictures of her, so...thanks, I guess."

Ernie's expression clouds over. He shifts uncomfortably in his chair. "Didn't know those were still around."

I study his face and find something there that I'd never noticed before. Regret. Something slides into place for me then, and in that moment I understand a little more about what had happened all those years ago.

Ernie loved her too.

He leans his chin on his hand, his expression sad. Unless I'm wrong, he'd had a hand in my parents' breakup all those years ago.

That stops my heart for a second. But I know Ernie is a good guy. And Frederick is a good guy. And my mother was a good person too. Even so, there was so much broken glass between them, a mess that had never been swept away.

What a waste.

"She was so unlucky," I say, echoing Aurora.

Ernie nods. "She was, and that meant you were too." His gaze is fixed on the tabletop.

I take in the flickering candlelight, and my friends gathered on the other side of the table. "You know what, Ernie? I don't feel unlucky right now." Wait—I've used a double negative. "I feel *lucky*, actually."

Ernie puts an arm around me. "Kid, that makes me happier than you know." Gently he clinks his Coke glass against mine and takes another sip.

———

Watching my father's performance from the audience is an entirely different experience.

From the minute he steps onto that stage, I feel the crowd surge around me, like a kind-hearted creature. As if five thousand people have made a pact of mutual affection.

He gives us his all, his fingers working the fret board at blur speed, and they give back to him all the love they'd paid a hundred dollars a head to express. Every time he plays the introduction to another song, there's a roar of approval.

The live-version experience is so *different* from the studio tracks I carried in my pocket my whole life. The concert acoustics are booming and ragged without the carefully edited balance mixed by a fleet of recording engineers. I can hear fret noise from Ernie's bass, and the occasional sound of my father drawing breath past his microphone. I can see all the sweat and effort and dropped guitar picks which are part of real life.

And it's perfect anyway. Perfect, loud, messy, and real. The crowd stands, swaying around me. Jake threads his arms around my waist and kisses me on the ear. The pulse from the subwoofers mingles with the warm thud of his heart.

Above me, my father beats out the rhythm guitar licks on "Much of Me" with a furrowed brow. He's literally up on a pedestal, several feet above eye level. How wild it must be to stand up there and hear people yelling your name. It must be a feeling that you can carry away with you afterwards. A guy can make a lot of stupid decisions in life, and still people will yell his name and throw flowers at his feet.

Weird.

After the final song in the set, people stamp their feet for more. The house lights stay off, and I picture my father backstage, toweling off his head, deciding what to play for an encore. Maybe he's taking a moment to give Norah a kiss. It only took him forty-one years to trust a woman enough to stick with her, so I suppose that would be a moment well spent.

When he comes back out on the stage, he comes alone, in front of the curtain. A techie scurries out with a chair and a microphone. Frederick sits down very close to the lip of the stage, and a spotlight makes a circle against the curtain behind him.

He strums his guitar while he speaks, looking out over the crowd. They're quiet, listening. "I don't know if you know this about me," he says. "But I have a beautiful daughter. Her name is Rachel, and she's the bravest person I know."

I gasp.

"Oh!" Aurora says, taking my hand. Jake squeezes my other one.

"She is, naturally, a genius," he says, and the crowd laughs.

"Recently she said something so clever and true that I couldn't let it go. So I wrote this song for her. I'm going to call it 'Double Negative.' It's a song that asks for her patience. I figure by the time she turns thirty I might figure out this fatherhood thing." He closes his eyes and begins slapping out a bluesy rhythm line on his guitar.

> I can't not love you,
> And I can't not care
> I won't take no for an answer,
> And I won't bow to despair.
>
> I don't stop hoping,
> But I won't forget to say
> That you're not wrong in anger,
> And I can't wish that away.
>
> You don't believe that I am true
> It took far too long for me to come through.
>
> But I am your double negative
> Where everything wrong turns right.
>
> You might say that I am trite
> But don't fight me, girl, on this tonight.
>
> I am your double negative
> Where everything wrong turns right.

I have to sit down when it's over. I fold myself into my seat and put my head in my hands. Eventually the theater empties out, leaving just the four of us in the third row.

Aurora fumbles in her purse for some tissues. "Here, sweetie."

"Thanks," I hiccup.

"You two! It's like duel of the tearjerkers," Aurora says. "Don't take this the wrong way, but I think Frederick won."

"He can keep the trophy." I sniff. I dig my phone out of my pocket. *Payback is a bitch*, I text to him.

"So what happens now?" Jake asks.

It's the question I've been asking myself for a year. But lately it seems less difficult to answer. I put my head on his shoulder. "After they pack up, there's a party somewhere. Probably at the hotel. We'll go ask Henry in a minute."

When we stand up, my phone buzzes with a response. It says only: *I love you Rachel.*

THE
END

Keep up with Sarina

Learn more about Sarina's titles at sarinabowen.com.

Acknowledgments

First of all I need to thank James Di Salvio for his permission to use a lyric from Bran Van 3000! I'm so flattered, and I love all your music.

Thank you to Mollie Glick for your help with this project way back when. How bumpy was this road? And to Patricia Nelson who is priceless.

And to Rosemary DiBattista and Sarah Stewart Taylor and Jess Lahey and K.J. Dell'Antonia who shored me up when things went wrong.

Thank you to Edie Danford for your editing wisdom and to Jo Pettibone for your sharp eyes. Thank you to my early readers: Becky Munsterer Sabky, Natasha Sinel Cohen, Sarah Mayberry, Tiffany Ing, and Jenn Gaffney. And to Miranda Kenneally and Ginger Scott for your support!

Made in the USA
Lexington, KY
08 March 2019